Animal Attraction
(Alaskan Werewolves Book 1)

PAIGE TYLER

Cover Design by Kim Killion

ISBN-10: 1499668252
ISBN-13: 978-1499668254

Animal Attraction

Not only are werewolves real, but they're damn hunky, too.

Frustrated when none of the real newspapers will hire her as a reporter, Eliza Bradley takes the only job she can get—at a paranormal magazine. Her first assignment takes her to Fairbanks, Alaska to investigate the rumors that a werewolf has killed two local men.

When she meets Hunter McCall, a local college professor and an expert on wolves, she finds herself irresistibly drawn to him and ends up spending more time in his bed than worrying about werewolves. That's when Eliza finds out Hunter isn't just an animal in the sack, he's an animal out of it, too—of the werewolf variety. Talk about a complicated relationship.

But Eliza can't dwell on Hunter's little shapeshifting issues for long. There's another werewolf out there with a taste for human blood, and she and Hunter are the only ones who can stop him. If they don't, they're likely to become his next victims.

EPIC Award Finalist

Best Book at Long and Short Reviews

"An Outstanding Read!" – Simply Romance Reviews
"ANIMAL ATTRACTION by Paige Tyler is one of those books that you just can't put down once you begin reading it, it is just that good. The story is very entertaining: the pace is fluid and the characters are extremely engaging. It is by turns fun, amusing, steamy and nail "biting" – no pun intended. There are quite a few twists and turns in the story, elements of the paranormal intermingle with the erotic and they are all rounded out with a very nice surprise ending to that mysterious werewolf plaguing the town throughout the entire book. Ms. Tyler knows how to paint a scene and prolong the anticipation, and the chemistry between Eliza and Hunter make turning each page a special treat. This is an exceptionally good story, one guaranteed to provide hours of enjoyment for its readers, and one that I can definitely recommend!"

5 Blue Ribbons from Romance Junkies
"ANIMAL ATTRACTION is one hot read. Ms. Tyler knows how to mesmerize an audience, she certainly kept mine. I'd love to have this in print so I could keep it always. My favorite paranormal subject housed perfectly.

Scene changes were as smooth as silk. The characters richly defined. I find nothing to complain about...I recommend this book if you love paranormal stories that hook you and hold you captive until the last page!"

"Wild for Animal Attraction" – Wild on Books

"ANIMAL ATTRACTION by Paige Tyler is scorching hot. More than once I blushed watching and being witness to the sheer animalistic attraction shared by Eliza and Hunter. Speaking of Hunter, he was a werewolf after my own heart. His complete infatuation with Eliza shined through and I wanted him so very badly to tell her that he was the very creature that she was looking to find. Eliza's character made me smile more than once. While she took the job as a reporter of a paranormal magazine because she had to and even scoffed at the possibility of werewolves, I loved watching her opinion on the possibility of werewolves change. The love scenes between Eliza and Hunter were erotic but romantic, forceful but sensual, and naughty but playful. The feelings and depth of emotions Eliza and Hunter felt for each other, almost immediately, were believable and so very sexy. After reading ANIMAL ATTRACTION I will never again look at a hot tub without remembering this risqué but thoroughly entertaining novel. Paige Tyler is now on my list of authors to watch for and I know that other readers will feel the same way!"

"Paranormal Romance At Its Finest" – Joyfully Reviewed

"ANIMAL ATTRACTION is paranormal romance writing at its finest. I really loved the interaction with Eliza and Hunter. They have this initial attraction that sizzles. Paige Tyler is an author with a knack for creating a werewolf who is sinfully sexy and she kept me totally engrossed right from the beginning. I am hoping for an additional story featuring Hunter's brother Luke. I also look forward to more offerings from Ms. Tyler in the very near future. I would recommend Animal Attraction to anyone who enjoys stories of werewolves and shifters!"

4.5 Pixies – Dark Angels Reviews

"ANIMAL ATTRACTION is a fun, lighthearted and humorous werewolf romance. The pace is quick, something is always happening. Eliza, our heroine, is bright, funny and yet wonderfully prosaic. Hunter, our hero, is handsome, educated and sincere. There are also some wonderfully quirky secondary characters as well as some very serious ones. Ms. Tyler does a great job of bringing her characters and setting to life. The romance between our hero and heroine develops quickly and the sex scenes are seriously hot. Attraction leads to heat, then to love and the emotions are very vivid in this tale. There are some surprises towards the end and I loved how things came together for the ending. ANIMAL ATTRACTION was a very enjoyable read and I hope to see more from Ms. Tyler!"

4.5 Hearts – Night Owl Romance Reviews

"I found this work by Ms. Tyler to be well thought out and developed. It contained plenty of humor to go with the mystery, and some smoking hot sex scenes. I even wanted a cigarette after a couple scenes, and I don't smoke. How will Eliza the skeptic and Hunter the werewolf have any kind of future together? Well you'll just have to read this wonderfully witty work to find out. You won't be disappointed you did!"

5 Cups – Coffee Time Romance Reviews

"Animal Attraction is a great story and I found the characters interesting and charming. Their relationship builds perfectly and the story flows wonderfully. Eliza and Hunter's interactions are fresh with just the right amount of humor. The background characters are good and fill in the blanks without taking the focus away from the couple. The Alaskan scenery is perfect for a werewolf story. The sex is hot and exciting, so having a cold drink handy is a good idea. I am so happy to be able to recommend this book!"

"An Amazing Story and One Hot Read!" – Paranormal Romance Reviews

"ANIMAL ATTRACTION was an amazing story! Ms. Tyler has an incredible ability to give life to her characters, and really make the reader feel as if they are in the story. Her descriptions are wonderful, her settings are well researched, and her writing is fantastic. The attraction between Eliza and Hunter was very believable, and led to scenes so hot that they could melt an iceberg. All in all, this was a great story, and I can't wait to read more from this author. Excellent job! Have the ice water handy, and turn on the AC, because this is one hot read!"

DEDICATION

With special thanks to my extremely patient and understanding husband. Without your help and support I couldn't have pursued my dream job of becoming a writer. You're my sounding board, my idea man, my critique partner, and the absolute best research assistant any girl could ask for!

Thank you.

And thank you to the wonderful fangirls on my Street Team. You all rock!

A Note from Paige Tyler:

ANIMAL ATTRACTION was originally published in 2008. It was an EPIC Award Finalist, was chosen as BEST BOOK of 2008 at Long and Short Reviews, and received amazing reviews. When I got the rights back from the publisher a little while ago, I decided to revise and rework the story, adding in new characters, a new story arc, and more suspense, action and adventure, which turned the original novella into a full-length novel, and I think made it even better. Hope you enjoy it!

Happy Reading!

"To look into the eyes of a wolf is to see your own soul."
— Aldo Leopold

Prologue

He watched his old friend Mark Dunham stomp through the woods, never realizing how incredibly noisy the big oaf was until now. Mark tripped, almost falling over a decaying tree trunk coated with a light dusting of snow. The big man was breathing hard by the time he got his feet back under him and picked up his rifle from the ground. From his place in the shadows beneath the large fir tree, he could smell Mark's alcohol-laden breath. The man was drunk – not surprising considering he'd been drinking during Jed's entire funeral.

He'd stalked and hunted Jed Matthews a month ago, but because it had taken weeks to find the body the funeral had just happened today. He was glad the timing had worked out that way. It meant he'd been able to attend the funeral of one of his tormentors in his demonic beast form. Appropriate, since that was the same form he'd been in when he killed Jed. Of course, he'd had to hide in the trees nearly a hundred yards from the service, but with his hearing and sense of smell, it was just like being there.

He hadn't expected to get a shot at any of the others for a while, figuring they'd stay out of the forest. But here Mark was, bumbling and stumbling around in a drunken haze only hours after putting Jed in the ground. He would have preferred to stalk Mark while his friend was in a more challenging frame of mind. But then again, he was going to kill him anyway, so why bother about the challenge?

A deer moved through the trees off to the left, and he almost laughed as Mark tried to swing his rifle in that direction and take aim at the animal. Of course, he couldn't laugh – not in this beastly form – any more than Mark could sight in on a creature he was likely too drunk to see.

Mark swore and started walking through the forest again, signing a song under his breath. He remembered *that song — the one about bowlegged woman. Mark had sung it the last time they'd gone hunting together.*

That memory, along with the flash of horrible pain that came with it, spurred him out of his hiding place and closer to the man he intended to kill. Though he had four enormous feet now — he was still shocked at their size — he moved more quietly than he ever had.

He followed Mark for a few hundred yards, moving close enough to almost reach out and touch him before slipping away to toy with him again. But he quickly grew tired of the game. Jed had been more fun. He'd been out hiking early in the morning and had immediately known something was stalking him. Jed had run like crazy and it had taken a while to catch him. He somehow doubted Mark would be nearly as satisfying. Hell, he doubted the man he used to think of as one of his closest friends would even see him until the very end.

To test his theory, he purposely stepped on a dead tree branch about the size of a two by four. His massive weight crushed the thing with a loud pop, causing Mark to spin around and lift his rifle.

Apparently, his old friend could see just fine because his eyes went wide and his jaw dropped.

Mark shifted the rifle he was carrying and snapped out a round at him. He wasn't angry that his friend had shot at him — he didn't exactly look like his old self.

Even if he had, Mark probably would have shot at him anyway.

He felt the bullet graze his shoulder, but he didn't pay much attention to it. Now that he knew Mark could see him, it was time to move things along. He never knew how long he'd stay in his demonic beast form and since he'd changed sometime late last night, he didn't want to chance it.

He trotted forward, baring his teeth in a snarl so Mark could see what was coming.

Mark moaned in fear and took another shot at him. This one wasn't even close, and Mark turned and took off running.

He could have caught Mark in ten steps, but he didn't bother. The reason he'd come back was revenge, and hearing Mark shouts of terror as waves of fear pheromones rolled off him was just about the best form of revenge he could imagine.

He knew why Mark was so scared. He was a beast, a demon, an instrument of hell unleashed on this earth. And Mark knew exactly why he was here.

Mark fired a few more shots at him, but they went wide just like the others. He let Mark think he might make it. He could almost taste the scent of hope on the air. Then, in three big bounds, he caught up to his friend and crushed him to the forest floor just yards away from the safety of his truck.

Mark's rifle flew into the brush, and the man scrambled a few feet after it before giving up and flopping over on his back. Mark held up his hands in supplication, but he leaped onto Mark's chest and closed his jaws over an arm. There was snap and a cry of pain. He let go, then did the same to the other arm. There was a lot more shouting now, but he ignored it. Just the same way Mark had ignored his cries of pain all those months ago.

Chapter One

If anyone found out she'd taken a job at *Paranormal Today*, her career as a serious journalist would be ruined. Eliza Bradley fought the urge to duck out the door and instead took her place at the huge conference table. But honestly, who was she kidding? She had no career to ruin. She'd never been more than a lowly fact checker. The most she'd ever gotten to write was the headline for someone else's article.

She probably shouldn't have complained about her job at the *San Francisco Chronicle*; it had paid the bills, after all. But after graduating summa cum laude from USC with a degree in journalism four years ago, she'd expected to move up the ladder at warp speed. That hadn't happened. Finally tired of checking for typos in other reporters' work, she'd given her boss an ultimatum. Determined to break into the ranks once and for all, she'd marched into his office and firmly told him that if he didn't find a job for her as a reporter, she was going to quit. She'd been so sure he would give in to her demands, but instead he called her bluff. Ten minutes later, she'd cleaned out her desk and left.

Finding a job as a reporter with another newspaper had been more difficult than Eliza thought it would be. While they'd been more than impressed with her college background, they'd been less than wowed with her lack of real world experience. It had been on the tip of her tongue more than once to ask how the heck she was supposed to get real world experience when no one would give her a job, but she'd restrained herself. Barely. That was usually the point during the interview when the person conducting it mentioned the newspaper had a position open for a fact checker, if she would be interested. *Right.*

No one would hire her—not the big papers, not the little papers, not even any of the locally published magazines. She'd been about to give up and take one of the fact checker jobs she'd been offered when she heard *Paranormal Today* magazine was looking to hire a reporter. The name alone sounded so ridiculous that her first instinct had been to say forget it, but then she remembered how desperate she was and decided to at least look into it. At that point, she hadn't cared what she wrote about, as long as she got the job.

She'd expected the interview to go the same as the others had, but Roger Brannick, the editor-in-chief of the magazine, hadn't been put off by her lack of experience in the field. In fact, he'd told her that she was just the kind of fresh, young talent the magazine was looking for. She'd been so stunned when he offered her the job that she'd taken it without hesitation.

In retrospect, Eliza was beginning to think she should have given the whole thing a bit more consideration. Working for a magazine like *Paranormal Today* could destroy her credibility and make it difficult to ever get a job with a reputable newspaper. In the world of journalism, it was as bad as working for a scandal sheet.

As Roger Brannick began handing out story assignments to the other reporters attending the staff meeting, Eliza found it hard to keep a straight face. He had them investigating rumors of vampires prowling New York City's Central Park, sightings of ghosts in a Miami hotel, tales of zombies terrorizing Los Angeles, even a sea . monster living in the Great Lakes. The list, which seemed to go on and on, only got more and more bizarre. But Roger was treating them as if they were seriously newsworthy. And he wasn't the only one. She looked around at the other reporters. My God, they were actually taking notes.

"Eliza," Roger said, finally coming to her. "The other day, we got an email from one of our long-time readers up in Fairbanks who says he has evidence of a werewolf in the area. It seems that a couple of locals have turned up dead recently. The authorities are calling it a wild animal attack, but I want you to go up there and check it out anyway. Undercover, though. I don't want people getting wind you're up there looking for a werewolf. We don't want to attract the competition. Say you're up there doing research for a book you're writing on wolves, or something like that."

Werewolf? He had to be kidding. She'd definitely go

in undercover. She sure as hell didn't want anyone knowing why she was really up there. If anyone found out, they'd think she was insane.

Before she could say anything, Roger continued. "I've already—" he began, but was interrupted by muttering coming from the opposite end of the table. Lifting his gaze from the notepad in his hand, the gray-haired editor turned his attention in that direction. "Is there a problem, Clark?"

"Damn right there is." The blond reporter at the far end of the table pushed his glasses higher up on his nose. "I've been working at this magazine for five years, and what do I get? I get a haunted house in Iowa while the new girl gets next month's cover story."

Eliza might have laughed if the other reporter didn't look so pissed off about the whole thing. She sat up straighter in her chair and cleared her throat. "I don't mind if he wants to switch assignments, Roger."

She really didn't mind. It was all the same to her whether she was investigating werewolves or ghosts. The idea that either one existed was ludicrous anyway. Her new boss, however, was shaking his head.

"That's not necessary, Eliza," Roger said, looking at her over the rim of his half-moon glasses. "I want you on the werewolf story."

At the other end of the conference table, Clark Emery picked up his spiral notebook and pushed back his chair. "Screw this!"

Eliza cringed as the man stormed out of the conference room. Great. She'd been working here for less than a week and she was already making enemies.

"Don't pay any attention to Clark. He's never happy," Roger told her. "I want you in Fairbanks ASAP. Go see Brenda in the travel department. She'll already have your flight, hotel, and rental car all set up."

Eliza blinked. She was impressed. For a magazine that published stories on the bizarre and ridiculous, it was certainly run efficiently. She opened her mouth to thank him, but Roger was already going down his list again, something about a fifty-foot boa constrictor in the sewers of Chicago. Thank God he hadn't given her that story. She hated snakes—and sewers.

She ran into Clark on her way back to her desk. He glared at her, but didn't say anything. That should have been her cue to keep walking, but the reminder that she had to work with this guy had her stopping to apologize for what'd happened in the meeting. She barely got two words out before the other reporter cut her off.

"Save it," he snapped. "Go to Alaska and chase after some stupid werewolf. I'm done with this rag anyway."

Eliza had to backpedal out of the way to keep from falling on her butt as he pushed past her. *Jerk.*

"Good riddance," said a male voice behind her.

She turned to see a tall, lanky man with shaggy, dark blond hair and wire-rimmed glasses. He was wearing faded jeans and a worn T-shirt that said *Property of the San Francisco 49ers* on the front.

"Clark's a crybaby. Don't worry about him," the man continued. "I'm Alex Decker, by the way, the staff photographer going up to Alaska with you."

The magazine was sending a photographer with her? Wow. It was almost enough to make her feel like she was a real reporter. Well, at least it would have if her first assignment didn't involve writing a story about something as silly as a werewolf.

* * * * *

Their plane landed at the Fairbanks International Airport a little after three-thirty the following afternoon. Even with the hour-and-a-half layover in Seattle, Eliza had to admit they'd made surprisingly good time. Then again, she supposed that had something to do with the time change. Fairbanks was an hour behind San Francisco.

Eliza had spent most of the flight and all of the layover digging up any information she could on the two the men who had been killed. This might be a make-believe article intended for a wacko paranormal magazine, but the journalist in her insisted on treating it like a real story.

Unfortunately, the articles she'd found on the internet hadn't said much really. Just that Jed Matthews and Mark Dunham had been killed by an animal while out in the forest. The various articles seemed to differ on exactly why the men had been in the woods in the first place. Some said the men were hikers while others said they were out hunting. There were even some who claimed the men worked for Big Oil and had been out fixing the pipeline.

The only thing the reports matched on was the dates of the animal attacks. Mark Dunham had been killed a week ago; Jed Matthews last month. One of the articles mentioned a few sheep had also been killed, but said local authorities didn't consider it unusual, especially since grizzly bears and wolves were known to attack farm animals from time to time. She'd noticed that *bear* was used in the articles just as many times than the word *wolf*—if not more.

When she didn't find anything useful about the killings, she'd decided to read the email from Nate Corrigan again—the guy who had contacted the magazine about the supposed werewolf. It was cryptic at best. He claimed he had proof that a werewolf killed the two men, but he didn't want to say too much in an email. Apparently, Nate didn't trust the internet all that much. No surprise there. He was probably a conspiracy freak as well as a paranormal nut. Then again, ever since discovering the NSA really was reading everyone's email, maybe the conspiracy freaks had a point.

By the time she and Alex got their luggage and picked up the rental car, it was well after four-thirty. After spending hours on a plane, all Eliza wanted to do was go to the hotel and fall into bed. But when her stomach growled in protest at that idea, she suggested getting something to eat first.

As they drove around looking for a restaurant, Eliza took in her new surroundings. She'd never seen so much nature in her life. There were tall trees everywhere, both evergreen and ones she thought might be birch, which made the whole place seem less citified somehow.

Of course, she would have enjoyed the view more if it was warmer. It was the middle of May and there was still a light frosting of snow on the ground. Well, she was in Alaska. And if the trees and the cold weather didn't convince her, the moose standing in the middle of the road would have. He just stood there in the center of the highway that ran along the forest, looking at them with his big brown eyes as if wondering why they were getting in his way. She might be a big-time reporter from the city, but that didn't stop her from demanding Alex take about a hundred pictures of the big, adorable thing.

While Fairbanks wasn't huge in comparison to San Francisco, it was still bigger than she'd imagined. The buildings ranged from one-story wood and brick shops that screamed Alaska to modern multi-story industrial looking places that seemed like they could have fit right in at home.

Eliza would have loved to do some sightseeing, but when her stomach growled again, Alex suggested they cut the tourist stuff short and find a place to eat. There were dozens of the usual fast-food restaurants to be found, but rather than go to one of those, they decided on the quaint diner down the street from their hotel. She wasn't much of a diner person, but there was something about the rustic-looking log cabin that seemed inviting.

The place had the same rustic feel on the inside. It was all exposed logs and hardwood floors, and Eliza found herself smiling as she took in the snowshoes, wood skis, outdoor photographs, and wildlife paintings that hung on the walls. She might be up here on a wild goose chase, but that didn't mean she couldn't enjoy the local sights. Though she could do without all the moose heads and mounted fish—they were just plain creepy.

"Two?" asked the teenage girl behind the hostess desk. At Eliza's nod, she grabbed a couple menus from the stack in front of her and gave them a smile. "Right this way."

As she read over the menu a few moments later, Eliza's mouth started to water, and she was relieved when the waitress finally came to take their order. She decided on a cheeseburger and fries. Alex ordered the same thing, though he opted for onion rings instead of fries.

Taking a sip of the iced tea the waitress brought to their table a few minutes later, Eliza looked at the photographer. "So, how long have you been working at the magazine?"

"Almost two years now."

That took her by surprise. "You must really like it then."

He laughed. "It's not bad. I get to travel to a lot of different places, and the pay is decent."

She nodded. "You don't really believe in all this paranormal stuff, though, do you?"

It had been something she'd wanted to ask the photographer all day, but with her spending most of the flight on her laptop, and Alex listening to his iPod, she hadn't gotten the chance.

Across the table from her, Alex shrugged. "I don't know. I've seen some things on this job that make me wonder."

Her eyebrows rose. "But werewolves? That's a little far-fetched, don't you think?"

"Maybe," he agreed. "Maybe not. I've learned to reserve my opinion until I see all the facts."

She wasn't so sure about that, but she kept her doubts to herself.

"Have you always worked for *Paranormal Today*?" she asked.

Photographers tended to bounce around a lot, so when he shook his head, she wasn't surprised.

"Nah. I've worked for a lot of papers, even some of the big boys in LA, New York, and Dallas. But they all bored me pretty quick. No matter where I went, they always wanted the same pictures—politicians, crime scenes, and car wrecks. It gets old. That's why I like working for *PT*—you never know what picture you'll be snapping next."

Eliza wanted to ask what kinds of things he'd photographed, but the waitress came by with their burgers. The older woman gave them a smile as she set down the plates.

"Anything else I can get for you folks?" she asked.

"Ketchup?" Eliza asked.

The woman nodded. "There's a bottle on the table right behind you, sugar. Enjoy your dinner."

Eliza had expected the woman to bring her a new bottle of ketchup, or at least grab the one from the other table for them but instead the woman walked away. Maybe it was a diner thing. Or an Alaska thing. Either way, it seemed she'd be going to get her own bottle of ketchup.

Taking her napkin off her lap and placing it on the table, Eliza pushed back her chair. When the waitress told her there was a bottle of ketchup on the table behind theirs, she figured it was unoccupied, so she was surprised to see a man sitting there. And not just the average, run-of-the-mill guy she'd expect to find in a diner either, but a mouthwatering specimen of a man. She remembered reading in *Cosmo* that there was something different about Alaskan men, that living in the great white north made them more hunky and sexy. Staring at the man seated at the table, she could well believe it.

Thank God he was intent on whatever he was reading on the laptop in front of him because he'd think she was a freak standing there staring at him with her mouth hanging open. But damn, with that dark hair, chiseled, stubble-roughened jaw, and sensual mouth, how could any woman not be mesmerized?

Abruptly realizing how idiotic she must look, Eliza finally forced her feet to move. As she neared his table, the man looked up from his laptop and she felt her breath hitch as his gaze met hers. She'd never seen eyes like his before. Not quite brown, but not really hazel, either, the only way she could think to describe them was gold. Regardless, they were the sexiest pair of eyes she'd ever seen. The heat from them captivated her, pulling her into their depths, and suddenly she found it hard to breathe. Talking was completely out of the question.

When he lifted a brow in question, she finally

managed to break out of her trance.

"I, um, was wondering if I could steal your ketchup," Eliza stammered, her face coloring. "We don't have any," she added, glancing back at her table.

The man followed the direction of her gaze, his gold eyes settling on the photographer for a moment before he gave her a smile. "Sure."

Picking up the bottle, he held it out to her. As she reached for it, her fingers brushed his and she almost gasped at the sensation that swept through her. It was like she'd just gotten completely and thoroughly kissed. Her knees felt weak and there was a delicious little flutter in her tummy that left her breathless. It was also entirely possible that a slight purr had started between her legs, but she was too distracted to know for sure.

It was then that she realized she hadn't actually taken the bottle of ketchup yet. She was just standing there touching him like a doofus. She tried to cover her bizarre behavior by grabbing the bottle, but ended up almost knocking it out of his hand. They both fumbled with the thing before she finally gained control of it.

Heat rushed to her face. Could she be any more lame?

"I think your boyfriend's waiting for the ketchup," he said when she continued to just stand there.

Eliza's brow furrowed in confusion at the word "boyfriend," but then she realized he must be referring to Alex. She forced her attention away from the pleasant warmth that was indeed swirling between her thighs and gave him a smile. "Oh, you mean Alex. He's not my boyfriend. We just work together."

One eyebrow rose. "Really?"

Oh, God. Did he think she was trying to come on to him? Crap, she really needed to go back to her table before she did something else to embarrass herself. But she couldn't seem to make her feet move. She had a crazy urge to reach out and touch him again to see if that same sexual spark happened again. Resisting the impulse, she instead tucked her long, dark hair behind her ear. "But you're right. He is probably waiting for the ketchup."

Giving the man another smile, she forced herself to turn and walk back to her table. She had to focus hard just to get one foot in front of the other. But halfway there she couldn't resist glancing over her shoulder to take one more look at him. He was still regarding her with those incredible golden eyes of his, and her pulse skipped wildly at the intensity in that gaze.

What was going on with her? She'd never experienced anything like this in her life. She had to get control of herself. Giving him one more look over her shoulder, she turned and stumbled back to her seat in a daze, clutching the bottle of ketchup in her hand.

Across from her, Alex looked at her as if to say, what the hell is wrong with you? "You just going to sit there and hold that bottle all night, or can I use some?"

She blinked. "What? Oh, yeah. Sorry," she mumbled, handing it to him.

Eliza watched as the photographer dumped ketchup on his onion rings, then dug into his meal. She knew she should do the same, but she couldn't stop thinking about what had just happened. Her heart was still racing as if she'd just come back from a run. Or just had some really fantastic sex. Damn, all of that was from a mere brush of the fingers? She couldn't keep herself from wondering what it would have been like if he really had kissed her.

It was a long time before Eliza could focus on her food, and by then, she realized she wasn't really hungry anymore, at least not for food anyway.

* * * * *

God, she smelled incredible, Hunter McCall thought as the woman walked back to her table and sat down. With her big, dark eyes, full lips, and long, silky hair, she was gorgeous, but with his werewolf senses, scent was always the first thing he noticed about a woman. The second and third things, too. And she definitely had it in that department. The pheromones pouring off her were so arousing that just one whiff of them had his heart pounding against his chest and his cock beginning to harden.

Get a grip, dude. Another minute and you'll be over there humping her leg.

He tried to go back to what he'd been doing before she walked up and asked to borrow the ketchup, but he couldn't make himself take his eyes off her for long. He couldn't ever remember being so drawn to a woman before, especially not one he'd only exchanged half a dozen words with. But there was something about her that was alluring. How the hell had he lived in Fairbanks and not noticed her before?

He hadn't meant to chase her off with that comment about her boyfriend, but he was glad the guy with her wasn't anything more than a coworker. Of course, if he'd been thinking straight, once he found out the guy wasn't her boyfriend, he would have asked her to join him.

Hunter's cell phone rang, interrupting his thoughts. Picking it up from the table where he'd left it, he checked the display, then held it to his ear. "Luke, what's up?"

"I was about to ask you the same thing," his brother said. "When were you planning on calling and telling me you've got a rogue werewolf on your hands?"

Hunter's mouth tightened. How the hell had his brother found out about that? "Do you have to be so dramatic? It's entirely possible it's just a normal wolf attack, you know."

"Sure it is." Luke's voice was sarcastic. "You don't believe that, and neither do I."

Hunter sighed. His brother knew him too well, and Luke was too sharp to make a mistake about something like this. Hunter only hoped his father hadn't seen the newspaper articles, too. He wouldn't even bother to call and ask if Hunter needed help—he'd just show up. Hunter appreciated the close relationship he had with both his father and brother, but sometimes he got the feeling they didn't think he could take care of himself. Maybe it was just the pack mentality that came with being a werewolf, but his human side preferred to take care of the situation on his own.

"No, I don't," he admitted.

When he'd heard about the first attack, Hunter assumed it'd been a regular wolf, maybe even a bear. Though it wasn't usual for an animal to attack humans, it did happen occasionally. But then the police had called him in to take a look at the man's body. Even as old and chewed up as the victim had been, all it took was one glance at the size and shape of the big bite marks and he knew it hadn't been a bear. It was a wolf—a damn big wolf. Which meant it was almost certainly a werewolf. Of course, he couldn't tell the cops that.

Werewolves usually didn't go around killing people, for one really simple reason—they didn't want to draw attention to themselves or their kind.

It wasn't like there was a set of laws or anything that werewolves followed, but they'd been hunted enough throughout the centuries to know that exposure wasn't good for any of their kind. So, they'd learned to hide in plain sight. And if a rogue wolf was found messing up things for all the civilized Weres, it was everyone's responsibility to deal with him. Every Were knew that if you made enough fuss to alarm humans, then every werewolf in the area would come down on your head—fast and hard. That was why trouble with rogue werewolves was rare.

But this one had obviously missed the memo. He'd killed two men for no apparent reason, then left the bodies where they could easily be found.

"Do you think this werewolf is there because he's looking to challenge you for your territory?" Luke asked, intruding on his thoughts.

"It's possible."

Hunter didn't know why it bothered him and every other werewolf he'd ever known to have others of their kind set up camp too close by—it simply did. Unless it was family, of course. He never minded having his brother and father around. But anyone else? That was a problem. And even though Fairbanks was a city, it was surrounded by enough wilderness to make it the perfect location for a werewolf to live. Hunter should know since he'd fought off two other Weres in the last five years looking to move into the area.

Both of those cases had been obvious, though. The Weres had shown up, made their presence known, then instigated a fight. And in both cases, the other Weres had moved on after the fight. They liked Fairbanks, but not enough to bleed to death over it.

This one didn't feel like a Were looking for territory.

"But with both attacks taking place around the full moon, my gut tells me that I have a recently turned Were on my hands—one that isn't in full control of himself yet," Hunter told his brother. "If he's new and doesn't have anyone to teach him the rules, he may not even realize he's on another Were's territory."

"What are you doing about it?"

"Since they think it might be a wolf, the cops have asked me to come in as a consultant, but there's not much I can do until he strikes again. I'm hoping that if I can get to the next scene soon enough, I'll be able to track him."

"Do you want some backup?" his brother asked.

"Thanks, but I can handle it."

On the other end of the line, Luke let out a sigh. "Well, if you change your mind, let me know. I'll be on the next flight up there. Seattle is just three hours away, you know?"

"I know," Hunter said. While he didn't need backup, he appreciated that his brother was willing to drop everything to come and help him.

He frowned as he realized that the dark-haired beauty was heading toward the door with her coworker. Damn, she had an amazing body, he thought, admiring the way her curvy hips swayed as she walked. He'd been so caught up talking to his brother that he hadn't realized she'd even finished dinner.

"Luke, I gotta go. I'll talk to you later."

Hunter hung up without waiting for a reply, but by the time he got his laptop put away and tossed some money down onto the table to pay for his meal, the woman and her friend were long gone.

Damn. You snooze, you lose, dude.

Chapter Two

After checking into the hotel, Eliza and Alex walked around downtown, making the most of the opportunity of being in Alaska. The night was cold enough that Eliza could see her breath on the air. She shivered and shoved her hands in her pockets. She might have to buy a heavier coat if they were going to be here a while.

"This is so freaky," Alex said, glancing at his watch. "It's almost ten and the sun is still up."

Eliza had to agree with him. She was definitely going to have a hard time sleeping tonight. Half of her was ready to fall in bed while the other half insisted it wasn't tired in the least. It was beyond her how anyone could get used to this crazy daylight schedule, but all around them people were going about their business as if everything was completely normal.

Up ahead a big man with a set of broad shoulders stepped out of a shop. For a minute, she thought it was that cute guy she'd seen back at the diner, but when he turned her way, she realized it wasn't. Of course not—she couldn't be that lucky.

Eliza glanced over her shoulder at the diner down the street. Was the dark-haired hunk still there? Maybe she should ditch Alex and go back to see. She knew it was crazy, but she hadn't been able to think of anything but that guy since she'd borrowed the ketchup. She shook her head. She was here to do a story, not hook up with Mr. Alaska, no matter how gorgeous here was. Besides, it's not like there'd ever be any long-term potential there. She was only going to be in Fairbanks for a few days—a week at the most.

She pushed her silly crush to the back of her mind where it belonged and focused on work—or more importantly the question she'd wanted to ask the photographer ever since they boarded the plane back in San Francisco.

"Alex, I need some advice," she said.

He gave her a sidelong glance. "Shoot."

God, she hoped he didn't take this the wrong way. "Does Roger really expect me to investigate this werewolf sighting and write a truthful story about it? Since werewolves don't exist, that's going to be a problem isn't it?"

Eliza braced herself—she wasn't sure how deep into this paranormal crap Alex really was. But he only laughed. Well, at least he hadn't accused her of blasphemy for so much as suggesting werewolves weren't real.

"Roger expects you to write an article that will grab our readers' attention, but he doesn't want you to lie," Alex said. "How you do both is up to you."

She frowned. That wasn't very helpful.

Alex pulled up the collar of his coat, then shoved his hands in his pockets. "I probably shouldn't be telling you this, but some of the reporters at *PT* write their stories on the flight, then just tweak them a bit to fit the details when they get on the ground. It's none of my business what they do, but I think it's pretty crappy of them. So, if you're asking my opinion, there are ways to write an honest story and still make it suitable for publication in a paranormal magazine."

Eliza wasn't sure if that really answered her question any better.

The photographer threw her another look as he sidestepped a streetlamp. "A couple months ago, I went to the Florida Everglades with another reporter looking for swamp monsters some of the locals said they saw. It turned out that the swamp monsters were nothing more than a new species of harmless lizard. Jackson could have made up some crap about Komodo dragons roaming the Glades and being responsible for every person who went missing in the local area for the last decade, but he didn't. Instead, he reported what he saw, then let the reader fill in the gaps. If they wanted to think those lizards were swamp monsters, he wasn't going to tell them otherwise."

Because if every reporter who worked for *Paranormal Times* did that, the magazine would be out of business. When he put it that way, it sounded easy enough. But it was still underhanded, wasn't it?

"So, why didn't you give your number to that guy back there?"

Eliza jerked her gaze away from an intricately carved

totem they'd stopped to admire outside a native arts and crafts store to look at Alex in surprise. She practically had whiplash from how fast he'd changed subjects. "What guy?"

He snorted. "The guy at the diner you thought was so hot. And don't try and tell me you didn't think he was. I have two sisters—I recognize the look."

She stifled a groan. Had she been that obvious? She was trying to come up with an answer that wouldn't make her seem like a total loser when something suddenly struck her. What if Alex had asked because he was jealous? Crap. That was all she needed. One coworker already hated her—she didn't need another to dislike her, too.

She gave Alex a sidelong glance. He didn't look jealous. He seemed genuinely interested in her answer.

Eliza sighed and went back to admiring the carved wood. A bear climbed up one side, his big paws wrapped around the other, while fish and birds made up the rest of the totem. "I'm crappy when it comes to meeting men," she admitted as she lightly ran her fingers over the wood. "I tend to overthink everything and before I know it, I'm standing there going over all the things I could have said in my head while a guy who could be Mr. Right walks away."

Or in this case, Mr. Alaska.

"Ah." Alex leaned one shoulder against the side of the building. "You froze huh? I get that—same thing happens to me. I usually only realize I messed up the chance to meet someone pretty cool after I'm on my way home. Then I'm kicking myself for being so stupid."

Eliza smiled. No doubt, she'd be doing the same thing on the trip back to San Francisco. Which sucked. It was almost enough to make her vow to eat at the diner every day until they left on the off chance she'd see Mr. Alaska again.

* * * * *

He expected the people in downtown Fairbanks to run when they saw him, but they didn't. Probably because the demon inside had allowed him to go back to his human form. These sheep had no idea what kind of monster walked among them.

He'd awakened in the forest several days ago naked, cold, in pain, and disoriented. He couldn't remember exactly when his body had started to convulse and shudder its way out the demon wolf form and into his frail humanlike shape. But he remembered the agony— that he would never forget. It was like the demon who possessed him had crushed every bone in his body as a way of reminding him that his torture wasn't over. That it wouldn't be over until every one of those bastards who'd betrayed him had been sent to hell first.

The first time he'd been released from his beast form, he thought it meant his ordeal was over. But he'd barely made it back from the place where he'd been abandoned to his house outside of Fairbanks when he'd caught Jed's stench on the doorstep. Knowing that traitor had been there sent the demon into a rage, and the excruciating pain that came with being possessed was a small price to pay for killing Jed.

That was when he knew why he'd been allowed to escape from hell for a short time and bound to a demon's form. He was here to be an instrument of retribution and revenge. And he was impatient to find the next person on hell's list.

Though it was far from the protective seclusion of the forest he preferred, his instincts had led him to this part of town because this was where he knew he'd find his next target. Aiken Wainwright had always liked to come here looking for some unsuspecting tourist to swindle—or take to bed. His lip curled.

He smelled Aiken before he saw him, but he trusted his nose, so he followed the scent for several blocks. It led him to a crowded street he remembered well.

Aiken was strolling down the sidewalk on the other side of the street as if he didn't have a care in the world. This man had betrayed him...hurt him. The urge to run across the street and rip out the bastard's throat was so overpowering he started to tremble. He grabbed the lamp post to steady himself. He couldn't attack until the beast inside him returned, and he had no idea when that would be.

He ran his tongue over his teeth and felt the prick of his sharp canines against the sensitive flesh. Perhaps it wouldn't take nearly as long as he thought for the demon to come out. It almost felt like his body was ready to change again. He'd been forced to wait nearly four weeks between Jed and Mark. But now he felt the burning itch in his muscles that told him it might be much faster this time.

He was wondering if he should go somewhere less crowded in case the demon came back when he caught a tantalizing scent on the cool night air. He turned in a circle, trying to pinpoint where the smell was coming from. His eyes locked on a dark-haired woman standing outside a store two blocks down that sold carved totems. She said something to the man beside her that made the guy laugh, then they both started down the street. He instinctively followed, pushing people aside who got in his way.

He'd almost caught up to them when he stopped short. What was he doing? He was sent back to get revenge, not to chase after some woman—no matter how good she smelled. He clenched his fists, fighting the urge to scour the streets until he found her. He needed to deal with Aiken first. Then he'd come back and track down the woman.

* * * * *

This was hopeless.

Hunter had been sitting in front of his laptop for two solid hours with nothing to show for it. So much for the lesson plan he was supposed to put together for next semester. The detailed study of the migratory patterns of Alaska's herd populations was a completely new class to the curriculum and he had to turn in his proposal to the head of the department in two weeks. Hunter had been one of the leading proponents of adding it to the program, but every time he tried to get his thoughts on paper, his mind refused to cooperate. Instead of focusing on how caribou and moose moved about the state throughout the year, all he could think about was the gorgeous woman he'd met at the diner earlier.

He pushed back from his desk with a growl. He couldn't understand what had him so geeked up. Sure, the woman had been attractive. But he'd met lots of attractive women and never had this kind of response. What made her so different? Maybe those exotic dark eyes, sexy voice, and the way her ass had looked in those jeans as she walked away. Then there was her scent. Just thinking about how delicious it was had his cock stiffening in his pants—again. Well, technically, it hadn't really gone down since he'd laid eyes on the woman. But when he thought about her, his erection got really hard.

Damn, he seriously needed to get laid more often.

He glanced at the clock and saw that it was midnight. Maybe he should take a cold shower before going to bed. Right. Like that was going to help. Not even sitting in a bathtub of ice water could make him forget the woman responsible for his current condition—or soften his hard-on. Yeah, well sleeping like this was out of the question.

That left him with only one other choice.

Getting to his feet, Hunter headed for the back door. The night was cool, but not bad compared to the winter months. He stepped out on the deck and took a deep breath, loving the feel of the cold air entering his lungs and the frost that hung in front of his face as he exhaled.

He scanned the area, his eyes adjusting to the darkness and allowing him to see as well as if it were daytime. He didn't expect anyone to be wandering around in the woods behind his house, but he always checked just the same. Even in a place like this where people went out of their way to keep to themselves, someone might take notice of him walking around the forest naked.

But both his eyes and his nose told him there wasn't anyone around. He took off his boots, then jogged down the steps and toward the tree line. Along the way, he stripped off his shirt and jeans, leaving them hanging on the partially opened doors of his work shed. The frigid night didn't do anything to cool his arousal, but at least shifting into his wolf form would force him to focus on something other than his damn hard-on.

It had been a week since he'd last changed—when he'd gone out searching the area where the latest victim had been found. Unfortunately, there'd been so many cops around that he couldn't really focus on tracking the killer's scent very well. To make matters worse, those same cops had also kept him from cutting loose and running like he normally did.

Which was probably part of the reason he was so damn keyed up right now—and likely why he'd been so affected by that woman's scent.

A few hours of running through the woods and he'd be so freaking exhausted he'd fall into bed when he came back—hopefully with his head screwed on straighter than it was now. Because he was definitely going to need to be sharp for the fight that his gut told him was coming. If he was right, and the other Were was an out-of-control newborn, Hunter would be going up against pure animal instincts. His human intelligence could mean the difference between winning and losing.

Hunter dropped to his hands and knees the moment he entered the forest, digging his fingers and toes into the loose, pine-needle covered dirt. He arched and bowed his back several times, then stretched his neck back and forth until he heard it pop. It was a ritual he'd established over the years, something that helped him relax before starting the change.

Even though he could already feel the itch crawling

over his skin and the heat in his muscles that told him the transformation was starting, he didn't push it. If he'd wanted to, he could rapidly accelerate the process, but that was hard on the body—not to mention painful as hell. Not that taking it slowly made the change any more enjoyable. There was no way to reshape every bone in your body and have it feel good. But it hurt a lot less if you let the changes wash over you gradually.

The part that always morphed first were his shoulders and chest, quickly followed by his hips. Those were the biggest bones that had to reform, and the cracking and popping that came with it seemed to echo in the night. Hunter closed his eyes and forced himself to keep his breathing slow and steady.

He remembered the first time he'd gone through this. He'd fought every step of the way to maintain his human identity and it had hurt like the seven levels of hell. Far worse even than trying to speed up the change. It had taken him a while to learn that the process was a tidal wave of force. There was no resisting it; just acceptance. Try to stand up to a tidal wave, and you'll only get crushed—that's what his father had told him.

As Hunter's muscles rippled to catch up to the bone structures changing around it, spasms slid up the back of his head and along either side of his jaw. The most amazing thing about the transformation was that the drastic changes to his face and head hurt less than the rest of the shift. Even though his head was easily twice the size it was when he was human, and his ears moved to the top of his head, for whatever reason, those changes

44

weren't nearly as uncomfortable compared to everything else going on in his body.

His dad had told him that howling during the change made some werewolves forget about the pain. Hunter'd always thought that was a stupid and dangerous habit to get into. He'd checked before starting to transform, but that didn't mean someone hadn't wandered into the area during the process. He wasn't exactly very aware of what was going on around him when he was shifting. And howling like an injured wolf caught in a trap would only make a person come running. Especially in Alaska. There were a lot of hunters who set a lot of traps.

The last part of the change—fur growing thick and fast over his body—wasn't painful as much as it was freaky feeling. And sort of itchy.

Even though he hadn't pushed the shift, the whole thing didn't take more than ten minutes. But because he hadn't forced it, he wasn't sore, tired, or out of breath. That was the true benefit to taking your time—you didn't feel like a rented mule afterward.

Hunter checked around again, this time with senses that were several orders of magnitude more perceptive. But while he immediately picked up the sounds and smells of hundreds of animals large and small, he didn't detect any people. It was safe for him to run.

He trotted deeper into the forest, the sound of his steps barely discernable to his sensitive ears, even though he now weighed more than three-hundred pounds. Luke had once asked their father how it was possible for them to weigh more in wolf form than they did when they were human. Their dad had simply asked him how it was possible for a human to turn into a wolf. So much for stupid questions.

Hunter ran harder the deeper he got into the trees. He didn't have a destination in mind. He didn't care where he went. He simply let go and enjoyed the sensation of the wind ruffling his thick fur. Running like this was the most exhilarating feeling in the world. It always allowed him to work through whatever problems plagued him in ways he couldn't when he was in his human form.

But tonight, that clarity wouldn't come—no matter how far or how fast he ran. He kept going back and forth between the beautiful woman at the diner and the rogue wolf that was killing on his territory.

It wasn't hard to figure out why the other werewolf bothered him. It didn't take a wolf's instinctive understanding of the world to realize that this Were wasn't behaving like any other werewolf he'd ever heard about. That same instinct told him this Were was going to be harder to deal with than the previous werewolves he'd gone up against.

What he couldn't get a grip on was why the woman—one he'd talked to for less than five minutes— was still having such powerful effect on him.

As the miles rolled by, the images of the dark-haired beauty grew more vivid. Shit. This wasn't normal, was it? Maybe he should to talk to another werewolf about it. Like Luke. Or better yet, his dad.

No, they'd think he was losing it.

So instead, he ran until he couldn't run anymore.

He got home a few minutes before sunrise. He changed back into his human form, then pulled on his clothes and jogged up the steps into his house. But while he might be exhausted as hell, he wasn't any more ready for bed than he'd been before.

Chapter Three

Eliza and Alex were supposed to be at the diner to meet with Nate Corrigan the next morning, but that didn't stop her from looking around for Mr. Alaska. She'd spent the better part of last night dreaming about the man, and she couldn't get dressed fast enough when Corrigan suggested meeting here. Unfortunately, the gorgeous golden-eyed hunk didn't make an appearance the whole time she and Alex were having breakfast.

Finally, she gave up on waiting for him to walk in the door and kept an eye out for Nate Corrigan instead. She'd been a little surprised he wanted to meet them at the diner. She assumed he wouldn't want to talk about man-eating werewolves in public, but apparently she'd been wrong.

She sat up straighter when she saw a heavyset guy with a beard enter the diner. Now he looked like a man who believed in werewolves. She was about to tell Alex their contact had arrived when the man made his way across the room to join some friends. Okay, so that hadn't been Nate. It'd be a heck of a lot easier if Corrigan had told them what he looked like. But when she asked how she'd know him, he laughed and told her that wouldn't be a problem—he'd find her. She didn't know whether to be impressed or creeped out.

Two minutes after ten, a tall dark-haired guy with a light beard and mustache walked into the diner and surveyed the room. The second his eyes came to rest on her and Alex, he headed in their direction.

This was Nate Corrigan? Eliza studied him, comparing him to the preconceived notion she had of a guy who'd email *Paranormal Times* and report a werewolf on the loose. He didn't fit the image she had in mind at all. While he wasn't as big and muscular as Mr. Alaska, he didn't look like the kind of guy who hid in his mother's basement wearing a hat made out of tinfoil, either. In fact, he was sorta cute—in an adorable way.

The man stopped a few feet from the table to give her and Alex a thorough onceover—like he was trying to decide if they were the people he was looking for. He must have decided they were because he came over.

"Eliza Bradley? I'm Nate Corrigan." He held out his hand. "Nice to finally meet you."

Eliza smiled as she shook his hand. "You, too." She gestured to Alex. "This is Alex Decker, my photographer."

Nate shook Alex's hand. "I saw those photos you took of the gators in the Chicago sewers in the most recent issue of the magazine. You know your stuff."

Gators in the Chicago sewers, huh? Alex hadn't told her that story. She'd have to remember to ask him later.

She looked up at Nate. "Why don't you have a seat and we can talk over coffee?"

He glanced around the diner before shaking his head. "If you don't mind, I'd rather go back to my place. It's a little too crowded in here to talk about...you know. I have some stuff there I need to show you anyway."

Eliza exchanged looks with Alex. Her photographer shrugged. Clearly he was leaving the decision up to her. Go with the adorkable werewolf-hunter or insist they talk in a public place?

She glanced at Nate as she reached for her purse. "We could have just met at your house if you're more comfortable there."

"Yeah, sorry about that." Nate gave her a sheepish look. "But to tell the truth, I wanted to get a look at you first—make sure you weren't a bunch of weirdoes, you know? Can't be too careful."

Considering she'd been having the same concerns about him a few minutes ago, Eliza could forgive the guy's caution. Of course, if she'd been by herself there was no way in hell Eliza would have agreed to go back to his house with him, but with Alex along for back-up, she didn't see why she shouldn't.

"Alex and I will follow you in our car."

As they walked out of the diner, Eliza glanced at Nate. "Mind if I ask a question, Mr. Corrigan?"

"Go ahead," he said. "And call me Nate."

"How did you recognize us when you walked in the diner? We don't look like paranormal reporters, do we?"

God, she hoped not.

Nate laughed as he dug his keys out of his pocket. "Nah. I Googled you and Alex. Like I said, you can't be too careful."

Damn, she didn't even know she had a picture on the internet. What kind of reporter was she?

Nate led them out of town in an old, rugged looking pick-up truck. The guy might be paranoid about making sure he talked to the right reporters, but at least he didn't drive them around town three times checking for a tail. Then again, if she was the one who thought there was a bloodthirsty werewolf stalking people, she guessed she'd be paranoid, too. She'd be lying if she said she didn't get a little nervous the farther away from Fairbanks they drove. Maybe going with him hadn't been such a good idea.

Eliza was about to say as much to Alex when Nate pulled his truck up outside a small log cabin. Crap, he lived in the middle of nowhere. But then again, she'd grown up in San Francisco, so pretty much every house out here seemed like the middle of nowhere to her.

As Nate unlocked the door to the cabin and led them inside, Eliza tried not to gawk, but it was almost impossible not to. Apparently, werewolves weren't the only thing Nate believed in. The walls were covered with photographs of every conceivable creature out of legend: Bigfoot, the Loch Ness Monster, aliens, even a zombie. There were some display cases along one wall containing stuff that looked like it had come out of a *Ripley's Believe It Or Not* museum, too.

Her gaze fell on a shriveled orb. Oh God, was that a real shrunken head? She started to take a closer look, but then turned away. She didn't want to know.

Focusing her attention on the wall over the fireplace instead, she saw a large *X-Files* poster with the phrase "The Truth is Out There" written in bold print across the bottom. Man, this guy was serious about this stuff. She could just imagine how the conversation was going to go. He'd probably swear the werewolf was really a secret government agent sent to kill people who were a threat to the current administration. Then he'd pull out a complete set of those tinfoil hats she'd thought about before and insist they put them on so the government couldn't record their thoughts.

Why did she take this job again? Oh yeah, a paycheck.

"Here, have a seat."

Nate gestured to the couch along one wall, only to flush when he realized it was covered with so many old newspapers and magazines that there wasn't any room to sit. Moving quickly over to the couch, he gathered up the periodicals and set them down on the floor.

"Sorry about that," he muttered.

As Eliza edged around the coffee table, she glanced at the stack of magazines on the table. Nate was indeed an avid reader of *Paranormal Today*, as well as another magazine called *Strange Times*. She vaguely remembered seeing the name before. They'd been even lower down on her list of prospective employment than *Paranormal Times*. Thank God she never had to sink that low.

Seeing the direction of her gaze, Nate hastily grabbed the stack of *Strange Times* off the table and gave her an apologetic look that was seriously cute.

"These are old," he mumbled. "I meant to throw them out, but I guess I forgot. I don't even subscribe to *Strange Times* anymore. Not since I found *Paranormal Today*, I mean."

Eliza saw Alex's mouth twitch with amusement as a red-faced Nate dumped the stack of magazines on the floor beside the recliner. She didn't know much about *Strange Times* other than the name and their bad reputation. But from the man's embarrassment, she got the feeling it was one of *Paranormal Today's* competitors.

"Can I get you anything to drink?" Nate asked as he straightened.

"No, thanks. I'm fine," she said.

Nate might be nice, but the faster she got this interview over with, the better.

He looked at Alex, who shook his head. "I'm good."

Nate sat down in the recliner to the left of the couch. "So, how does this work? Do you ask me questions, or should I just tell you what I know?"

Eliza took her notebook and pen out of her purse. She probably wouldn't need to write anything down, but if she was going to be a reporter, she wanted to look the part.

"Let's start with the basics," she said. "What makes you think that the recent attacks were the work of a werewolf?"

Had she really just said that out loud?

Nate leaned forward in the recliner, his hazel eyes full of excitement. "How much do you already know about the attacks?"

"Just what I read online. Two men had been killed, supposedly from animal attacks."

He nodded. "Then you probably didn't know that both attacks took place during the full moon."

Huh. None of the articles had mentioned that. "Actually, I didn't," she admitted. "But go on."

"Well," he continued. "Animal attacks happen up here occasionally, so I didn't think too much about it—until I noticed that the attacks lined up with the lunar cycle. That's when I started doing a little investigating."

Getting up, Nate walked over to the bookcase and took down a cardboard box from one of the shelves. "I couldn't get near the site of the second attack where Mark Dunham was killed because the place was crawling with cops, so I went to the place where the first attack happened instead. As you might expect, there wasn't much there—not after a month. But I did find this."

He reached into the box and came out with what looked like a tuft of dark fur. At least Eliza thought it might be fur—it could have just as well been a piece of an extra fuzzy toupee.

"I found this in a tree about five feet up. Only way a piece of wolf fur gets that high is if you're dealing with a seriously monstrous-sized beast—at least twice the size of any normal wolf you see around here."

He held out the piece of fur—or whatever it was—but she waved him off, so he handed it to Alex instead. At least her photographer was nice enough to seem interested.

Now that she looked at it more closely, she realized the chunk of hair definitely hadn't come from some poor guy's toupee. It was too silky looking for that. But she wasn't ready to admit that it was werewolf fur, either.

"How do you know that's not a piece of bear fur?" she asked. "They're big, right?"

Nate frowned. "It's not bear fur. Anyone can see that."

Her skepticism must have shown because Nate snorted.

"Playing the doubting reporter, huh? I get it. Well, I have to admit that I wanted to make sure myself. I figured the werewolf might come back to the scene of the crime, so I set up a camera with an infrared trigger. When I went to check a couple days later, this is what I got."

He reached into his box of goodies again and whipped out an 8x10 photograph, then handed it to her. Eliza wasn't sure what she expected to see, but she was surprised to find herself gazing down at a slightly blurry picture of a gray wolf.

She lifted her gaze to Nate. "It's a wolf."

"A werewolf," he corrected.

Eliza gave him a dubious look. "How can you be sure it's a werewolf?"

He held out another picture. "Because *this* is a wolf taken a day later at nearly the same location."

Beside her, Alex leaned in for a closer look.

Eliza went back and forth, comparing the two photos. The second wolf was lighter in color than the first and easily half the size. If the trees around it were any indication, the wolf was still bigger than most dogs she'd ever seen, but nothing like the first beast. That one was huge in comparison.

"I also found tracks." Nate took out a third photo and handed it to her. "The things were as big as my hand. Deep, too."

She glanced down at the picture of the wolf again. "Nate, don't you think if this were a werewolf, it would look more like—"

"The Hollywood version?" He shook his head. "I know that *Paranormal Today* was probably hoping for a full-on Lon Chaney Jr. show, but that's not the way it works. Sorry to burst your bubble, but when a werewolf changes into a beast, it's a complete transformation—man into wolf."

Eliza glanced at Alex to see what the photographer thought of all this, but he was sitting there with a completely neutral expression on his face that suggested he heard this kind of stuff every day. Then again, Alex had been working for the magazine a long time. He'd probably heard hundreds of stories way freakier than this one.

The only problem she had now was trying to figure out where to go with the interview. Unless Nate had more pictures to show them, they were done here. Damn, maybe she should have done some background research on werewolves so she'd have more to talk about. She didn't want Nate to think she was dissing him.

"You seem to know quite a bit about werewolves," Alex prompted, giving her a small smile.

"With our Native Alaskan population, we have our fair share of shapeshifter and skinwalker legends. Stories of men and woman who can change directly into wolves is pretty common up here."

Eliza took notes as he told them some of the local legends. Nate was clearly knowledgeable about the stuff and she figured she might need the background information to help write the story Roger expected her to deliver when they got back to San Francisco. And the way Nate spun, it sounded fascinating.

"Fortunately for us, there are a few ways to identify a werewolf when he's in his human form," Nate said, drawing her attention back to him. "For starters, his brows will be heavy and will likely meet over the bridge of his nose. As you can probably image, he'll have a lot of excess body hair. His canines will be elongated. His eyes will be strangely compelling, almost mesmerizing, and women will be hopelessly drawn to him, regardless of the body hair issue."

Eliza had a hard time suppressing a laugh. It was hard to believe that a guy who was as intelligent as Nate seemed to be could believe all this stuff. "Really?"

"Definitely," Nate said. "While in human form, the man will have a nearly insatiable sexual appetite—women will literally be following after him in a daze. And it goes without saying that he'll eat lots of red meat and be prone to violent rages."

Eliza didn't bother to write that last part down, seeing as the werewolf was supposedly going around killing people. But she nodded anyway. Except for the legends about shapeshifters and skinwalkers, the interview had gone pretty much as she feared. They were now officially on the lookout for a hairy, horny hunk with hypnotic eyes, a unibrow, a harem of women, and a tendency for violence.

She held up the photos. "May I keep these?"

He glanced down at the pictures. "Sure—it's why I printed them."

She tucked her notebook and pen in her purse, then got to her feet and extended her hand to Nate.

"We can never thank you enough for all your help," she said as he walked them out. "You've definitely given us a lot to work with."

"I'm glad I could help. But if you don't mind me asking, were you planning to investigate this sighting any further, or will you be writing your story based purely on this conversation?"

His question caught her off guard and for a moment she stood there staring at him like a near-sighted opossum. Mostly because she'd been wondering the same thing a little while ago. She couldn't admit to that to him, though, especially since the idea of doing that still didn't sit right with her.

"Um…no. Of course we're planning to look deeper into your story," she finally got out. "I was just thinking about digging into the two victim's background a bit, perhaps talk to the police and see whether they've established a connection between the two men who were killed."

Nate eyed her appraisingly, then nodded. "That's a

good idea. I actually never thought about the possibility that the werewolf might be going after specific people. It's an interesting angle."

From where he stood slightly behind Nate, Alex was smiling at her. What the heck did he think was so funny?

"Thank you," she told Nate, ignoring her amused photographer. "*Paranormal Times* prides itself on doing a complete and thorough job when we cover a story."

"I know." Nate grinned. "That's why I prefer your magazine over all your competitors. So, do you have any contact in the local police department?"

Once again Eliza was left speechless by a question she hadn't seen coming. Behind Nate, Alex was trying hard to hide the smile threatening to overwhelm his face.

"Um…actually, no," she admitted. "I thought I'd just stop by and flash my press ID."

"That's one approach," Nate said. "Or I could head over with you and introduce you to a few friends in the department who will actually talk to you."

Eliza was hesitant to involve Nate any further in her story. He was a nice guy, but he seemed a little out there. But what choice did she have? She might have come up with the idea of talking to the cops on a whim, but in reality, it *was* a good plan. And unless she wanted to go back to the hotel and write the story now—which she didn't—talking to the police was the most logical thing to do next. Hell, for all she knew, she might actually find a real story buried underneath all this werewolf crap.

But she had no contacts in Fairbanks and it sounded like Nate did, which meant she needed his help.

"You really know some people in the department?" she asked. "Not like a dispatcher or secretary, but someone who really has information on the victims and the case?"

He grinned again in a way that told Eliza he probably knew he had her off balance at the moment. "Uh-huh. And some of them actually carry weapons and do police work. My offer to introduce you stands. Unless you'd rather try your cold-call approach."

Was he calling her bluff?

Eliza stifled the urge to scream. She should just go ahead and write the stupid story with the information she had and be done with it. Alex wouldn't judge her and Roger wouldn't even know. She could legitimately describe the murders, weave in the bits about the legends Nate had told them, then drop in a judicious mention of the wolf fur and the photographic evidence and let the magazine's readers draw their own conclusions. Like the other reporters at *Paranormal Times* did.

But the journalist in her wouldn't allow it. She didn't want to be that kind of reporter—even if she did work for a paranormal magazine.

She smiled at Nate. "I'd love if you could introduce us to a few of your contacts at the Fairbanks police department."

Chapter Four

As they walked into the police station, Eliza wished she had a real press ID—one with a newspaper name not related to ghosts, werewolves, and Elvis sightings. If Nate really didn't have any contacts down here, she'd be forced to flash her ID and pray nobody actually took the time to read it.

But within thirty seconds of stepping inside, their paranormal sidekick introduced them to several officers—all of whom honestly seemed to know Nate. He was asking one of the men how his pregnant wife was doing when he caught sight of someone behind her and Alex.

"Hey Tandi," he called. "I've got someone I want you to meet."

Eliza turned to see a uniformed female officer walking into the main room, a mug of steaming coffee in her hand. Tall, with dark eyes and a pretty smile, she wore her dark hair in a bun.

"Tandi, this is Eliza Bradley and Alex Decker. They're reporters from San Francisco," Nate introduced as they walked over to her desk. "This is Tandi McGee."

Tandi regarded them curiously over the rim of her mug as she sipped her coffee. "Reporters from San Francisco, huh? That's a first."

"They're hoping to get an inside look at the recent murders," Nate explained, lowering his voice. "I mentioned that I know some people at the station who might be able to help them out."

Eliza didn't get a chance to see what Officer McGee thought of Nate's blatant request because just then a man in a suit and tie came out of a side office and walked over to them. Dark-haired and tall, he carried himself like he was a man used to being in charge.

"You're not bothering my officers again, are you, Nate?" he asked.

"He wasn't bothering me, Lieutenant," Tandi said quickly. "Nate just met these reporters on the front steps and was nice enough to show them in. They're up from California to do a story on the animal attacks."

Tandi made the introductions this time, telling the lieutenant—Fred Newman—that they were from one of the big papers in San Francisco.

"Lieutenant Newman is in charge of the investigation," the female officer told them.

While Eliza was thrilled to have a chance to talk to the cop investigating the killings, she was also a little worried. If there was ever a person who would immediately demand a reporter's identification, it was this guy. But Lieutenant Newman was not only ready to take her at her word, but was more than willing to talk to her, too. That was a shocker. Hadn't anyone ever told him that cops were supposed to distrust reporters?

Before she knew it, Tandi was leading Alex and Nate off to a break room for coffee while Newman took Eliza into his office.

"I have to admit I'm a little surprised that a paper from San Francisco would send a reporter all the way up here for a story," he man said as he motioned for her to sit down in one of the chairs in front of his desk.

Eliza took a few seconds to come up with something that wouldn't sound like she was there to sensationalize the death of those two men. She wanted Newman to think she was after something deeper than that—which she supposed she really was.

"Northern California has had a few animal attacks of their own recently, and it was devastating for the communities where it happened," she lied. "My editor thought our readers would be interested in hearing how a place as rugged and remote as Fairbanks deals with these kinds of events. Not just at the emergency responder level, but also at the community and individual level. Sort of a lessons learned approach."

He nodded. "That sounds like a very worthwhile effort. I'll be glad to help in any way I can."

Eliza pulled out her notebook and collected her thoughts, pushing aside the fact that she worked for a paranormal magazine and trying to think of this as a real story. If she was writing the article she'd just described, what would she ask a cop like Newman?

"I know from other news articles that the deaths were attributed to animal attacks, but none of those articles ever specifically mentioned what kind of animal," she said. "Was it a wolf?"

Newman sighed. "One of our local experts says it's a large wolf, though I think it could just as likely be a bear. The wounds seemed too large for any wolf I've ever seen around here."

Eliza's mind momentarily flashed on the image of the big wolf Nate had shown her. That thing had certainly seemed big enough to leave a devastating bite. Just the thought of it practically had her shuddering.

"Do animal attacks like this happen often here?"

"Probably more than in other places," Newman admitted. "But that's because we're so close to the wilderness out here. Overall, it doesn't happen a lot, though. And when attacks do occur, they rarely result in a fatality. I guess that's why these two deaths are drawing so much attention."

She jotted a quick note about that. "Is this a case of humans encroaching in areas where animals aren't used to running into them?"

Newman shook his head. "I wish it was that simple, but no. It seems like those men were just in the wrong place at the wrong time."

"But the attacks occurred in the same general area, right?"

"Not really. The first victim—Jed Matthews—was out on a morning hike. The second victim—Mark Dunham—was out hunting in an area nearly thirty miles away. Both attacks happened miles north of town, but that's about the only thing they have in common as far as location."

Eliza tried to imagine what it would be like to be out in the open with so much wilderness around you. It sounded scary to her. "That seems like a large amount of territory for a single animal to roam."

"At first, we thought so, too," he said. "We initially thought the attacks were completely unrelated, but our expert is pretty adamant that both men were killed by the same animal. Unlike us, he wasn't surprised by the large separation between the attack sites."

She frowned. "What would make an animal attack a person like that, do you think?"

Newman shrugged. "Maybe it was injured. Or the men backed it into a corner and provoked it in some way."

That really didn't make a lot of sense to her. The beast had obviously been healthy enough to cover a thirty-mile range, and if there was so much wilderness out there, how could those men corner it?

"Those are the only reasons?" she persisted.

"I'm sure there are a lot more, but I'm not an expert on the subject," he said. "If you want some better insight into the behavior of wolves, you probably need to talk to Dr. Hunter McCall. He's a zoology professor in the university's wildlife biology department. He's the expert we've been using as a consultant on the case. He's pretty smart about the wildlife in these parts."

She wrote the name down in her notebook. "I'll do that. Thank you."

They talked for little while longer about animal

attacks in general, and the kind of steps the local emergency responders took to deal with them before Eliza led the conversation to the one area she was really interested in—whether there was a connection between the two dead men.

Newman lifted a brow as if he thought that idea was the dumbest thing he'd ever heard. "A connection between two men attacked by animals?"

She shrugged. "I thought that if there was, it'd resonant with the readers and allow them to think of this in terms of more than just two random acts of violence."

The lieutenant considered that. "I guess I'll just have to take your word on all that. I'm a cop, not a reporter. But as far as a connection between the two victims, about the only link I know of is that both men occasionally worked part time for a local company called Wild Alaska Adventures. They served as tour guides and instructors for people hiking and camping in the area."

Eliza sat up straighter. "So they knew each other?" And no one thought that was strange?

He let out a short laugh. "Most people in Fairbanks do. We've only got about thirty thousand residents in the town itself. And most people involved in outdoor activities tend to move in the same circles. Hell, I've been hunting and fishing with both those men a couple times myself."

Coming from a big city like San Francisco, she couldn't image what it'd be like to know everyone in it. Newman gave her the address and directions to the wilderness outfit where the men had worked, though he admitted he wasn't sure what they'd be able to tell her.

Eliza thanked him, then went looking for Alex and Nate. She was on her way to the break room she'd seen them heading for earlier when a door along the hallway opened and Tandi stuck out her head.

"There you are." She grinned. "We thought Newman was going to keep you half the day. Come on in."

Eliza expected to walk into a break room, so she was surprised when she saw that it was a small office of sorts, complete with filing cabinets and computers. Alex and Nate were seated at the small table in the center of the room poring over what looked like incident reports and photos from the crime scenes.

Huh. She hadn't thought the cops would let them get a look at the official police records, regardless of what Nate said.

"Get anything useful out of Newman?" Nate asked.

"Maybe." Eliza chewed on her lower lip as Alex picked up a photo and looked more closely at it. She glanced at Tandi. "Not that I don't appreciate you letting us look at this stuff, but I'm not used to police being so open with reporters."

"I'm only doing this because Nate vouched for you and said that none of this information would end up in your story," Tandi said.

Apparently, Nate had more clout with the Fairbanks PD than she'd given him credit for. Tandi must have seen her shock because the female cop smiled.

"Most of the cops in the department think of Nate as sort of a quasi private investigator. He's helped us out on a few cases—missing persons, kidnapping, runaways, burglary, even a few murders."

When Tandi's gaze slid to Nate, there was admiration in her dark eyes, along with something that looked an awful lot like fondness. If Eliza didn't know better, she'd think the cop had a thing for Nate.

"He just has a way of figuring things out that the other cops and I miss," Tandi continued. "If he thinks there's more going on with these animal attacks than it appears, we're willing to listen to him."

Eliza regarded Nate again, trying to look at him through Tandi's eyes. Could this paranormal conspiracy nut be onto something?

"Go ahead," Tandi said, jerking her head toward the table. "I'll guard the door."

Eliza couldn't look at the photos of the victims without feeling sick, so she stuck mainly to the written reports. They were concise and to the point. The two men had been attacked by a large animal in the woods, end of investigation. Besides working for the same company and knowing the same people, there was nothing else linking Mark Dunham and Jed Matthews.

"This is a waste of time." Across from her, Nate closed the folder, then looked at the cop. "What we really need is to get a look at the second crime scene." He gave her a grin. "What do you say, Tandi?"

Eliza didn't think that was such a bright idea, but at least Nate had a plan. She, on the other hand, didn't have a clue what to do next. She supposed she could go back to the hotel and write a completely fabricated piece of crap story dripping with werewolf innuendo like the other reporters at *Paranormal Today*. Or she could write a real story about how two men in a city like Fairbanks could end up dead from a wolf attack, and how the whole world passed it off as back luck and kept on going. Were they living in a world so jaded that even two deaths like these were considered so commonplace that they barely merited more than a line or two in a few papers?

Roger wouldn't think much of that kind of story, but maybe if she played this right, she could write one story for *Paranormal Today* and still put together another piece she'd be proud to put her name on, then sell it freelance somewhere else. At least that way, she could look herself in the mirror after this trip was over.

But if she was going to write a real story, she was going to need a lot more information. She wondered if she should talk to this Dr. McCall first and get some serious background on wolf behavior, or whether she should check out Wild Alaska Adventures and find out how well Jed Matthews and Mark Dunham knew each other.

She decided on the latter. She wanted to put off the boring task of stopping by the university to hear some old, fuddy-duddy professor ramble on about animal behavior as long as possible.

By the time she checked back in mentally, Nate had somehow convinced Tandi to take him out to the scene of the second attack. He'd even talked Alex into going with them. She thought Alex would have been smart enough to point out how foolish—and potentially dangerous—Nate's plan was.

"You're not seriously going with them, are you?" Eliza asked in a low voice as they followed Nate and Tandi outside.

"Yeah. I need to get some photos for your story anyway," Alex said. "Trust me, you'll be glad to have them when the time comes."

Eliza wanted to tell him she could do without the photos, but she knew he'd just go do it anyway. Alex was a guy, and guys could be so dense sometimes.

"Just be careful out there, okay?" she said softly. "It might not be a werewolf, but there's definitely something out there killing people."

* * * * *

While Newman's directions to Wild Alaska Adventures were easy to follow, navigating roads that had partially frozen slush in some places was difficult. Eliza almost put the rental car in the ditch more than a few times.

Fortunately, the drive out to the wilderness camp was worth it. There were quite a few people there who'd known both Jed Matthews and Mark Dunham. Every one of them told her how shocked they'd been to learn the men had been killed by an animal considering they'd been such skilled hunters. Dunham had even been carrying a rifle at the time. While that was interesting, Eliza was more curious about how well the men knew each other.

"Jed and Mark?" The bearded man she was talking to

snorted. "They were practically best friends."

And the cops hadn't considered that relevant? Why would they? The men had supposedly been attacked by a wild animal. But the more people she talked to, the harder it was to accept the coincidence of two men who knew each other so well being killed by the same wild animal—on different days, miles apart. There had to be a story here that the cops weren't seeing.

"Do you know where Jed and Mark hung out when they weren't at work?" Eliza asked a blond man with a goatee.

His brow furrowed as he considered that. "They used to go hunting, mostly. But they had a few bars in town they went to regularly. And a barbeque place called Buck's, too."

"Do you know which bars?"

The man named a few places in the section of town where she and Alex had gone sightseeing last night. Maybe they could hit up a few of them tonight.

"The last few weeks, though, Jed and Mark stopped hanging out together as much," the blond man added.

Eliza looked up from her notepad. "Did they have some kind of fight?"

He shrugged. "Don't know for sure, but something happened between them."

That sounded like it needed further investigating. When she got back to the car, Eliza texted Alex to let him know what she'd learned and that she was heading over to the University of Fairbanks to talk to Professor Fuddy Duddy.

Chapter Five

Hunter swore under his breath as he realized he'd been staring down at the same essay paper for the past ten minutes. He was supposed to be grading the tests he'd given that afternoon in his animal behavior class, but he was still thinking of that woman. She'd grabbed hold of him and wouldn't let go no matter how hard he tried to shake her.

After his midnight run, he'd fallen into bed hoping to get an hour or two of sleep before coming to work. But every time he closed his eyes, all he saw was her. If it wasn't that long, dark hair, it was her lush, curvy body. When it wasn't either of those two things, it was those full, pouty lips of hers that begged to be kissed. Even her mind-blowing scent had refused to fade away. Like her image, it seemed destined to be locked in his mind forever. Just the memory of how good she'd smelled was enough to make him uncomfortably erect.

He'd ended spending the few hours before coming to campus staring up at the ceiling fantasizing about making love to the woman of his dreams. He'd had one erotic vision after the other—her on her hands and knees in front of him while he took her from behind; her on top, riding up and down on him for hours on end; him on top with her legs wrapped around him while he drove himself deep inside her.

It had been pure torture. When the alarm finally went off, he'd been grateful the night was over so he had an excuse to get up and go to work.

Unfortunately, his distraction hadn't ended just because he had a job to do. Hunter shook his head as he stared down at the essay paper on his desk. Oh, the hell with it. He marked an "A" on the top of the paper and moving on to the next. But he didn't pay any more attention to it than he had the first.

He bit back a growl. What the hell was wrong with him? He'd been attracted to other women before, especially when he was younger and just learning how to deal with his change. But it had never been like this.

Maybe he should call his dad to ask if this was some kind of bizarre werewolf mating thing. What if he was going through the male version of being in heat? This had to be some sort of chemical reaction. What else could be this strong?

Shit. He could smell her pheromones even now.

His dad had never really talked about werewolf mating stuff, but Hunter knew enough about wolves in general to know that bonding was a huge issue for them. The beasts were known to mate for life and absolutely no one had ever figured out how they chose their mates.

What if he and the woman from the diner had some kind of wolf-based connection? It wasn't that much of a stretch. Because right now it seemed like his body wasn't going to let him rest until he saw her again.

Like that was ever going to happen. The woman could have been a tourist. If so, chances were good that she wasn't even in Fairbanks any longer.

He tossed down his pen. God, he'd been so stupid. He should have said the hell with his laptop and the bill and gone after her. She'd been attracted to him. He had seen it in her eyes, smelled it on her skin. So, why had he let her get away? Because he was a moron, that's why. Of course, if he had chased after her, he probably would have only embarrassed himself. What would he have said? *You smell better than any woman I've ever met. Want to come back to my place so I can hump your leg?* She would have looked at him like was some kind of pervert.

A knock on the door jerked him out of his misery. Thank God.

"Come in," he called.

He must be worse off than he realized because when the door opened, he could have sworn he saw the woman from the diner standing there. Not only was he imagining her scent, but he was seeing things now, too.

Only he wasn't seeing things. She really *was* here. How the hell had she found him?

Hunter had always thought his brother was full of crap when he said werewolves gave off a pheromone that made them irresistible to some females. But maybe Luke was right. Maybe she'd subconsciously followed that pheromone back to him.

Or maybe she was here for another reason entirely.

Right then, he didn't care which. This time, he wasn't letting her get away.

* * * * *

Mr. Alaska—the gorgeous hunk of a man she'd borrowed ketchup from at the diner last night—*was* Dr. Hunter McCall?

Eliza took in his golden eyes, chiseled features, and broad shoulders. Damn, he was even more handsome than she'd remembered. The attraction she'd felt back at the diner was just as intense, and she had to fight the uncontrollable urge to run over and touch him to see if they'd give off that same spark.

"May I help you?" he asked.

She felt her face color as she realized she'd been standing in the doorway staring at him like the same ditz she'd been last night. Sheesh, he was really going to think she was an idiot. "Um, you're Dr. McCall?"

"That's me." He gave her a half smile. "Were you expecting someone else?"

Actually, she had. "No... I mean yes... Well... It's just that I thought you'd be...older."

His gold eyes danced with amusement. "I see. Well, I hope you're not disappointed."

Disappointed? Hardly. "No, of course not," she said quickly. What was she here for again? Oh yeah, the story. "My name's Eliza Bradley. I'm a reporter doing a story on those men who were killed out in the woods. Lieutenant Newman suggested I talk to you. He said you'd be able to give me some insight as to why an animal might have attacked them."

The corner of his mouth edged up. "And here I was hoping you'd been so fascinated with me after we'd met at the diner last night that you'd spent the entire day tracking me down just so you could see me again."

Eliza let out an embarrassed little laugh. If she could have figured out a way to track him down, she would have.

Before she could say something suitably witty in reply, he continued. "So, are you with the *Miner* or the *Sun*?" he asked, referring to the local papers.

Though still deep and sexy, his voice had taken on a more professional note, which reminded Eliza again of the real reason she was there to see him. Closing the door behind her, she walked across his office to sit down in the chair in front of his desk. She took a deep breath and forced herself to focus on the story instead of how absolutely incredible he looked.

"Neither, actually. I'm with the *San Francisco Chronicle*."

The name of her old newspaper slipped out before she realized it. But even if she could take it back, she wouldn't. He'd never talk to her if he knew she worked for a magazine that specialized in monsters and freaks.

Hunter lifted a brow. "And they sent you all the way to Alaska to cover an animal attack? It must have been a slow week for news in San Francisco."

She gave him a small smile as she took out her notebook and pen. "It seemed like it was newsworthy, I guess."

He nodded. "So, what kind of information are you looking for?"

It was difficult to concentrate sitting this close to him, and it took her a moment to gather her thoughts. "The police mentioned you believe the two victims were attacked and killed by a wolf. Why do you think that?"

He sat back in his chair. "I told them that a wolf was the most likely scenario. Some people suggested it was a bear because the wounds were so large. To someone who hasn't seen a lot of animal bites, the bite pattern of a very large wolf could certainly resemble that of a bear. But when you look more closely, the wounds are very different."

Eliza was so hypnotized by his deep voice she almost forgot to ask him the next question—the same one she'd tried to get Lieutenant Newman to answer.

"What would prompt a wolf to attack a person?"

Hunter was silent for a moment. "Wolves only usually attack if they're provoked or if they feel threatened in some way. A female would attack to protect her pups. A male would attack to protect his pack. But even then they'd have to be backed into a corner. Because while they may be predators themselves, their natural instinct is still to run from humans."

Eliza frowned. That sounded exactly like the explanation Newman had given. "How do you back a wolf into a corner in the middle of the woods?"

He shrugged. "It's impossible to say. One would have to think like a wolf to answer that question."

Well, that wasn't any help. "The police reports said the bite marks were extremely large. How big would a wolf have to be for a bite that size?"

"Extremely large. Female wolves are usually about four- to five-and-a-half feet in length. Males tend to be around six-and-a-half feet. The bite marks indicate it was a much bigger animal than that, perhaps somewhere in the eight-to-ten feet in length. Wolves that big are rare, and never come this close to a major city."

Eliza tried to image what a wolf that large would look like, but she didn't have any basis for comparison. "Do people have to be concerned that this wolf is going to become a man-eater now that he's attacked humans?"

His mouth twitched. "You've seen a few too many movies. Aged and injured lions have been known to turn into man-eaters in Africa, but there's never been a case of that happening with a wolf. Besides, according to the autopsy reports, the two men weren't eaten—just mauled and killed."

That didn't sound any more pleasant to her. She chewed on her lower lip thoughtfully. "But if the wolf isn't a man-eater, don't you think it's an odd coincidence that two men who knew each other were attacked miles and miles apart? What's the likelihood of both of them backing the same wolf into a corner?"

He frowned. "I hadn't realized the men knew each other. But I'm not sure it's really a factor. Wolves rarely attack humans, and when they do, it's even rarer that they kill. The fact that the two men knew each other and were killed miles apart simply make something statistically rare even more rare. Wrong place, wrong time."

Maybe. But it still seemed odd to her. Eliza glanced down at her notebook and saw that she'd asked Hunter all her questions. Well, damn.

She eyed those broad shoulders of his from beneath her lashes as she tried to come up with another question. For a college professor, he was seriously built. Maybe he went to the gym a lot. Suddenly, images of him all hot and sweaty from a vigorous workout flashed into her head. She had a mini-fantasy of walking up to him as he lay back on some piece of exercise equipment and straddling him. Now that was a workout she wouldn't mind getting.

On the other side of the desk, Hunter was still talking about wolves and their behavior in the wild compared to wolves in captivity. Crap. She hadn't heard a word he said.

Eliza closed her notebook. "Thank you for taking the time to speak to me, Dr. McCall. Your insight has been very helpful."

He flashed her a grin. "Anytime. And please call me Hunter."

She smiled back. "Okay. Hunter, then."

Reluctantly stowing her notebook in her purse, she got to her feet. Hunter stood and came around the desk. She was tall for a woman, but even with the added inches from the chunky-heeled winter boots she was wearing, the top of her head didn't quite reach his chin. This close, he seemed even more muscular, too. It was hard not giving in to the urge to reach up and give his shoulders a squeeze.

She held out her hand instead. "It was nice meeting you."

Eliza had to bite her lip to keep from moaning as his hand closed over hers. If she thought the current that passed between them yesterday had been amazing, it was nothing compared what she was feeling now. As the warmth from his touch seeped into the palm of her hand, she swore she felt a tingle between her legs. But that was crazy. It wasn't possible to get aroused from shaking hands, was it?

As she gazed up into his incredible gold eyes, she saw her own arousal mirrored in their molten depths, and she realized that he felt the connection, too. For one wild moment, she thought he was going to kiss her, but instead, he roughly cleared his throat.

"Um, do you want to grab something to eat?" he asked.

"Eat?" she echoed.

The corner of his mouth edged up in a sexy smile. "Yeah, eat. As in dinner."

Eliza flushed. How could one man put her so off balance like this? "I'd love to."

"Great. I just need to send an email, then we can go."

While Hunter did that, Eliza shot off a quick text to let Alex know she wouldn't be around for dinner, then spent the rest of the time looking around Hunter's office.

A floor-to-ceiling bookcase filled with everything from books on animal anatomy to those on philosophy took up one whole wall, while another had framed photos of wolves in their natural habitat. Looking at the beautiful animals, it was hard imagining them killing a person.

"Ready to go?" Hunter asked.

She turned to find him standing behind her. His nearness made her pulse go haywire, and it was all she could do not to reach out and grab his arm to steady herself.

"I should probably ask before we leave." He glanced at her as he locked up. "You eat meat, right?"

She nodded. "As a matter of fact, there's this place in town called Buck's I wanted to check out."

Actually, she'd planned to go there with Alex so they could do some investigating, but he wouldn't mind if she went with Hunter instead. Besides, in between asking the locals what they knew about the two dead men, Hunter could give her some more information on wolves and how they acted. That would come in handy—on both stories she was going to write.

That was her excuse, and she was sticking to it.

Chapter Six

"I have a confession to make."

On the other side of the table, Hunter gave her a curious look as he tipped back his bottle of beer. "What's that?"

"I didn't really want to come to Buck's for the food." Though the smoked chicken she'd ordered was delicious. "I wanted to come here because I heard Jed Matthews and Mark Dunham hung out here. I thought I could ask around and see if anyone might know anything."

"Ah." Hunter set the bottle down on the table. "You really think there's a connection between their deaths?"

Eliza shrugged. "I know it sounds crazy considering they were attacked by wolves, but yeah."

He regarded her thoughtfully. "I could ask around if you want. The locals are more likely to talk to me than a reporter from San Francisco."

"I appreciate the offer, but that wasn't why I told you."

He smiled. "I know. That's why I offered. Besides, I'm just as curious to see if there's a connection as you are. Who told you that Jed and Mark came here anyway?"

"The guys who worked with them at Wild Alaska Adventures. They said Jed and Mark hung out together all the time. The two men had some kind of falling out a couple weeks ago, but no one knew what it was about." She had the glass of iced tea halfway to her mouth when a thought hit her. "That makes me wonder. According to them, Jed and Mark used to go hunting together all the time. What if they tried to kill this wolf when they were out on one of their hunting trips, and the animal remembered them?"

Hunter glanced at her as he speared a piece of steak with his fork. "And you think the wolf is out for revenge?"

She sipped her tea. "I know that sounds insane. I mean, animals don't think that way, do they?"

"No. Revenge is strictly a human thing."

"That's what I thought." Eliza sighed. "I guess I'm back to square one then."

She and Hunter continued to speculate as they ate. And although their server had waited on Jed and Mark a few times, the woman didn't know much more about the two men other than that they were good tippers.

"Sorry that wasn't much help," Hunter said as the waitress left with their empty plates. "I hope you don't think the evening was a complete waste."

Looking at the sinfully attractive man across from her, Eliza decided that any time she spent with Hunter definitely wouldn't be a waste.

She smiled at him over the rim of her glass. "Not at

all. I'm having a great time."

He grinned back at her. "Me, too."

The same heat she'd seen in his eyes earlier was back, and Eliza felt her breath hitch. "So, are you originally from Alaska?"

He nodded. "My brother and I grew up in a tiny town to the southwest of here called McGrath."

She scrunched up her nose, trying to place the name. "I don't think I've ever heard of it."

"When I say it's tiny, I'm not exaggerating. There are only about four-hundred people. You can't even get there by road."

"You're joking."

His mouth twitched. "I'm not."

"Then how do people get to the place?"

"Plane," he said. "Or dog sled."

Crap. He was serious.

She shook her head. "And I thought Fairbanks was remote."

He chuckled. "You really are a city girl, aren't you?"

"It's that obvious, huh?" she teased. "Do your parents still live in McGrath?"

"My dad does. He loves the place."

"What about your brother?"

"Nah. Luke lives down in Seattle."

Eliza rested her chin on her hand, studying him from across the table. In the restaurant's soft lighting, Hunter's eyes looked even more gold. "What was it like? Living in a place that small, I mean."

"I thought it was great," he said. "Life there was like

one long snow day. Well, except for the fact that school never closed. But that was okay because we got to take a snowmobile there and back."

"Snowmobile, huh? Sounds like fun."

"You've never been on one?" he asked.

She shook her head.

Hunter grinned. "Not much call for those in San Francisco, I guess. I could take you riding while you're here, if you want?"

Was that his way of asking her out on a second date? "I'd like that."

Despite being a city girl—as Hunter put it—Eliza had to admit that growing up in McGrath sounded like a ball. Or maybe he just made it sound that way. Being snowbound and isolated from the rest of the world didn't seem so bad when he talked about it. Eliza couldn't help but notice that while he mentioned his father and his brother several times during the conversation, he didn't say a word about his mother. Eliza wanted to ask, but didn't want to pry into something he obviously didn't want to discuss.

"Have you ever been down to the states?" she asked instead.

"A few times," he said. "Washington State and Oregon mostly. I even made it down to California once. But Alaska is the only place that feels right for me, so I always come back."

She could understand that. If there was ever a man built for this rugged frontier, it was Hunter. Cold weather looked good on him.

As they finished their second cup of coffee, he smoothly maneuvered the conversation around to relationships. Eliza casually mentioned that she wasn't seeing anyone at the moment.

"What a coincidence," he said. "Neither am I."

She had no idea why that thrilled her so much. It wasn't like they were going to date long distance or anything. But hearing there wasn't another woman currently in his life made her pulse do a little happy dance anyway. And if the way his eyes glinted was any indication, he was equally pleased that she wasn't seeing anyone, either.

Eliza didn't realize how long they sat there talking until the waitress pointedly slid the check she'd left earlier a little closer to the center of the table and asked if there was anything else they needed—before they headed out.

"Do you want to stop by some of the other places where Jed and Mark hung out?" Hunter asked as they left the restaurant.

Eliza wasn't sure if it'd be worthwhile, but with Hunter along for company, it would at least be fun.

She was right on both accounts. While everyone they talked to remembered Jed and Mark, no one knew what the two men had fought about, or even if they'd fought at all. And although she didn't learn anything useful, she enjoyed herself more than she had in a long time. Who knew she'd have to come all the way to Alaska to find a guy she clicked with?

She and Hunter were heading to the last bar on her list when they ran into Alex, Nate, and Tandi coming up the sidewalk from the opposite direction. The cop had changed out of her uniform and was wearing jeans and a sweater. She looked different with her hair loose around her shoulders.

The photographer's gaze darted briefly to Hunter before he gave her a knowing grin. "Got your text and thought you might be down here. Find out anything useful."

Eliza shook her head. "Not really."

She made the introductions, starting with Alex and finishing with Nate.

He nodded his head in Hunter's direction. "Hey, Professor. Good seeing you."

Eliza looked from Nate to Hunter and back again. "You two know each other?"

"I've audited a few of his classes," Nate said. "He does a whole series on predator behavior that I find really fascinating."

Eliza tightened her grip on the shoulder strap of her purse. Crap. What if Nate started talking about werewolves and his crazy X-Files theories? Even worse, what if he told Hunter that she wrote for *Paranormal Times* and that they were all working together to find the beast? She'd be so mortified she'd likely melt into a puddle on the spot.

Thankfully, Nate controlled himself and waited until the pleasantries were over with before politely pulling her aside to tell her what they'd discovered out in the woods. Tandi wandered over to listen in, leaving Alex to entertain Hunter on his own.

"We found the place where the werewolf killed Dunham pretty easily," Nate said.

Even though he spoke softly, Eliza still glanced over her shoulder to make sure Hunter hadn't overheard. But he and Alex were deep in conversation.

"Did you find anything interesting?" she asked.

"More than I expected," he said. "I'm starting to think you might be onto something with your idea that these were targeted attacks. The werewolf stalked Dunham through the woods for nearly two miles before he chased him. Even then, the beast kept toying with him. That doesn't sound like a raging monster that simply attacked the first human it stumbled across."

Eliza looked at Tandi, trying to figure out how to ask her if Nate was exaggerating without actually *asking*. Luckily, the cop read her mind.

"I wouldn't have believed it if I hadn't seen it, but Nate found the wolf's tracks about fifty yards off to the side of Dunham's trail. It was pretty obvious that this big-ass thing was shadowing Dunham for a long time."

Eliza turned wide eyes on Nate. "You can track a wolf—and a person—through the forest for two miles?"

He shrugged. "I had a lot of Native Alaskan friends growing up. We practically lived in the woods. Tracking a monster-sized wolf and a man who'd been hitting the bottle pretty good isn't all that hard."

It would've been hard for her.

Eliza glanced at Hunter. He and Alex were talking as if they'd known each other for years. Hunter must have felt her eyes on him because he turned and flashed her a grin. She smiled back.

"Maybe Dunham saw the beast. Or maybe the werewolf just got bored following Dunham," Nate continued. "Either way, once it decided to finally go after him, the poor guy didn't have a chance."

"The evidence tags showing where Dunham had shot at the wolf were still out there," Tandi said. "Even drunk, the man got off at least a half dozen shots at the thing before the wolf took him down, but the gunfire didn't look like it slowed the creature at all. Even I have to admit it's more than a little weird that this thing wasn't afraid of gunfire. That's not how animals behave."

"Neither was the way this monster went at Dunham," Nate added.

Eliza frowned. "What do you mean?"

Tandi was the one who answered. "Once Nate pointed out what the tracks meant, it was easy figuring out how the last few moments of the attack went down. The thing disarmed Dunham first, then viciously attacked him. The blood was still there—and it was everywhere. The wounds weren't severe enough to kill Dunham right away, though. Just maim him so he couldn't get away."

Eliza shuddered, but Nate picked up the story before she could say anything.

"Then the werewolf sat back on his haunches and watched as Dunham tried to drag himself to safety. " He shook his head. "The guy was tough. He made it a good hundred feet across the forest floor."

"While the wolf played with him the whole time," Tandi said, not even bothering to hide her revulsion. "We found large blood splatters every twenty feet or so. It was like the creature tore into him again and again."

"Dunham died within a hundred yards of his truck," Nate finished. "And the ending was just as vicious as the rest. This wasn't an animal attacking a person—this was a monster murdering another human being in the most cruel, painful way he could come up with."

Chills ran down Eliza's back. She didn't know much about animals, but this didn't seem like a traditional attack to her. Maybe it was her imagination, but there seemed to be a menace to these killings that sounded all too human. She wasn't ready to believe there was a werewolf running around the Alaskan wilderness, but her gut told her a human was behind this.

"We ran across an old woman living in a small cabin not too far from where Dunham was attacked," Tandi said. "No one in my department even knew she was there, so we never talked to her, but she said there's been something strange running around those woods out there for well over a month—since before Matthews was killed."

"Whatever it is, it scared all the other animals away," Nate put in. "She hasn't seen a raccoon, mink, deer, or rabbit since the werewolf moved into the area. Which means it's probably living nearby."

Eliza shuddered. "Will the old woman be safe out there?"

Tandi sighed. "I tried to talk her into staying with family or friends until we catch the wolf, but she refused to leave. I'll make sure someone checks on her regularly."

That was something, Eliza supposed. She only hoped the poor old woman wasn't the wolf's next victim.

Alex, Tandi, and Nate left a little while later, saying they were going to grab something to eat at the diner. The sun had started going down while they'd been talking and darkness was settling over the downtown area. Eliza looked at her watch in the glow of a street lamp and saw that it was almost eleven. This really was the land of the midnight sun.

Hunter must have taken her time check to mean she was tired. "You want to hit some more bars, or would you rather go back to your hotel?"

Eliza couldn't help but wonder if that was a come-on line. Hunter wasn't looking at her as if he expected her to invite him back to her room, though. She was pretty sure they weren't going to learn anything more about the two men who'd been killed no matter how many bars they went to. But she didn't want the evening to end yet. She was enjoying Hunter's company way too much.

"I think I'm done investigating for tonight," she said. "I'd rather just walk around some, if you don't mind?"

He smiled. "I don't mind at all."

Now that the sun had gone down, it was even colder than before, and Eliza shivered.

"Cold?" Hunter asked.

She nodded and shoved her hands in her pockets. "I think I'm going to have to buy a heavier coat."

"Well, until you get one, let's see if I can keep you warm," Hunter said.

Eliza was about to ask what he had in mind when he

wrapped one muscular arm around her shoulder.

"Better?" he asked.

She smiled and snuggled closer to the warmth of his body. "Much."

Most of the stores were closing up, but Hunter didn't seem to mind when she stopped to window shop on the way. Eliza was so caught up in how right being with him felt that she didn't realize he hadn't said anything in a while. She looked up from the painting she was admiring in the gallery's front window and saw him staring off into the distance. No, not staring—sniffing the air.

She took a quick sniff, but couldn't smell anything. Hunter sure as hell looked like he could, though—and he didn't seem to like it.

"Is everything okay?" she asked.

He jerked. "What?"

"You look like you smelled something."

"Oh." He gave her a smile. "I thought I smelled something burning."

Eliza sniffed again, but still couldn't smell anything.

"It was nothing." His arm tightened around her. "You're starting to shiver. Come on. Let's get you back to your hotel."

She would have preferred to spend more time with Hunter, but she *was* getting cold. Hunter turned the heat in his SUV up to high the moment they got in, and while the toasty air warmed her up, it also made her suddenly realize how tired she was. She stifled a yawn.

"How long are you going to be in Fairbanks?" Hunter asked, pulling onto the street.

"I'm not sure," she admitted. "At least a week."

He glanced at her. "Maybe we can get together again? Go for that snowmobile ride, or something."

Or something. She smiled. "I'd like that."

"Me, too." He flashed her a grin. "I'll call you."

Even though Eliza told him he didn't have to, Hunter walked her to her room when they got to the hotel.

"I had a good time tonight," she said.

His mouth curved. "So did I."

She chewed on her lip, toying with the keycard in her hand. Should she ask him in? God, it was tempting. But she'd always been crappy at one-night stands and wasn't about to embarrass herself by asking Hunter to spend the night only to fall asleep on him. She stifled a moan. That image was definitely going to give her very sweet dreams.

* * * * *

He was leaning against a building waiting for Aiken to finally drag his drunk ass out of the bar across the street so he could kill the asshole when he picked up that same captivating female scent he'd smelled last night. It didn't take him as long to lock on which direction it was coming from, and he swore under his breath when he saw she was once again with someone. It wasn't the man from last night, though. This man was taller and more muscular. He had no idea why, but seeing them together made the demon possessing him let out a snarl.

He ground his jaw and forced himself to take a deep breath. That was when he picked up the man's scent. It was vaguely familiar, but he couldn't remember where he'd smelled it before. His memories were a tangled mess—like a movie reel of someone else's experiences that had been spliced together all out of sequence. He could barely make sense of the images most of the time—darkness, rocks, falling, cold so complete that he couldn't feel most of his body, pain so horrible that just the memory of it made him want to beg for death.

The only thing he ever seemed to be able to remember for very long was the violent urge he had to kill the people he'd come back for.

But those urges receded into the background and instead, he followed the couple. The man led the woman around several blocks in way that made the demon inside him think the stranger had picked up his scent and was trying to locate him. He wasn't sure how that could be—unless the man was possessed like him. Is that why he was with the woman? Did she somehow have a scent that made her alluring to demons like him?

He would have tracked them all night if it meant finding out the answer to that question, but a few minutes later, the man and woman got in an SUV and drove off. He watched through narrowed eyes as they disappeared around a corner. It was probably just as well. He didn't want to risk a confrontation with the other demon until he'd done what he came here for. Unfortunately, Aiken wasn't making that easy on him. Unlike Mark and Jed, Aiken didn't look like he'd be venturing into the forest anytime soon. That meant he was going to have to go after the man on his own turf. After Aiken, that would leave only one more person to kill.

He crossed the street and headed for the forest. For the first time since this nightmare started, he began to think there might be some purpose to his tortured existence—other than getting revenge.

The dark-haired woman was meant to be his. No doubt, he would need to kill the other demon to have her, but what was one more death on his hands?

* * * * *

It was damn hard not inviting himself into Eliza's room when they got back to the hotel, especially when he could smell her arousal. The scent was so intoxicating, it felt like he was drunk. But he'd picked up the rogue Were's scent when they'd been walking around downtown and he needed to track the guy while it was still fresh. So, he'd said goodnight when all he really wanted to do was lose himself in Eliza's heady scent and hauled ass back downtown.

Unfortunately, both the rogue werewolf and his scent were long since gone.

Shit.

Hunter drummed his fingers on the steering wheel. What the hell had the werewolf been up to? The damn thing had been tailing him and Eliza for at least thirty minutes, but had been too smart to let Hunter get a look at him. It wasn't like the guy was going to challenge him—not in the middle of town.

He cranked the engine and headed out of town. He'd already checked out the scene of the werewolf's second kill, but after overhearing everything Nate and Tandi had told Eliza earlier, he wanted to take a closer look at the surrounding area. The drive took almost an hour, and when he got there, he parked his SUV in the closest pullout, then hiked into the forest on foot.

It wasn't hard to find that small cabin where the old woman lived. She was right when she said something had been roaming around out here. The rogue werewolf's scent was all over the place. That meant he hadn't just wandered through the area on his way somewhere else. He spent time here—a lot of time. The woman was right about the werewolf scaring off the other animals, too. Hunter couldn't smell another living creature for miles.

It was like the werewolf was living out here. But why? It didn't make any sense.

Hunter turned to head deeper into the woods when a ragged howl coming from the east stopped him in his tracks. He spun around, the hair on the back of his neck standing up. That wasn't the howl a regular wolf made. It was the sound a werewolf made in mid-change. The strained sounds coming from partially formed vocal cords were unmistakable.

Hunter stripped off his clothes as he ran toward the sound. He hated to force his body to change quickly—it hurt like hell—but he didn't have a choice. If wanted to get a look at this killer—maybe even end it right now—he needed to get there before the thing was fully formed. If he was a newborn, it would take a long time for him to change. That would give Hunter the advantage.

Hunter let as much of the shift happen as he could while he ran. Only when his arms, legs, and spine began to crack and twist did he drop to the ground. Even then, he pushed hard, forcing his body to take the shape it was used to assuming at a more sedate pace. Pain tore at him, but he ignored it and clambered to his four feet to keep moving as soon as he could.

His nose led him straight to the other werewolf, a big black beast standing in the middle of a fir-shrouded clearing. Hunter had come in downwind, but it didn't matter since the other Were could hear him coming. While the beast might be gasping for air and drooling saliva, it had completed the change and was standing there ready to fight. He was smaller than Hunter, but had the whipcord appearance that meant he'd be fast as hell.

Hunter bared his teeth at the other werewolf. Across the clearing, the black beast did the same. After this creature had prowled his territory for nearly two months and killed two men, it was finally going to come down to a fight.

Hunter launched himself a split second before the other Were did the same.

The moment they met in mid-air, Hunter knew without a doubt that the guy had just recently turned. It fought by pure animal instinct, biting and clawing without thought. Only it was like no animal Hunter had ever seen. Even the most savage animal calculated its best options. This werewolf didn't do any of that. There was no rational thought, no reasoning, not even an attempt to set Hunter up for a good strike. It simply snarled and snapped at him. It was like the human half of the pairing had completely disappeared.

It wasn't until Hunter skipped aside, then darted in to sink his fangs deep into the black werewolf's flank that the creature seemed to finally realize it was fighting another werewolf that could kill it.

That was when the man inside finally came alive. Without hesitation, the beast turned and ran.

Hunter followed, but the black werewolf ran like it fought—without reason and without thought. It smashed through tree branches thick enough to tear open its flesh and jumped from rocky heights tall enough to break bones. Somehow, it managed to do neither.

Hunter wanted to end this, but he wouldn't kill himself to do it.

Still, he had more skill than this creature when it came to running through the woods. He also knew that this could turn into a long chase, so he conserved his energy and chose the best route that would allow him to catch up to the psychotic beast.

He actually started to close the distance, but then the other Were turned aside from his previous course and bolted in a completely different direction—away from Hunter—and straight toward the nearest highway.

What the hell was the thing doing? The route ahead was a logging and mining road. Hunter could hear the big trucks and heavy equipment moving up and down it, even at this time of night.

Intelligent animals, including werewolves, avoided heavily congested highways. Even a three-hundred pound werewolf would lose a fight against a ten-ton truck. Worse, the men and women who made their living driving these roads were a tough bunch. Most carried guns and they knew how to use them.

Hunter couldn't catch the other Were before he

reached the highway, so instead, he slid to a stop and watched as the crazy thing ran right through the middle of the oncoming trucks.

Horns blared and tires squealed as trucks slid every which way. Unbelievably, the creature somehow made it all the way across the wide road despite getting his hindquarters clipped at least once.

The black werewolf disappeared into the thick trees on the far side of the road as pissed off drivers climbed down from their trucks, shouting and cursing the animal.

Hunter ducked deeper into the woods on his side of the road. He didn't want some sharp-eyed trucker seeing him and taking a couple of shots at him. He had enough trouble. He wasn't simply going up against a rogue werewolf that enjoyed killing—he was going up against an *insane* rogue werewolf that enjoyed it.

PAIGE TYLER

Chapter Seven

Eliza woke up to the sun shining through the curtains. Damn, she'd forgotten to close them last night. Apparently, she'd also forgotten to set the alarm on her phone. Squinting against the brightness, she rolled over to see how late she'd slept and groaned when she saw the time—four-thirty. There should be a law against the sun coming up this early.

She turned her back to the window and snuggled into her pillow to get some more sleep, but it was useless. Her body was ready to get up regardless of the time on the clock. She might as well get some work done.

She took a quick shower and was just opening her laptop when her cell phone rang. Guess Alex couldn't sleep, either.

But the number on the call display didn't belong to Alex. It had a Fairbanks area code. Not Hunter, though. His number was programmed in her phone. Nate, then?

She held the phone to her ear. "Hello?"

"Eliza? It's Tandi McGee. I didn't wake you, did I?"

"No. I've been up for a while. What can I do for

you?"

"Good. Nate told me that you and Alex were having a hard time adjusting to all this daylight, but I wasn't sure," Tandi said. "I have a couple hours before work and thought you might want to grab a cup of coffee."

Eliza grinned. It might be too early for the sun to come up, but it was never too early for coffee. "I'd love to."

"Great." Tandi named the same diner where she and Alex had met Nate the other day. "That way we can grab breakfast, too. See you in thirty minutes."

After she hung up, Eliza almost went to her contacts list to call Alex and tell him she was using the car, but stopped herself. She didn't want to wake him if he was sleeping, so she sent him a text, then shoved her laptop in her messenger bag and grabbed her coat.

Thirty minutes later she was in the diner sitting across from Tandi, breathing in the rich aroma of coffee.

"So, what time did the sun wake you up?" the cop asked, looking at her over the rim of her mug.

"Four," Eliza said. "I don't know how you stand it."

Tandi laughed. "You get used to it. Just be glad you're not here in winter when we only get a few hours of sun a day."

Eliza groaned. She hadn't thought about that. That much darkness would be miserable.

Tandi studied her as she set down her mug. "Nate told me that you work for *Paranormal Today*."

Thank God the waitress appeared with their breakfast because Eliza didn't know what to say to that.

She wasn't sure if she was more embarrassed that the cop knew what she was really there to investigate, or more angry at Nate for telling Tandi.

On the other side of the table, Tandi smiled. "Hey, I'm not judging here, okay? I mean, I hang out with Nate. He's shown me a lot of things over the years I can't explain, that's for sure."

That sounded a lot like what Alex had said the other night. Eliza poured maple syrup on her waffles. "But a werewolf? That's what Nate thinks killed those men."

"I know." Tandi spread orange marmalade on her toast. "I like to think I'm the kind of cop who does things by the book. If the evidence suggests those guys were killed by a big wolf, that's probably the answer I'd go with."

"But?"

Tandi hesitated before she continued. "But I've seen some really strange stuff since I've been on the job, and what Nate showed me in the woods doesn't match with the department line that we're dealing with a rabid wolf. That damn thing stalked and tortured Dunham. It did the same to Matthews."

"So, you do believe there's a werewolf out there," Eliza said.

"I trust Nate's instincts, but I'm still not ready to go that far. Yet." Tandi sighed. "But I definitely think there's more going on here than my lieutenant thinks. And I'm not the only one. Some of the other patrol officers aren't buying it, either."

Eliza sipped her coffee. "What are you going to do

about it?"

Tandi shrugged. "I'm going to keep helping you, Nate, and Alex dig into this case and hope you find something the rest of the police won't be looking for."

Eliza doubted very much it was going to be a werewolf, no matter what Nate's instinct's said. But she didn't tell Tandi that.

She speared a piece of waffle with her fork and ran it through the extra syrup on the plate. "Can I ask you something?"

Tandi nodded.

"What's the deal with you and Nate? I know you're friends, but I get the feeling there's something more between you two."

Tandi froze, a forkful of scrambled eggs halfway to her mouth, a stunned look on her face.

Eliza sat back. Oh, crap. Being a reporter meant sticking your nose where it didn't belong some of the time, and this was one of those times.

"I'm sorry," she said quickly. "I shouldn't have asked you something so personal. Let's just forget I said anything and go back to talking about werewolves."

Which would lead right back to Nate. Damn.

Tandi shook her head. "No. It's okay. You're right. Sort of." Her lips curved into a small smile. "Nate and I have known each other since we were kids."

"And you've always liked him," Eliza said.

The cop nodded. "Yeah. But in some ways, the man can be so clueless. I think it's because we've been friends for so long. Nate just doesn't see me as a woman."

Eliza doubted that. She'd seen the way Nate looked at Tandi. More likely he was too nervous to make a move on a woman as confident and outgoing as Tandi. Especially if things were complicated by an existing friendship.

"Maybe he just needs a nudge," Eliza said.

"More coffee?"

Eliza smiled at the waitress. "Thanks."

"Okay, enough about me and my friend without benefits," Tandi said after the waitress left. "What about you and the hunky professor?"

Now it was Eliza's turn to pause. "What about us?"

"Don't try and deny it." Tandi popped the last of the toast in her mouth, then pushed her plate away. "I'm a cop. I'm trained to be observant. And I saw the way you were looking at him last night. You're dying to get him into your bed."

Tandi didn't pull any punches, did she? Then again, Eliza had asked about her and Nate first. She hadn't realized she'd been so obvious about being attracted to Hunter.

"Do you think Hunter knows?" she asked.

"Probably not. Men are clueless when it comes to women, remember?" She picked up her mug. "If we don't hit them over the head with stuff, they never figure out anything out."

Eliza couldn't argue with that, though in Hunter's case, she got the feeling he'd eat her right up if she gave him the okay.

"Are you going to hit Nate over the head with it and

let him know what you want?" Eliza teased.

Tandi sipped her coffee. "Maybe—if you agree to make a move on Professor McCall."

Eliza stuffed another piece of waffle in her mouth so she wouldn't have to answer. She'd already milked this assignment far longer than her boss had probably intended. She and Alex probably weren't going to be up in Fairbanks much longer. Did she want to start a fling with a guy—even one as hot as Hunter—if she was going to leave in a few days?

"You should go sit in on one of his classes," Tandi suggested.

"Right." Eliza snorted. "Nothing says stalker like showing up where a guy works and staring at him while he does his job."

Tandi laughed. "Okay, maybe. But this is different. Everyone does it around here. Just say that you're doing more research for your story."

More like research on the perfect male body.

Tandi glanced at her watch. "I gotta get to the station. Go sit in on a class the professor's teaching. The university puts the schedule up on their website."

"I'll think about it," Eliza said.

As she sat there finishing her coffee, Eliza had to admit Tandi's suggestion had its merits. She could use a little more background information on wolves for her story. At least that's what she told herself as she pulled up the university's website on her phone.

* * * * *

Eliza was pretty sure that at least a third of the people sitting in on Hunter's class weren't officially on the roster. She could tell because they were all woman, they weren't taking any notes, and they were staring at the professor in dreamy contentment.

She'd actually written stuff down in her notepad, so she only qualified for two out of three of those characteristics.

It was no surprise that women flocked to his class. Between his good looks, gorgeous body, and mesmerizing voice, Hunter probably had women lining up for days to get in here.

Hunter's topic for the day was wolves and pack behavior. It was some fascinating stuff, especially the part about what happens when a pack tosses out a male wolf for misbehaving. According to Hunter, when a wolf lost his pack, he could essentially go nuts. Wolves needed a pack, even a loosely aligned one, to maintain their balance. Could that explain why this wolf had killed those men?

After class was over, Eliza waited patiently while Hunter talked to a group of girls who hung around to discuss a project due later in the semester. The girls were so busy gazing into his eyes they probably didn't hear a word he said. Not that it mattered. Eliza had a sneaking suspicion the whole thing was just a ploy. Kind of like her sitting in on his class? She cringed. When she put it that way, it was kind of embarrassing. Hopefully, Hunter was as clueless about women as Tandi seemed to think.

"I didn't expect to see you here."

Eliza jerked her head up to see Hunter grinning at her. The girls had left. They were alone.

She smiled and tucked her hair behind her ear. "I remember you saying you were teaching a class about wolves this morning, so I thought I'd stop by and get some more details for my story."

He nodded. "And did you?"

"Definitely. I never realized wolves were such social animals."

"They're a lot like dogs in that regard," he said. "Wolves, and wild dog packs for that matter, have a social structure a lot like primates. They have leaders—male and female—soldiers, hunters, scouts, nurturers, protectors, and teachers. In many ways they're more advanced than primates, but people just refuse to see it."

Eliza opened her mouth to ask how he'd learned so much about wolves, but before she could get the question out, Hunter posed one of his own.

"Want to see some wolves up close and personal? I have a friend who runs a private wolf recovery sanctuary just north of town. You'll learn more in a few hours there than I could teach you in a year."

She'd gladly go anywhere with him if it meant getting to spend more time with him. "I'd love to. If you're free, I mean."

He closed his laptop. "I have class later, but I'll let my teaching assistant take over. He's been begging for me to let him teach more on his own anyway."

They were just heading out to the parking lot when

her cell rang. Eliza dug it out of her purse and thumbed the answer button as quickly as she could. God, she really needed to change that ringtone. Downloading LMFAO's *Sexy and I Know It* had seemed like a cute idea back when she was a fact checker buried deep in the bowels of the *Chronicle*, but it wasn't nearly as cute having it play in front of someone she wanted to impress—like Hunter.

It was her editor, wanting to get a status update on the story. She put her hand over the phone and looked at Hunter. "I have to take this."

At his nod, she smiled her thanks and moved further down the sidewalk for some privacy. She definitely didn't want him hearing any of this conversation.

"How's the story coming?" Roger asked.

Eliza chewed on her lip. Crap. He wanted an update, and she didn't have a clue what to tell him. Did she think there was a werewolf killing people up here? Hell, no. But if she told Roger that, he'd fire her in five seconds flat and she'd be walking all the way home from Alaska. She wished she could tell him the truth. The problem was, she didn't know what the truth was in this situation. But if she wanted to stay up here long enough to actually figure out what was really going on, she was going to have to put the best *Paranormal Today* spin on the situation.

"I don't think we're dealing with two random werewolf attacks," she told him.

"We're not?"

"No." She took a deep breath. "I don't know how to say this without sounding crazy, but I think this werewolf is targeting very specific people. Those two men weren't killed on a whim. They were hunted down and torn to shreds. This was personal."

There was silence on the other end of the line. "Do you have proof?"

"Not exactly. More like a hunch," she said. "The two men were supposedly good friends up until a few weeks ago. No one knows what they fought about, but it was obviously something big if it broke up a friendship."

"So, where does the werewolf come in?"

"I'm not sure yet," she admitted. "But he tortured both men before he killed them. Which also sounds crazy, I know, but I've seen the crime scene photos."

"You have?" Roger sounded genuinely surprised.

"Yeah. I have a police contact who thinks there's something going on and is helping me."

"Good work. Anything else?"

"Nothing concrete," she said. "According to an old woman who lives out the woods, this thing has been hanging around the area for at least a month and a half. Yet the only two people who have even seen it are the dead men. My gut tells me there's something going on here."

"I knew you were a real go-getter." Eliza could almost see her boss grin. "What's your next move?"

"I'm meeting with an expert on wolf behavior right now—a professor at the university. I thought he might be able to give me insight into how this werewolf thinks. My plan is to figure out who this thing is going after next and be there to get it on film."

That wasn't exactly the plan, but it sounded like

something a reporter for *Paranormal Today* might do.

"Be careful," Roger warned. "You're there to report the news, not be part of it."

Eliza assured him that she and Alex would be careful, then hung up. God, she felt like she needed a bath. She'd just lied her ass off without even thinking about it. What was she turning into?

Chapter Eight

"Was that your editor from the *Chronicle*?"

Eliza breathed a sigh of relief. Hunter hadn't heard anything. Good. She nodded, dropping her phone in her purse. She felt awful about lying to him, but what could she say? That she was really up here looking for evidence that werewolves existed?

They dropped her car at the hotel in case Alex needed it. The photographer wasn't in his room, so she gave him a quick call to let him know it was parked outside. But Alex was out with Nate getting some pictures of the area where the first victim had been attacked.

"Be careful," she told him. "That thing might come back."

"I will, Mom." Alex laughed. "Later."

Eliza made a face and hung up.

Hunter took Sheep Creek Road out of town, then a smaller road called Murphy Dome. After that, the roads didn't have names, so she just trusted that he knew where he was going and admired the scenery. It truly was beautiful up here. Rugged and cold, for sure, but beautiful nevertheless. She supposed she could understand how a person could fall in love with the place the way Hunter had.

They drove until they reached a driveway with a big security gate across it. Tall fences ran along the road in either direction for as far as she could see. Hunter got out and punched a code into the lock to open the gate, then climbed back in the SUV and drove inside. As he got out to lock the gate behind them, she noticed him scan the wooded area. Like he thought something was going to charge them. She looked around, too. Did the wolves run free here?

But as they continued along the dirt road, she didn't see any wolves. For some reason, the thought that they might be caged instead of roaming free bothered her even more.

They drove for another ten minutes before finally reaching a sprawling place that looked like a farm. As they got out, the front door of the house opened and a tall man came out, a huge dog by his side. Eliza's breath caught in her throat. No, not a dog—a wolf. It wasn't as big as the one she'd seen in the photo Nate had shown her, but it was bigger than any dog she'd ever seen.

Before she could ask Hunter if the wolf was a pet, the animal was off the porch and running toward them through the snow.

She started to backpedal only to freeze when she saw Hunter running at the wolf, plowing through the snow like a crazy man to reach the animal. That was when she noticed the wolf was missing almost all of his front right leg. Even so, the animal still ran way faster than she ever could.

Hunter and the wolf came together in an explosion of snow, barks, and laughter. Both disappeared into a snow bank, only to reemerge covered in fluffy powder and rolling all over each other. Eliza stared in disbelief as Hunter wrestled with the handicapped wolf. Men in Alaska really *were* different than men everywhere else. Watching them, she couldn't help but smile.

The man who'd come out of the house with the wolf walked up to her and put out his hand.

"I'm Mitch Hanson," he said. "I run the wolf sanctuary here. You must be Eliza. Hunter said he was bringing a reporter from San Francisco out to see the place."

Eliza shook the man's hand, but most of her attention was still focused on Hunter and the three-legged wolf playing around in the snow. While it was completely adorable, they seemed to be *playing* really rough. Mitch must have seen the concern on her face because he laughed.

"You don't have to worry about Rusty, ma'am. If it was any other man out there in the snow with him, I'd be a nervous. But Rusty and Hunter roughhouse like this all the time—like they're some kind of pack mates or something. All the wolves out here accept Hunter—even the wild ones."

Hunter tossed the big wolf off him and into the snow drift. Still laughing, he got to his feet and jogged over to her and Mitch before the beast had a chance to dig himself out.

The wolf surfaced with a chuffing sound and trotted up behind Hunter. Eliza expected the wolf to launch himself at Hunter's back so they could wrestle some more, but he didn't. He simply hobbled slowly beside him like he'd somehow gotten the memo that playtime was over.

Hunter had brushed most of the snow off his clothes by the time he reached her and Mitch, but she still couldn't believe he wasn't freezing. There had to be piles of the frozen white stuff inside every piece of clothing on his body.

"I see you've already met Mitch," Hunter said. "I guess that just leaves Rusty to introduce."

Even though Eliza had just seen the wolf and Hunter playing around in the snow like a kid and his big, fluffy dog, it was hard to stand there and let the wolf walk right up to her. His head practically reached her waist, and even with its jaws only partially open, all she could see were teeth.

Hunter took her hand and gave it a squeeze. His touch sent tingles through her. "Rusty, this is Eliza—a friend. Eliza, this is Rusty—another friend." He glanced at her. "Hold out your hand. He won't hurt you."

She slowly extended her free hand, horrified to see that it was trembling. They said animals could sense fear—and that it made them uneasy. That was when they usually attacked, right? But Rusty only sniffed her hand, then looked up at her with his beautiful blue eyes before turning his gaze on Hunter. After a moment, he chuffed and walked away. Apparently, Rusty didn't think she was as interesting as Hunter. She wondered if she should be offended.

"Well, I guess the introductions are over," Mitch announced with a laugh. "Can I get you two some coffee."

Hunter gave her a questioning look.

She shook her head. "I'm fine, thanks."

Mitch gave Hunter a nod. "Go ahead and show Eliza around. I'll be inside if you need me."

"What happened to Rusty's leg?" she asked as Hunter led her around to the back of the house.

Hunter frowned. "He lost it in a trap. Mitch found him and brought him to the sanctuary. He can't fend for himself in the wild anymore, but he gets along okay here."

Eliza felt a pang as the wolf lowered himself onto the back porch and began to lick his good paw. "Does that happen a lot? Wolves getting caught in traps, I mean?"

His frown deepened. "More than it should." He gave himself a shake, then smiled. "Come on. Let's go meet the rest of the pack."

Despite meeting Rusty, Eliza was still a little wary of the wolves roaming free as she and Hunter walked among them. But after a while, her fear was replaced with awe. They were truly beautiful animals inside and out. She could see why he'd spent his life studying them.

"So, what the story with this girl?" she asked, running her fingers over a female's thick gray fur. The wolf had come out of a nearby shelter to greet Hunter, but kept glancing back at the building every few seconds. "Why does she keep looking over there?"

Hunter's mouth twitched. "She has pups in there."

Eliza blinked. "Babies? Can I see them?"

"Depends on Luna." He reached out to scratch behind the wolf's ears. "What do you think, girl? Want to show Eliza the pups?"

Luna regarded Eliza with a thoughtful expression, as if considering the question. Then she chuffed and trotted toward the shelter.

"Is that a yes?" Eliza asked Hunter.

He grinned. "That's a yes."

Luna was waiting for them just inside the doorway. The moment they entered, she led them over to where four wolf pups were rolling around on the straw-covered floor, wrestling with each other not unlike how Hunter and Rusty had roughhoused earlier. Eliza wasn't sure what was more precious—the way the little balls of fur tackled each other or the yipping sounds they made as they did it.

As if just realizing they had visitors, the pups stopped playing and ran over to her and Hunter. Mitch Hanson hadn't been exaggerating when he said all the wolves accepted Hunter. They climbed on him like he was their big brother the moment he kneeled down.

Eliza dropped to her knees beside him. She wanted to pet the pups, but didn't dare do it with Luna watching them. So instead, she knelt there and lived vicariously through Hunter.

He scooped up the pup playfully tugging at the laces

on his boot and held the little guy out to her. "Want to hold him?"

She threw Luna a quick look. "Are you sure it's okay?"

"I'm sure."

Eliza laughed as Hunter carefully handed over the baby wolf. The little guy was so soft and warm that she couldn't help cuddling him. He gazed up at her with so much trust in his eyes that her heart squeezed.

She glanced at Hunter and found him watching her intently. A slow grin curved his mouth and she couldn't help returning his smile. She was going to start giggling like a kid in a minute. She probably would have, too, if the wolf pup hadn't gently pawed at her coat. She looked down to see him snuggling up against her like he was ready to take a nap.

"He's so cute, I want to keep him," she said softly.

Hunter chuckled. "I'm not sure Luna would go for that."

Probably not. And it would be wrong to take him from his mother. But still… He was just so adorable.

She caressed the pup's soft fur. "Will they stay here at the sanctuary?"

"Until they're old enough to fend for themselves," Hunter said. "Then Mitch will introduce them into the wild."

Even though Eliza knew that was the right thing to do, she wasn't sure she could do it.

"I never knew wolves could be so gentle," she said, running her fingers over the pup's fur again.

"Most people don't. They think of the wolf that attacked and killed those two men, and assume all wolves are like that."

After coming here and interacting with the wolves, she was even more convinced than ever that Jed Matthews and Mark Dunham hadn't been killed by some random wolf. Of course, after seeing how big a wolf could be, she wasn't ready to go along with Nate's werewolf theory, either. So, where did that leave her?

Eliza could have spent the rest of the day right there in the shelter, but after a little while, the wolf pups got restless and ran off to play again. She pulled out her phone and took dozens of photos of the happy family before they left so she had something to remember the visit. It wasn't as good as taking one of the cute pups home with her, but it was close.

Eliza had such an amazing time at the sanctuary that the feeling should have lasted, but as they drove off the property and turned onto the main road, all she felt was guilty. Hunter has been nothing but wonderful to her and she'd been lying through her teeth to him the whole time. Would admitting that she worked for a paranormal magazine really be that awful?

"Hunter, I have a confession to make," she said softly.

He gave her a sidelong glance. "Yeah, what's that?"

She took a deep breath. Admitting she worked for a paranormal magazine might not be so awful, but telling him she'd lied might be. There was a good chance she'd ruin whatever this was she had going with Hunter. But she couldn't deceive him anymore.

"I don't work for the *San Francisco Chronicle*. I work for a magazine called *Paranormal Today* and I'm in Fairbanks looking for a werewolf."

She let it all come out in a rush, then held her breath as she waited for Hunter's angry response. What if he accused her of playing him to get her story? Worse, what if he laughed at her?

But he didn't do either of those things. "I assume Nate is the one who started this?"

"He's the one who wrote to the magazine and suggested that the deaths were the work of a werewolf, yes." Eliza cringed as the words came out of her mouth. They sounded exactly like something a reporter for a paranormal magazine would say. "How did you know?"

His mouth quirked. "That Nate was involved, or that you really work for a magazine that specializes in monsters and the supernatural?"

She slumped down in the seat, wishing it would swallow her. She should have told Hunter who she worked for the moment she walked into his office. He probably wouldn't have talked to her, but it wouldn't have made her feel nearly as badly as she did right now.

"To answer your question, I know Nate has a reputation for believing in that kind of stuff and since your photographer is hanging with him, it wasn't that hard to figure out." Hunter glanced at her. "But I appreciate you telling me."

Eliza did a double take. "You're not mad that I lied to you?"

"Not really." He shrugged. "Let's just say that I can understand why you wouldn't want to mention something like that the first time you meet someone. Keeping secrets isn't so bad—as long as the truth comes out when it's time."

Either that was the biggest line of bull she'd ever heard or Hunter was way more understanding than most men. If it was the latter, she should seriously consider marrying this guy on the spot.

"I do have a question or two, if you don't mind me prying," he said.

She was hardly in a position to mind. "Pry away."

"What about Tandi? Don't tell me the police actually believe Nate's werewolf angle?"

"Not really," she said. "There are a few cops who think there's definitely something strange going on, and Tandi is one of them. But she's hanging around mostly because she likes Nate and wants to make sure he doesn't do anything crazy."

"What about you?" He glanced her way again. "Do you think there's a werewolf out there attacking people?"

"No," she answered without hesitation. "But I also don't think this is as simple as the police are making it out to be, either. Nate is kind of out there with his werewolf theory, but he's right about a lot of things. Besides the fact that the men knew each other, he figured out they weren't just attacked by a wolf—they were tortured."

Eliza chewed on her lowed lip, wondering if she was actually answering the question or simply trying to convince herself she didn't believe in werewolves.

She sighed. "In the end, it doesn't matter what I think happened. I still have to write the story...unless I want to get fired from a job I've only had a couple weeks."

"Well, in that case, I won't hold it against you if you have to include werewolves in your story. You gotta do what you gotta do."

"Thanks, but you might not think that when you see the article. It has the potential to be epically bad." She groaned. "Not to mention put a stake in my career."

Hunter made no comment.

Eliza gazed out the window. So, if death by werewolf was off the table, how did she explain the fact that a wolf tortured those men? Especially after she and Hunter had just spent the afternoon at the sanctuary. Heck, she was this close to begging Mitch to let her take home one of the pups.

Eliza sat up straighter. Maybe that was it.

She looked at Hunter. "Do you think a person could train a big wolf to kill for them?"

* * * * *

Hunter had already known that Eliza was in Fairbanks looking for werewolves because he'd overheard both her recent phone call with her editor and the conversation she'd had last night with Nate and Tandi. But he was still glad she'd come out and told him. He wasn't sure why she'd lied in the first place. Or maybe he did. She was clearly embarrassed she worked for a rag that had her out here looking for werewolves.

Considering he was a werewolf, he probably should be insulted.

But her question made him consider something he hadn't. Not the stuff about teaching a wolf to kill. That'd be no different than teaching an intelligent dog to do it for you. Though there weren't many humans who could get a wolf to follow their commands. Wolves didn't do something to please a human, not unless they regarded you as their alpha—which was the way Rusty and the other wolves at the sanctuary thought of Hunter.

No, what he wondered was whether the werewolf was targeting his kills with a purpose in mind. Considering the two men he killed had been friends, that actually made sense.

If the werewolf was targeting certain people, how was that going to help Hunter figure out who he was? Hunter wasn't a cop or an investigative reporter. He was lousy at tracking people down with anything but his nose.

He slid Eliza a sidelong glance. She, on the other hand, was a reporter, which meant she was probably very good at tracking down people.

"If a person is behind killing those men, how would you go about finding him?" he asked her.

She chewed on her lower lips as she considered that. "It had to be someone who knew the victims well."

"But you already talked to the people who worked with Jed and Mark out at the wilderness camp," Hunter pointed out. "And we both talked to all those people downtown. Nobody seemed to think the men had any enemies."

"I know." Eliza let out a sigh. "Normally, I'd talk to wives, girlfriends, or family—they're the ones who'd really know what was going on in the men's lives. But neither man had any family or close friends—other than each other."

Damn. He turned onto the main highway. "Wait a minute. Jed and Mark practically lived outdoors— hunting, fishing, hiking, camping—maybe we should talk to the people at the places where they purchased their supplies."

"You mean, like a camping store?"

He nodded. "We call them outfitters up here, but yeah. There are a couple big ones in town. As much time as Jed and Mark spent outdoors, they had to be regular customers. The people in those stores would almost be like their families."

The first two stores they went to were a bust, but they got lucky at the third one. Hunter frequented the store himself, so chatting up the people who worked there was easy. And since Eliza had experience at this kind of thing, he let her take the lead when it came to asking questions. He had to admit, she was good at getting people to talk.

"I thought Jed and Mark were killed by a wolf," the gray-haired clerk said when Eliza asked if the men had a falling-out.

She nodded. "I know, but my story focuses more on the two men being friends and how tragic it was that they were both attacked by a wolf within weeks of each other."

"Ah, I see." The older man shook his head. "Well, I don't know how friendly they were with each other lately. You were right about there being some kind of rift between them. They hadn't been in here together since they came back from that latest hunting trip they went on."

"Do you know where they went hunting?" Eliza asked.

"I sure don't," the man said. "But some of the worst fights I ever saw were over who was going to make that trophy shot when it came time for it. Something like that can turn the best of friends into enemies."

And if that trophy shot was a werewolf, the two men would have made another enemy.

"Do you know if anyone else went on this hunting trip with them?" Eliza asked.

The old man thought about it for a while, then nodded. "Now that you mention it, another guy did come in with them that day. He was definitely going with them. I don't remember ever seeing him before, though."

"Do you remember his name?" Hunter asked.

The man made a face. "I'm not very good with names. Let me think about it a minute." His brow furrowed. "Altman. Anders. Something like that. No, wait—Aiken. That's it. Aiken."

It was Hunter's turn to frown. "Is that his first or last name?"

The old guy shrugged. "No idea. Hell, it could be a nickname for all I know."

Great. Well, it was more than they had to go on

before.

"If he was going hunting, he probably bought something." Eliza looked at the clerk. "How hard would it be to go through your old sales receipts?"

The man gave her a look over the top of his glasses that as good as said, "Are you kidding me?"

Eliza sighed. "Okay. I suppose we can Google him. There can't be more than a couple hundred people in the Fairbanks area with that name." She looked at Hunter. "Right?"

Hunter hoped.

"Actually," Eliza said as they walked outside, "it might faster to ask Tandi. I'll give her a call."

Hunter gave her an appraising look as he opened the passenger door for her. "You've only been here a couple days and you already have contacts inside the police department. You reporters from the *Paranormal Today* don't mess around, do you?"

She climbed into the SUV with a laugh, then fixed him with a look that made his inner wolf stir. "I never mess around when I want something."

Neither did he. So why was he doing it now?

Keeping one hand on the top of the door, he braced the other on the back of her seat. "Have dinner with me?"

She blinked. "Dinner?"

He chuckled. "Yeah—dinner. It's what people eat at this time of the night."

Eliza looked down at her watch and groaned. "I'm never going to get used to this much daylight. It's after seven, but my head thought it was like two or something."

"It does take a while to get used to," he said. "If you're hungry, I know this great place just outside of town that makes a fantastic steak."

She nodded. "Okay, sure. I'd love to."

Hunter's heart kicked into gear as he walked around the SUV to the driver's side. Five minutes ago, all he could think about was tracking down this guy Aiken. Now, all he wanted to do was lose himself in Eliza. They had to wait for Tandi to track down this guy Aiken anyway. Besides, they had to eat.

But instead of heading to the steak place he knew, he turned right off the main road and headed north—to his place. He wasn't the mood for a crowded restaurant right then. He'd rather spend a little quiet time getting to know Eliza better.

Chapter Nine

Eliza was so caught up in trying to figure out if she imagined the heat she'd felt between her and Hunter a few minutes ago that she almost forgot to call Tandi. It took the cop a while to answer and when she finally did, she sounded out of breath.

"Didn't mean to make you run for the phone," Eliza said.

"You didn't," Tandi said with a laugh. "What's up?"

In the background, Eliza heard a male voice telling Tandi to get the heck off the phone and finish what she started. Eliza frowned. "Is that Nate?"

"Yeah." There was a sharp intake of breath on the other end of the line. "Nate, behave!"

Eliza smiled. "I guess you gave him that nudge we talked about."

"It was good advice," Tandi said. "What about you? Did you make a move on the professor yet?"

Eliza glanced at Hunter out of the corner of her eye. The day had been fun, and that had definitely been some heat she felt before—she was sure of it now—but she wasn't sure if that would qualify as making a move on him. "Not yet. I don't work as fast as you."

"So, why'd you call—if not to gloat about shagging Hunter?"

Eliza felt her face warm. She was so damn happy Hunter couldn't hear what Tandi was saying. Eliza quickly explained her theory that someone might have trained the wolf to kill for him, then related what she and Hunter had learned at the outfitter store. "Do you think you can track this guy Aiken down?"

Tandi started to say something, then giggled before finally answering. "I should be able to. If I can stop Nate from nibbling on my neck long enough to get dressed."

Eliza heard grumbling in the background. She laughed. "It probably won't turn into anything but a wild goose chase anyway."

"Maybe, but it's actually an interesting idea," Tandi said. "And I'd rather know for sure, especially since it looks like Newman is planning to close the case on this one and chalk it up to two random animal attacks. I think he figures the odds are in his favor against this happening again. I'll drag Nate down to the station to help me look through our records."

"Call me if you find out anything. And feel free to call Alex for help if you need it. He's probably bored back at the hotel with nothing to do."

Eliza shoved her phone in the pocket of her jeans. "Tandi's going to check out the lead we got."

She reached out and turned the heater vent more her way. The wind had picked up since they'd left the outfitter and the snow swirled around them as they drove. The new coat she'd gotten at the mall earlier might be warmer, but she wasn't designed for cold weather. San Francisco might not be known for its balmy springtime weather, but it wasn't anywhere nearly as cold as Fairbanks. It was the first week of May for heaven's sake and there was still snow on the ground. It had to be in the thirties without the wind. Beside her, Hunter seemed unaffected by the frigid temperature. He didn't even have his coat buttoned. Then again, he had rolled around in the snow with a wolf that afternoon. That should tell her everything she needed to know.

"Is it always so cold up here this time of year?" she asked.

Hunter glanced her way. "Short answer—yes. We get some days that are warmer, but this is about the average spring temperature. It's a small price to pay for living in a place this gorgeous."

She looked out at the snow-capped mountains of Denali National Park in the distance. "It is beautiful. Even if it is cold enough to freeze my fingers off."

Hunter chuckled and Eliza felt her pulse flutter as the sexy sound rumbled from his broad chest. She suddenly had the urge to see what he looked like beneath that flannel shirt he was wearing. She didn't know how she could go from talking about the weather to fantasizing about him naked, but she had to tighten her grip on her purse to keep from leaning over to unbutton his shirt and running her hands over all that muscle. God, she hoped they got to the restaurant soon. Another minute and she'd be crawling across the console to straddle his lap. That vivid image made her pussy tingle, and she was glad when they finally pulled off the road and into a driveway.

Forcing her gaze away from Hunter, she looked out the window and was surprised to find that they weren't at a restaurant at all, but a house. A very nice house, but a house nonetheless. She gave him a sidelong glance. "Is this your place?"

He pulled to a stop in front of the two-car garage and clicked a button on the remote attached to the visor, but didn't drive in. "Yeah. But if you're uncomfortable having dinner here, we can go back to town. I didn't mean to trick you, but I really do make the best steaks in town."

Eliza hesitated. She should be alarmed that a man she barely knew assumed she'd want to have dinner at his place, but she wasn't. There were no alarm bells going off and her female intuition told her that Hunter was about as far from being a serial killer as a guy could get. For some reason she couldn't explain, she felt safe with him. And then there was the undeniable fact that he turned her on like crazy. Heck, last night, she would have invited him into her hotel room if she hadn't been so exhausted.

"No, it's okay," she said. "Dinner at your place sounds good."

While far from being a log cabin, the exterior of the house definitely had a rustic feel, so she was surprised to discover how modern it was inside. She'd half expected lots of exposed beams, Adirondack chairs and animal heads mounted on the walls, but Hunter's style leaned more toward stainless-steel appliances and granite countertops. There was even an indoor grill built into the cook-top—that must come in handy in Alaska.

"Can I get you something to drink?" Hunter asked as he took her coat and tossed it on the back of the couch along with his. Thanks to the open floor-plan, the kitchen and living room were really one, and it made the house seem even larger than it was. "A glass of wine?"

"That sounds great."

She leaned back against the island in the center of the kitchen as Hunter poured two glasses of red wine. Damn, he even looked sexy doing something as mundane as that.

"Can I help you with anything?" she asked.

"You can make the salad, if you want." He handed her one of the glasses. "Everything's in the fridge."

Even though she enjoyed cooking, she didn't do it much, but putting her culinary skills to use in a fabulous kitchen like his was definitely her idea of fun. Doing it alongside the hot college professor made it even better. Every time his arm brushed hers when he reached around to grab something from the fridge or take something out of the cabinet, little sparks of desire shot through her. While it was a huge turn-on, it made it difficult to focus on the salad she was making.

"So, how'd you get into journalism?" he asked as he worked on the steaks.

"My granddad was one of the great journalists in California history. He worked at all the big papers in San Fran, Sacramento, and LA." She reached for another tomato and began cutting it. "He started as a paper delivery boy and worked his way up to senior editor, doing every possible job in between. He had a million stories and I heard them all a dozen times. When I was a kid, I'd sit on the couch beside him and listen to him talk for hours. He had such passion for the truth that it was impossible not to get hooked." She added the diced tomatoes to the bowl. "He died while I was still in college, but I promised him that I'd make it in the business."

Hunter flipped the steaks on the grill. "And here you are."

She snorted. "Granddad is probably turning in his grave right now knowing I sunk so low that I took a job at *Paranormal Today*."

"Somehow, I doubt that," Hunter said. "You know what they say—there are no small jobs, just small people. I think he'd admire your determination to be a journalist, no matter what."

Damn, this guy was good for her ego.

Hunter cooked the steaks just the way she liked them, and while they were probably as fantastic as he'd claimed, she really couldn't say because she spent the entire dinner completely mesmerized by the chef, not the meal. She'd never been so fascinated by a man before. And there was definitely a lot to be fascinated with.

Like his hands. She'd never really looked at a man's hands before, but every time Hunter picked up his wine glass or gestured with his fork, all she could think about was what those big, strong hands of his would feel like caressing her naked body. She imagined them gliding up her midriff to firmly cup her breasts while he suckled on her nipples. The idea was enough to make them harden beneath her bra, and she quickly reached for her glass of wine as she felt her face color.

Eliza tried to banish the erotic image from her mind and focus on what Hunter was saying, but all that did was draw her attention to his wide, sensuous mouth. She almost moaned as her thoughts headed in another, even naughtier direction. She let herself fantasize about lying back on the kitchen table while Hunter did all sorts of delicious things to her body with that incredible mouth of his. Then—when she was totally on fire for him—he'd pull off his clothes and show her the rest of that fine body before climbing up on the table with her.

Wow. She almost had to fan her face with her hand to cool off. She'd always had a vivid imagination, but this was amazing. It was all she could do not to slide her hand beneath the table and touch herself. How was it possible to get so aroused by a man simply from being in the same room with him? It must be the wine, because she'd never gotten this aroused without some serious foreplay first. But here she was practically drooling from a few harmless fantasies. She'd never been so attracted to man before. She practically had to physically restrain herself from jumping him.

Somehow, she managed to keep her fantasies—and her urges—at bay enough to actually carry on an intelligent conversation. She was amazed at how much they had in common and how easy it was to talk to him.

She felt like she'd known him for years.

Hunter told her to sit while he cleared the table after they'd finished dinner, but Eliza insisted on helping. She put the salad dressing in the fridge, then picked up the restaurant-style pepper mill.

"Where does this go?" she asked.

He dried his hands on a dishtowel. "In the cabinet behind you, but I can get it."

Tossing the towel on the counter, Hunter took the pepper mill and opened the cabinet above her head. His nearness was doing crazy things to her pulse, and Eliza found herself leaning back against the counter and holding her breath as he reached up to put the pepper mill away. She very nearly moaned out loud when she felt his chest brush against the tips of her breasts. God, she could feel the heat from his body through their clothes.

Eliza expected Hunter to finish loading the dishwasher after he put the pepper mill away, but instead, he gazed down at her with those incredible gold eyes of his. This close, she could see that they were flecked with green and edged with a light brown. He really did have the most gorgeous eyes she'd ever seen.

Her pulse quickening, Eliza tilted her head back and licked her lips, silently begging Hunter to do what she'd been longing for him to do since she'd first met him, and finally kiss her.

She imagined him threading his fingers in her hair and tilting her head back so he could plunder her mouth. The fantasy was enough to make her sway on her feet, and she found herself reaching back with one hand to grab the countertop. Dear God, how would she react if he actually did kiss her? She couldn't believe how turned on she was. She didn't even care that she barely knew Hunter. Her body craved his touch so completely it felt like she would die if he didn't kiss her right then.

As if reading her mind, Hunter bent his head to cover her mouth with his. The kiss was gentle, his mouth moving over hers tenderly, almost experimentally, and she melted against him with a little sigh. He tasted of wine and steak sauce, and something else that was difficult to put a name to. But it was decidedly male and unbelievably intoxicating.

All at once, Hunter deepened the kiss, his mouth moving more urgently over hers as if he suddenly couldn't seem to get enough of her. His tongue invaded her mouth, claiming hers as its mate even as he slid one hand into her long hair to tilt her head back further. Eliza let out a soft moan of pleasure. She'd been kissed by a lot of men, but never like this. When it came to kissing, Hunter McCall was in a class all by himself.

"God, you taste sweet," he said hoarsely, his breathing ragged from their kisses, his mouth hovering temptingly over hers. "I want you, Eliza."

"Yes," she breathed, the word a husky whisper on her lips as she pulled him down for another kiss.

This time, it was her tongue that sought his, intent on exploring every inch of his tasty mouth. She didn't care that she'd just met him two days ago. She wanted him and right then that was all that mattered.

With a groan, Hunter swung her up in his arms and

headed for the stairs. She didn't know how he managed to find his way out of the kitchen, through the living room, and up the steps while still kissing her. He must have an uncanny sense of direction because before she knew it, they were in his bedroom. Only then did he lift his head and set her down on her feet.

In the light coming from the hallway, Eliza saw his eyes smolder with the same passion she was feeling. Her pulse skipped a beat, and she moaned at the fire racing though her. She'd never experienced this kind of desire with another man.

Eager to see if he really was as well-built as she thought, Eliza ran her hands over his shoulders and down the front of his shirt, but her fingers stilled on the button she'd been about to open as Hunter slid his hands beneath the hem of her top. Her skin tingled beneath his fingers as they glided up her stomach, and she couldn't help but let out a husky, little sound when he cupped her breasts through the thin material of her bra. Her nipples strained against the garment, begging for his touch, but he barely brushed the turgid peaks with his thumbs before his hands were on the move again. Urging her shirt up her arms, he lifted it over her head and carelessly tossed it aside.

The look on Hunter's face was almost predatory as he gazed down at her breasts, and Eliza felt her nipples tighten beneath her bra. She'd never ached so badly for a man's touch before. The thought of Hunter fondling and caressing her breasts had her breathless with anticipation. Thank God, he didn't make her wait long.

Eliza gasped at his touch, her hands automatically gripping the front of his shirt to steady herself. Hunter teased her nipples through their lace covering, making tiny circles with his thumbs even as he bent his head to kiss the curve of her neck. She arched against him, her head lolling back as she let out a soft sigh of pleasure. As wonderful as what he was doing with his hands felt, she was impatient to feel them on her bare breasts, and was just about to reach around to unhook her bra when she felt his fingers on the clasp. It came away easily at his touch, her breasts spilling into his waiting hands, and she could only murmur her appreciation as he trailed a path of hot kisses down her neck to feast on one pink-tipped nipple.

She let out a little whimper as he closed his lips over the stiff little peak and drew it into his mouth. He slowly swirled his tongue round and round the outside before flicking it across the sensitive tip. She tightened her hold on his shoulders, afraid that if she didn't she might collapse.

Hunter suckled hungrily on her nipple, torturing her until she thought she would melt. Only then did he turn his attention to her other breast and do the same glorious thing to that nipple. When he finally lifted his head, Eliza automatically opened her mouth to protest, but then closed it again when he began to unbutton her jeans. But rather than take them off right away like she expected him to do, Hunter eased them down just enough to slide his hands inside her panties and cup her ass. She always liked it when a guy paid attention to her bottom, and she couldn't stifle the moan of approval that escaped her lips as Hunter squeezed and caressed her ass cheeks. Damn, the man certainly knew his way around the female anatomy.

But she wanted to do some sightseeing of her own, and he was falling too far behind in the let's-get-naked race. She reached out and hurriedly began undoing the buttons of the sexy flannel shirt he was wearing, only to let out a groan when the broad expanse of his smooth, muscular chest came into view. *Daaammmmmnnn*, he was built. Her imagination hadn't even come close to how gorgeous he was.

Suddenly wanting to do more than just look, Eliza leaned forward with the intention of doing a little nibbling, but before she could, Hunter slid his hand into her hair and pulled her close for another soul-searing kiss. She was still dizzy from that when he urged her backward.

"Hey, no fair!" she protested as he nudged her back onto the soft bed. "I was just getting started."

He chuckled softly. "Don't worry. There'll be plenty of time for you to do all the exploring you want. Right now, it's my turn. I've been dreaming of your naked body since I first saw you at the diner. It's time to see how my fantasies compare to the real thing."

Eliza blinked. He'd been having fantasies about her? She opened her mouth to ask, but Hunter was already unlacing her boots and pulling them off. Then he grabbed the cuffs of her jeans and yanked them off in one smooth motion to toss them aside. Her panties followed, though not nearly as quickly since he took his time wiggling them down over her hips. Not that she was complaining. She adored the feel of his fingers as they brushed the skin of her bare legs. When she was completely naked, he stood back to gaze down at her with those molten-gold eyes of his.

Leaning up on her elbows, Eliza gave him a sultry look. "So, how do I compare to your fantasies?"

Where had that come from? She wasn't usually so bold with a guy, but she just couldn't seem to help herself around him.

His mouth curved into a sexy smile as he lazily looked her up and down. "My fantasies pale in comparison. You're absolutely perfect."

The compliment warmed her all the way to her toes. That was exactly the answer she'd been hoping for.

Shrugging out of his shirt, Hunter tossed it on the floor, and Eliza took the opportunity to let her gaze run over his well-muscled chest and washboard stomach. The man would put a professional athlete to shame.

Eager to see the rest of him, Eliza waited breathlessly for him to make quick work of his jeans and join her on the bed, but instead, he cupped the heel of one foot in his hand and lifted her right leg. Staring hotly into her eyes, he leaned over and, starting at her ankle, began to slowly kiss and nibble his way up the inside of her leg. She let out a little sigh. She might be eager to see the rest of his naked body, but she couldn't deny that being treated to his warm mouth was a great way to pass the time while she waited for the rest of the reveal.

Hunter seemed content to take his time working his way up to her pussy, and she shivered as much from the stubble on his jaw against her skin as she did from the anticipation of what his tongue was going to feel like on her most sensitive region.

Even when he reached the juncture of her thighs, Hunter still seemed intent on teasing her. Eliza caught her lower lip between her teeth, her breath coming in excited, little pants as his dark head edged closer and closer to her pussy. Just when she thought she might have to thread her fingers into his thick hair and put his mouth exactly where she wanted it, he ran his tongue along the slick folds of her pussy.

Eliza gasped, her entire body tingling in response. Giving in to the urge she'd had before, she reached out and slid her fingers into his hair, holding his head in place. Now that she finally had him where she wanted him, she wasn't about to let him go back to tormenting her again, no matter how delightful it had been. And yet somehow, he still managed to tease her anyway, slowly running his tongue up one wet fold and down the other, but never touching her clit. He was going to drive her insane. But as he continued to run his tongue over and over her pussy lips, she had to admit that it was the most pleasant torture.

Just when she was sure she would scream from the teasing, his mouth closed over her throbbing clit and he made slow, little circles with his tongue around the sensitive nub. She writhed on the bed and clutched the sheets as pleasure surged through her. She let out moan after moan as his tongue magically found the exact spot she wanted him to lick. It was like he could read her mind.

Her fingers tightened in his hair. "Right there. Don't stop. Please don't stop!"

Hunter didn't stop, but rather began to move his tongue faster and faster over her clit. Eliza automatically moved her hips in time with his tongue, rotating them round and round until she felt the first waves of an orgasm flow through her. She was seized by a rush of sensation so intense it almost made her dizzy and she threw back her head and let out a scream so primal it seemed to come from the very core of her being as it echoed around the room.

As the tremors from her orgasm finally began to subside, Eliza lay there unmoving and panting for breath. That had to have been the most amazing orgasm any man had ever given her, she was sure of it. The one thing she wasn't as sure of, was whether she had the strength to move after coming so hard. Perhaps she'd simply lie there and let Hunter have his way with her. But when she felt him press a gentle kiss to the inside of her thigh, she managed to lift herself up on her elbows and gaze down at him.

He leaned back to regard her silently, a grin tugging at the corner of his mouth. "You seem to have enjoyed that."

She smiled. "You're very good at what you do, Professor. But now it's my turn."

Forgetting all about her earlier lethargy, Eliza pushed

herself into a sitting position and ran her hands down his six-pack abs to his belt. "I think it's time these came off, don't you?"

Without waiting for an answer, she tugged open his belt, then made quick work of the buttons on his jeans. Eager to finally get a look at the hard cock she'd felt pressing up against her when they'd been kissing before, she quickly pushed down his jeans and underwear. As his hard shaft sprang free in front of her, Eliza could only stare. Long, hard, and thick. Just the way she liked it.

Reaching out, she wrapped her hand around his thick cock and leaned forward to take him in her mouth. Hunter groaned as he slid down her throat. Letting out a little moan of her own, Eliza slowly slid her mouth along the length of his shaft and back down again. She would have immediately repeated the motion, but Hunter slid his hand in her hair and gently pulled her away. Curious, she looked up to find him gazing down at her, a glint in his gold eyes.

"Any more of that and you're going to make me come sooner than either of us wants," he growled.

Eliza only let out a husky, little laugh and leaned back on her arms, watching hungrily as Hunter shoved his jeans and underwear down the rest of the way. There wasn't anything on him that wasn't perfect, she thought as she took in his long, powerful legs. As he rolled on a condom and settled himself between hers, Eliza felt her pulse quicken in anticipation. She might have been content to explore his cock with her mouth before, but now she couldn't wait to have him inside her.

But to her dismay, he didn't enter her right away. Instead, he braced himself on one strong arm while he rubbed the head of his cock up and down the opening of her pussy. Even though it felt wonderful, she needed more.

"Please," she begged. "Stop teasing me."

The head of his cock still poised at the opening of her pussy, Hunter lifted his gaze to meet hers, and for a moment, Eliza thought he'd ignore her entreaty and continue teasing her instead. But then, inch by delicious inch, he slowly slid his cock into her waiting pussy.

Eliza gasped. He was hot and hard inside her; the perfect fit.

Letting out a hoarse groan, Hunter bent his head to claim her lips in a passionate kiss. Reaching up to loop her arms his neck, Eliza wrapped her legs around his waist and pulled him into her even deeper. They stayed like that, his cock buried in her pussy, his mouth plundering hers, his strong, hard body pressing her into the soft mattress. Then abruptly, he slowly started to move inside her. She whimpered against his mouth, lifting her hips to meet his. Every time Hunter thrust, his cock seemed to find that secret place deep inside of her that no one else had ever even come close to discovering.

Just when it seemed she would go insane with ecstasy, Hunter suddenly rolled over onto his back, taking her with him so that she was now the one on top. Breathless, Eliza could only sit there and gaze down at him.

"Ride me," he commanded huskily, the hands on her

hips urging her to move even as he spoke.

Eliza didn't need to be told twice. Placing her hands on his chest, she made slow, rhythmic circles on his cock. In this position, she could grind her clit against him perfectly, and as sensitive as she was from the orgasm he'd given her earlier, she knew it wouldn't take long for her to come again. No sooner had the thought crossed her mind than she felt the familiar tingling that always preceded her orgasms. As it continued to build, she rotated her hips faster and faster, moaning as she came for the second time that night.

When she slowly drifted back to earth, Eliza opened her eyes to find Hunter looking up at her with a hungry expression. She leaned forward to kiss him, moving her hips in a way she instinctively knew he'd like.

Hunter growled against her mouth. Tightening his grip on her hips, he began to pump in and out of her, his cock going deeper and deeper with each push. The first tremors of another orgasm approaching, Eliza broke free of the kiss and buried her face in the curve of his neck. She felt Hunter shift his grip so he was cupping her ass. Grasping her cheeks firmly, he thrust hard and fast until she was crying out in one long, continuous scream of pleasure.

As her orgasm went on and on, she knew in her heart that no matter how many other men she made love with after tonight, this would truly be the most perfect and complete sexual moment of her life. And when his deep, hoarse groans of satisfaction joined her cries of ecstasy, she almost wept at how perfect the moment was.

Gasping for breath, Eliza collapsed on his chest afterward, utterly spent. She wanted to say something, to tell Hunter how wonderful it had been, but his arms were so warm and comforting around her that she allowed drowsiness to overtake her and let her eyes drift closed instead. The last thing she remembered before she fell asleep was Hunter pulling up the blanket and throwing it over both of them.

Chapter Ten

At first, Eliza didn't know what woke her, but as the familiar strains of *Sexy and I Know It* continued to play over and over in her head, she finally realized it was her cell phone ringing. Who would be calling her at this ungodly hour? Hoping it would stop if she ignored it, she cuddled closer to Hunter. But it didn't. She wasn't sure exactly what time she and Hunter had finally gotten to sleep, but it had to have been late. She'd only been lying there for what seemed like a few minutes after making love for the first time before his hardening cock had awakened her for round two. While the first time had been wonderful, the second had been absolute perfection. God, he was good in bed.

Beside her, Hunter groaned. "What the hell is that?" he asked, his voice sleepy in her ear.

"My cell phone," she mumbled.

Throwing back the blankets, she reluctantly left the warmth of Hunter's arms and got out of bed. That ring tone was really irritating at this time of night. Not to mention kind of embarrassing. She'd told herself she was going to change it to the standard ringtone after it had gone off in the university parking lot, but she'd completely forgotten.

Finding her jeans in the dark and unfamiliar room while she was still half asleep was much easier said than done, and the song continued to play. Following the sound of the ring tone, she grabbed her jeans off the carpeted floor and dug out her cell phone.

"Hello?"

"Hey, Eliza, it's Alex. I'm with Tandi and Nate. Sorry if I woke you, but I thought you'd want to know. We found that guy you were looking for—Aiken Wainwright. Turns out he was an old hunting buddy of the first two victims."

She was barely awake, but she was still thrilled with the news. "That's great. We can stop by in the morning and see what he has to say."

There was silence on the other end of the line and that was when she heard the unmistakable sound of police sirens.

"I don't think anyone is going to be talking to him," Alex finally said. "He's dead."

That was enough to completely startle her out of her sleepy stupor. Across the room, Hunter turned on the bedside lamp, then got out of bed and walked over to her naked. He was beautiful beyond belief, but right then she was kind of distracted.

"What happened?" she asked Alex.

"He was attacked by that wolf a few minutes before we got here. Eliza, the thing smashed into his house and killed him in his bedroom."

"Oh, God." She covered the phone and turned to Hunter. "There's been another attack."

"I thought you'd want to come out and take a look," Alex was saying. "Do you need me to come by and pick you up at Hunter's place?"

How did Alex know she was with Hunter? Tandi must have told him. Brushing her disheveled hair back from her face, Eliza glanced over at Hunter to see him already pulling on his clothes, though she wasn't quite sure why. "Um, give me the address, I'll meet you there."

"The place should be easy enough for you to find," he said after he gave her the address. "Just look for the small cabin in the middle of the woods surrounded by every police car, fire truck, and ambulance in the city. I know you don't believe in this werewolf crap, Eliza, but the cops down here are freaking out. Whatever kind of creature attacked Wainwright, he tore the damn door to shreds to get at him."

Eliza frowned at that, but made no comment. Hunter handed her a pencil and a piece of paper so she could write down the address.

"I'll see you in a little while," she told Alex.

Hanging up, she turned to find Hunter standing there with her clothes in his hands. Even considering the news Alex had just given her, Eliza couldn't help feeling a little aroused standing there naked in front of such a sexy man—who just happened to be completely clothed.

Giving herself a mental shake, she forced herself to focus as she reached for her underwear. "That was Alex.

That guy Aiken was attacked and killed tonight. I'm going to call a cab and meet him there."

"You're not taking a cab," Hunter said. "I'll drive you."

Since he'd gotten dressed already, she'd figured he'd make the offer, but that still didn't change the fact that she appreciated it. "Are you sure? It's so early."

Or late. She wasn't even sure what time it was.

"The cops will want me to take a look at the scene anyway." He waited until she wiggled into her panties, then handed over her bra, his eyes slowly roaming her body and making her shiver. "Especially since the guy got attacked in his house."

She started to nod, then frowned. "Wait—you heard that?"

Hunter looked at her in confusion for a moment, then shrugged. "Yeah. Your phone's really loud."

Eliza didn't think it was that loud, but she supposed it must be. It wasn't like he could have guessed that kind of detail.

As she pulled on the rest of her clothes, she couldn't help glancing over at him from beneath her long bangs. Damn, even with his hair all tousled and disheveled from sleep, he looked good enough to eat. Of course, that thought brought with it a flood of images from last night's sexcapades. To say the sex had been mind-blowing was an understatement. It had absolutely, positively, been the most amazing experience of her life. She was pretty sure Hunter had just ruined it for every other man she might ever be with.

149

But the funny thing was, she couldn't help but think there was way more to Hunter than just great sex. Sure she'd only known him for a few days, but there seemed to be a connection between them. Everything just felt *right*. She'd always overanalyzed everything when it came to men, but right now her head was screaming at her that there was something unique and special about Hunter McCall—and to not screw it up.

She only hoped she'd be able to stay up here in Alaska long enough to have a chance to explore how special he really was.

* * * * *

The address Alex had given Eliza was for a house just on the outskirts of town. It was situated on the edge of the industrial area, right where the warehouses and equipment storage yards left off and the forest began. It didn't exactly look like the part of town you'd want to put your quaint little cabin in the middle of. In fact, it looked a little creepy with all the dark, windowless buildings and densely wooded areas. She could just imagine a big wolf lurking out there among the trees waiting to attack. And if her theory was right, there could be a person out there with him, one that was somehow able to control the beast enough to get it to kill for him. Three men—who all knew each other—dying from wolf attacks? That was stretching the boundaries of coincidence, and the only thing that made sense to her was that there was a person behind all of this.

Alex was waiting for them at the end of the street when she and Hunter arrived. He was standing behind the yellow police tape along with a handful of other onlookers, and he walked over when he spotted Eliza.

"Hey," he said, then glanced at Hunter. "What's up, Professor? Sorry to drag you guys out of bed, but I knew you'd really want to see this."

"What happened?" she asked Alex.

"Nate and I were helping Tandi dig through old police records for most of the night. We found an old complaint filed under Jed Matthews' name for disturbing the peace. He and a friend got drunk about six years ago and were driving up and down the highway, shooting up the speed limit signs. The friend turned out to be Aiken Wainwright. We figured it was too much of a coincidence to ignore, so we looked up Wainwright's address and headed out here. The cops were already here when we arrived. Tandi got inside, but then they sent her back out to help secure the perimeter. She said it's really bloody in there, and you can't miss the ripped up door. Nobody will confirm anything, though, not even the victim's name."

If it was as bloody as Tandi said, they might not be able to confirm the victim's name, Eliza thought.

Hunter glanced at her. "I'll never get Alex in with his camera, but I might be able to get you in. I'll tell them you're my assistant."

"Thanks," she said, grateful for the offer.

Giving Alex an apologetic look, she followed Hunter over to the yellow police tape and the uniformed officer standing just inside the cordoned-off area. The officer held up his hand to stop them until he recognized Hunter.

"Dr. McCall. I heard they were going to call you. Go on in. But watch out for the blood. It's a mess in there."

When Hunter held up the crime-scene tape so she could duck underneath it, the officer frowned. "She can't go in. Lieutenant Newman just mentioned you."

"It's okay," Hunter said. "She's my assistant."

The cop's frown deepened and Eliza thought for sure he was going to insist she stay outside, but Tandi hurried over and said something in the man's ear. The officer looked at Tandi sharply, who simply shrugged and nodded. What the heck had Tandi told him?

The man motioned them forward. "Go ahead. Like I said, be careful in there."

There was another uniformed officer posted outside the front door, but he merely gave Hunter a nod as they walked inside. He must have figured if they got past the cops on the perimeter, they were good.

Eliza didn't know what to expect, but she wasn't prepared for the massive amount of destruction that greeted her. It was shocking and unsettling. She wasn't some kind of hardened reporter from the streets of the big city. She was a fact checker working for a paranormal magazine one step up from a scandal rag. That kind of work hadn't prepared her for this.

Not only had the front door been torn to shreds as if someone had gone at it with a chainsaw, but the entryway and living room were in complete shambles, too. The couch had been knocked over and shredded, along with the coffee table. A lamp and what looked like the end table it had been sitting on had been tossed across the room, and now lay broken to bits in one corner. Even the carpet hadn't escaped damage. It was covered with long claw marks that dug deep into the wood underneath and led straight from the shattered door to the hallway off the room. Could a wolf really do all this?

Still looking around in disbelief, Eliza followed Hunter out of the room and down the hallway. When they reached what was left of the door at the far end, Hunter turned to her.

"Maybe you should wait out here until I see how bad it is," he suggested. "Tandi said the scene was bloody, but if it's like the other attacks, that's going to be an understatement."

Eliza suddenly tense stomach tried to raise a hand in agreement with that idea, but she ignored it. She'd wanted to come in here, and if she was going to be a real reporter, she was going to have to get used to this kind of stuff.

She shook her head. "No, I'm good."

Following behind him, she edged closer to the shattered doorway to get her first look.

If she'd thought the living room had been a mess, it was nothing compared to the bedroom. It looked like a bomb had gone off in there. It was the blood that captured and held her attention, though. She'd never seen so much of it—and it was so...red. The stuff was everywhere—the walls, the floor, the windows, the bed, even the ceiling.

Then the odor smacked her in the face so hard it almost drove her out of the room like a physical assault. She'd never smelled anything like it in her life. The stench of blood—and other things—was so thick in the air she could almost taste it on the back of her tongue.

Feeling bile rise in her throat, Eliza tried to block out the smell as she forced her gaze away from the sickly red smears to focus on something else. Unfortunately, it seemed that the only other thing in the room her attention wanted to focus on was the body lying on the floor. Someone had covered Aiken Wainwright with a sheet, but it was so saturated with blood that it clung to him like a second skin. Worse, the sheet did absolutely nothing to conceal the huge pool of thick, dark blood congealing on the hardwood floor around the body.

As Hunter crossed the room, the two men who'd been standing beside the body glanced up, and Eliza recognized one of them as Fred Newman, the lieutenant she'd met yesterday.

"Hunter. You're already here. Good," Newman said. "I'm praying you can telling me something to convince me we're not dealing with the same animal as in the first two attacks. It's a long shot, I know, but if the public starts thinking we're dealing with some kind of man-eater, the shit is going to hit the fan."

Newman looked like he was about to say more, but then he caught sight of her and stopped. "Who let you in here, Ms. Bradley? This is an active crime scene. You can't be here."

"I asked her to come," Hunter said. "I thought you

154

might want to talk to a reporter who's dealt with animal attacks in San Francisco. She might be able to help you come up with what you're going to tell the local press— something that can keep the heat off you until we can catch this thing."

Newman's mouth tightened, but then he nodded. "That's actually a good idea. I wouldn't have thought of it." He gave Eliza a hard look. "You understand that you won't be able to print anything you see here, though, right? Not until after the case is closed."

She was so shocked the lieutenant had actually bought the line Hunter was selling she just stood there. God Lord, if Newman knew she worked for a paranormal rag and not a legitimate newspaper, the man would have a cow. But she couldn't worry about that now. Hunter had put his own standing with the cops in jeopardy to give her an in. All she had to do as go with it.

So she gave Newman her most sincere and professional look—a task made infinitely more difficult with the body on the floor. "Certainly, Lieutenant. I wasn't sent up here to write a sensationalized story about animal attacks." That was true enough at least. "I'm here to do an in-depth article on how a community copes with the tragedy of those attacks. My article won't even be printed until the investigation has been resolved."

Damn, that actually sounded really good. She almost believed it herself.

Newman apparently did as well. "Good. We can talk later then."

Eliza was so busy congratulating herself on her

composure and well thought out response that she didn't notice Newman had pulled the sheet away until he and Hunter crouch down beside Wainwright.

Fortunately, Hunter was blocking most of the body, but she still saw a lot more than she ever wanted to. There didn't seem to be a single part of the man that wasn't chewed and mangled beyond recognition. Completely unconcerned with her desire to be a real reporter, her stomach suddenly started doing cartwheels. Oh God, she was going to hurl.

She quickly turned her attention to a relatively clean section of the wall and pretended to be very interested in it. But she kept her ears open, figuring at least she could listen in on what the men were saying.

"Stupid question, but do you think we're dealing with the same wolf?" Newman asked. "I'm not asking for a definitive answer here. I just need to know what your gut is telling you."

Hunter was so quiet, she turned around to see if he was okay. He was hunched over the body, his shoulders tight.

"I hate to say it, but I think we are," he finally said. "The bite patterns are too similar to be any other animal. See the way the attack started with the arms and the legs—only moving on to the chest and throat after the victim was immobilized? It's him."

"Shit. I could explain the two attacks out in the woods, but this? What the hell would make a wolf break into a house and attack a guy?"

Hunter shook his head. "I don't know. I've never

seen anything like this before. Wild wolves simply don't behave this way."

The lieutenant dropped the sheet and stood. "Well, we've got to find this animal, and soon. I've arranged a meeting with Fish and Wildlife to see what we need to do about organizing a hunt to go after this thing."

Even with the sheet back in place, Eliza couldn't escape what she'd seen. Suddenly, the smell and all the blood were too much for her and she hurried out of the bedroom.

She waited out in the hallway, staring at the deep gouges made in the hardwood wood while listening to Hunter and Newman talk.

"You look kind of pale," Hunter said when he came out. "Are you okay?"

She tried to nod, but it was halfhearted. What she'd just witnessed in that room was the most horrible thing she'd ever seen. She'd never done well with blood—and she'd just seen enough to last a lifetime. She had a right to feel faint.

"Here," he said, taking her arm. "Let's get you outside."

Eliza allowed him to guide her down the hall and through the living room, then out the front door. She took a deep breath, grateful for once that the air was so frigid.

"Better?" Hunter asked.

She nodded. "Sorry. It's just that I've never seen anything like that before."

"Nothing wrong with that. Few people could look at

what we saw in there and not be affected." He glanced at the house, then back at her. "I hate to do this, but I'm going to have to hang around here for a while. Maybe you should get Alex to give you a ride back to the hotel so can get some sleep. You look exhausted."

Eliza would much rather have gone back to Hunter's place and spend the rest of the night cuddled up to him. "Oh…okay."

"I'll call you tomorrow," he said.

"Yeah. Sure."

She tried not to hold it against him—the cops needed him here, after all. And she knew he was only looking out for her when he suggested she go back to the hotel.

Mumbling a quick "good night," Eliza turned to walk back toward the group of onlookers still gathered behind the police tape, but Hunter caught her arm.

"Tonight was amazing," he whispered softly in her ear.

His breath was hot on her skin, and she shivered, forgetting that only moments before she'd felt like he was somehow dismissing her. "It was for me, too."

The heat in his eyes told her in no uncertain terms how much he still wanted her. With a smile, he gave her a wink, then turned and walked back to the house.

Eliza made her way over to where Alex stood. Ducking beneath the yellow tape, she glanced at the house to see Hunter talking to one of the uniformed police officers.

"So, did it look like it was another wolf attack?" Alex

asked.

She turned her attention to her coworker. "Yeah. And it's one vicious wolf, too." Her stomach churned again at the memory of what she'd seen in the house. She didn't want to admit to Alex that she'd gotten a bit queasy, so she focused on something else. "Look, there's not really much more to do here, so we might as well go back to the hotel."

"You go on. I'm going to hang around. See if I can get any pictures of them bringing out the body—that's always good for the story. I'll have Nate drive me back to the hotel."

She frowned. "Where is he? I haven't seen him around."

Alex jerked his head to the right. "He was off looking for clues about which way the werewolf came when he attacked the house, and which way he went when he left. He came back a little while after you and the professor went inside. He's been talking to Tandi ever since."

Eliza turned her gaze in the direction Alex had gestured. Sure enough, Nate was there talking to Tandi. Hearing a jingle behind her, she turned back to find Alex holding out the car keys.

"I had to park down the street a little, but you can't miss it," he told her.

Taking the keys from Alex, Eliza told him to have a good night, then started down the street in the direction of the car. She couldn't resist glancing over at the house to see if Hunter was still standing outside, but to her disappointment, her hunky lover was nowhere in sight.

Stifling a yawn, Eliza unlocked the car, then climbed in. Starting the engine, she immediately turned on the heater, sighing as the warm air enveloped her. She was just about to pull out onto the road when she noticed a man walking away from the house toward the more industrial end of the street. At first she thought it was Nate, but then realized there was only one guy out here as big as this guy was—Hunter. What was he doing?

He crouched down and examined something on the ground, then got to his feet again. Rather than continue on his way, he stood where he was, looking first in one direction and then the other, as if trying to decide which way to go. After a moment, he headed across the street toward the warehouses. A moment later, he disappeared around one of them.

Eliza frowned. What had Hunter found so interesting on the ground? More importantly, where was he going? If she didn't know better, she'd think he was trying to track the wolf. But that was ridiculous. There was no way he could track a wolf in the dark. And even if he could, what the heck was he planning on doing if he found the beast? Pull his best wolf whisperer on the thing and ask him to come along peacefully?

Curiosity getting the better of her, Eliza turned off the car, then got out and dashed across the street. She needed to know what Hunter was up to.

Chapter Eleven

He was extremely satisfied with the night's work. Another one of the betrayers was dead, and he was one step closer to finishing the task he'd been assigned.

He'd been watching the house for most of the day and had seen Aiken go in hours earlier. He would have killed the bastard right then, but he had to wait for the demon to come out. So, he'd seethed and raged, waiting until the right time to get his revenge. Finally, a few hours after dark, he'd felt the burning, tearing sensation come over him that announced the demon's arrival.

The change had been just as painful as ever, but he'd barely noticed it in his excitement. He could he extract his revenge tonight—that was all that mattered. The strange thing was, the pain seemed somehow less when he thought of what he'd be able to accomplish once the transformation was complete.

The attack had been beyond satisfying. Aiken had screamed louder than Mark or Jed. He'd been able to control the beast inside him much better this time, enjoying every crunch and tear as he went about his work.

Then he'd sat in the woods across from the cabin and the industrial buildings, watching all the pathetic police, EMTs, and reporters arrive at the house. He would have laughed at them if his beast form allowed it. He was a monster and he knew it. He was doing what monsters were meant to do, and doing it well. There was some small part of him that gloried in that fact.

Then the other demon and his woman had come. Even from as far away as he was, he could smell the way their scents were comingled together—they'd had sex very recently. The thought infuriated him for some reason, even more than the sting he felt at the knowledge that the other demon had chased him like a mangy mutt the night before.

The other demon had sent his woman away, then followed his tracks through the warehouses. He'd been considering heading into the industrial complex to get another chance at the gray beast that was so much like him—but so different as well—when the woman with the amazing scent climbed out of her car to follow her mate. But she turned the wrong way almost immediately, heading farther and farther from the safety of the other beast

That's when the strange urge that appeared every time he smelled the woman reared up again. The need to follow her was irresistible, stronger even than the need to fight the other demon. He found himself on his feet, running in the direction the woman had gone. He wasn't sure what he was going to do when he caught the woman, but he knew he was going to enjoy it. As her scent grew stronger in his nose, a growl began growing deep in his chest. Killing the other demon would be thrilling, but even more so if he took the creature's woman first.

* * * * *

Eliza didn't want Hunter to see her following him, but if she didn't stick close, she'd lose sight of him down one of the dark alleys and backstreets that weaved around the warehouses.

When she got to the corner of the building he'd disappeared around, Hunter was nowhere in sight. *Damn!* Frowning, she rounded the corner of the building and cautiously made her way down the street as quickly as she could. It was a hell of a lot darker back here than up by the main road. Maybe she should call out Hunter's name. Or maybe not. She'd already had to apologize for lying to him, she didn't want to add stalking to the list.

She walked for a couple blocks in what she hoped was the right direction, making several turns along the way and trying to follow sounds she hoped were his footsteps. After a few minutes, she not only lost Hunter's trail, but was also unsure exactly which way she'd come. All of the warehouses seemed to look alike in the dark, and there were no streetlamps back here. She couldn't even see the glow of the flashing lights from the police cars near Wainwright's cabin.

Eliza whirled at the sound of crunching gravel behind her, her heart leaping into her throat. But there was nothing there. She held her breath, listening, but didn't hear anything. She turned around and quickened her step. As she passed each building, she glanced down the street running between that one and the next, hoping to spot Hunter, but they were all deserted. Where the hell was he?

Stopping, Eliza lifted her cold hands to her mouth

and blew warm air on them. This was a waste of time. For all she knew, Hunter had already gone back to his SUV and was on his way home. Shaking her head at her stupidity, she turned to go back to the car—praying it was the right way—only to stumble to an abrupt halt. There, standing no more than ten feet in front of her was the biggest wolf she'd ever seen.

Oh, crap. He had to be almost twice as big as Rusty, maybe larger, with thick black fur and eyes as dark as night. As she watched, his lips curled back to show long, white teeth, and he let out a low snarl. The canines on the thing looked as long as her fingers.

This black beast didn't look like the gray shaded creature that Nate had gotten the picture of, but something in her clenched insides warned her that this was the killer.

She quickly looked left, then right. If this big wolf was being used by a human to commit murder, wouldn't the person be somewhere nearby? But she didn't see anyone. Just that great big wolf—who looked like he was ready to eat her.

Heart thudding, Eliza slowly backed away. The wolf followed, his movements slow and deliberate as if he was waiting for the right moment to attack. Well, she wasn't going to stand there until he did. She might not be able to outrun the animal, but she was damn well going to give it her best shot.

Biting back a scream, she turned and ran as fast as she could.

Eliza had no idea where she was going, and she

didn't care. All she knew was that she had to get away from the wolf. The terror that surged through her was so complete she could barely make her feet work, but she kept moving forward.

Even though she jogged regularly back home in San Francisco, she wouldn't be fast enough to outrun a wolf for long. It didn't help that the cold night air made her lungs feel like they were on fire. She just had to hold out long enough to get to the main road. If she did that, she'd be safe. She threw a quick glance over her shoulder at the wolf still pursuing her, only to trip and lose her footing on the loose gravel.

Eliza went down hard, the stones digging into her palms as she broke her fall with her hands, but she ignored the pain. She glanced over her shoulder, expecting to find the wolf in mid-air ready to tear her to pieces, but instead he was approaching her slowly. His teeth were bared in a snarl again and that same low growl was coming from deep in his throat. Her heart was beating so fast she thought it might explode in her chest. She looked around wildly for an escape route, but there was nowhere to go. Her rapidly beating heart sank lower. There was no way she was going to get away.

* * * * *

When Hunter had picked up the other Were's trail back at Wainwright's house, he'd followed in his human form to begin with, but then stripped down and changed once he'd gotten off the main road and into the pitch blackness enveloping the metal sided buildings. He didn't hold out much hope that the other Were would still be around, but if he was, Hunter didn't want to run into him while walking on two feet.

Hunter followed the werewolf's meandering trail through the warehouses, not surprised when it had taken him closer and closer to the forest's edge. He'd assumed the trail would lead him deep into the forest where it would end right beside a fresh set of vehicle tracks. That's what had happened when he tried to follow the tracks after the first and second killings. Even if this particular werewolf was insane, he still apparently possessed the ability to drive a vehicle.

Hunter was surprised when the trail made a sharp turn and headed back toward the house where the attack had taken place. It only took a minute to find the place where the killer had sat on his haunches and watched the house. The psycho had treated the scene of his latest savage killing like it was some kind of fucking dinner theater. Damn, this guy was messed up.

Hunter checked the area. The smell was fresh—really fresh. Like the thing had only left a few minutes ago.

Hunter continued following the black werewolf, sure this time the creature would head off into the woods and make good his escape. But once again, Hunter was caught off guard as the trail took another sharp turn and headed back toward the warehouses.

Afraid the Were was going back for another attack, Hunter had quickened his pace. That was when he picked up another scent on the breeze, an extremely familiar one—*Eliza*.

Hunter froze in his tracks, unable to believe what his nose was telling him. Eliza said she was going back to the hotel. But his nose couldn't be that wrong, which meant she was nearby.

Shit.

Terrified at what he might find, Hunter took off running at full speed.

When he came tearing out of the alley, the scene that met his eyes confirmed his worst fears. Eliza was on the ground, the black werewolf approaching her menacingly. Hunter didn't even slow down as he rushed the other wolf.

* * * * *

The black monster was only a few feet from her—so close she could see the saliva dripping from its fangs and smell the odor of blood coming off it. Every instinct she had told her to scream, but her vocal cords wouldn't respond. Hell, nothing would respond. She couldn't move a muscle. All she could do was lie there on the ground and stare into those glowing eyes, knowing this thing was going to kill her.

That knowledge finally spurred some primal instinct and she crab-walked backward. She wanted to get away, but she was too terrified to take her eyes off the wolf.

The wolf's mouth leered open, like it was amused by her futile efforts. Then it crouched down and Eliza knew the thing was about to launch itself at her. She backpedaled faster, but it wasn't going to matter. This thing could probably leap further in a single bound than she could run in ten seconds.

Suddenly, a huge shape came hurtling out of the darkness to slam into the big, black wolf. The impact from the collision sent the black wolf tumbling across the gravel, and for a moment, Eliza couldn't understand what was happening. Then, as she used the distraction to put more distance between her and the thing that wanted to kill her, she realized a second wolf had arrived on the scene. This one was gray and just as large as the first—actually, it might have been a bit bigger.

The black beast was up in a flash and threw himself at the recent intruder. The movements were violent and almost faster than she could see. But even in the darkness, she could make out the flash of teeth as they snapped and ripped at each other. The growls were deep and ferocious as they fought, rolling and tumbling across the ground. She couldn't believe how vicious the wolves were as they tried to rip each other apart. These two were nothing like the wild wolves Hunter had shown her at the sanctuary. As imposing as those wolves had been, they seemed like gentle puppies in comparison to these battling giants.

Every instinct Eliza possessed told her to run while she had the chance, but she was afraid if she moved she'd attract the attention of the fighting animals. The last thing she wanted was for two of the huge creatures to come after her. So instead, she stayed where she was, waiting to see what would happen.

As fast as the fight started, it was over. With a loud yelp, the black wolf turned tail and ran down one of the alleys. The gray wolf started to follow, but then stopped. Eliza tensed as the animal slowly turned toward her. Just because he'd chased the black wolf off didn't mean he wasn't planning on making a late night snack of her himself. But as he gazed at her, she didn't see ferocity in his gleaming, gold eyes. Instead, he seemed to be regarding her with what could only be called interest. She had no idea how, but she knew the gray wolf wouldn't harm her. Then again, maybe that was just wishful thinking.

As the wolf stood staring at her, his breath frosty in the cold night air, she realized he hadn't come out of the encounter unscathed. Blood ran down his shoulder and matted his thick fur. The wound looked deep, and she had to fight the urge to see for herself how badly he was injured. What was she thinking? It wasn't too bright to go poking and prodding a wounded animal, especially a wild one, even if he had just saved her bacon.

The wolf stood and stared at her for several long moments more before abruptly turning and loping off in the direction the other wolf had gone.

Still too stunned to move, Eliza stayed where she was. Then her head finally woke up enough to point out that maybe now would be a good time to leave.

She scrambled unsteadily to her feet and ran through the maze of streets back to the car. Luckily, she found her way there without getting herself too turned around in the warren of warehouses. Once at the car, she wasted no time getting inside, but rather than starting the engine, she just sat there, tightly gripping the steering wheel in her trembling hands. She must have sat there for fifteen minutes thinking about what had happened and how lucky she was. My God—she'd almost been killed back there. If that gray wolf hadn't come along when he did...

Which brought up the obvious question. Why the heck had that wolf come along? She realized now that the second wolf was the one in Nate's picture, but she really couldn't imagine how he was the one responsible for the recent deaths. But that black one—she could certainly see that beast killing those three men.

But what she'd seen tonight seemed to contradict her theory—that this wolf was attacking people at the direction of a human. There hadn't been anyone around that she could see, and if there had been, why would he want the beast to attack her? And now there was the second wolf—could a human control two creatures like that?

That thought brought another problem with it. When she'd assumed the wolf was Rusty's size, it seemed feasible that a human could control it. But could any person—no matter how skilled—control a monster that size?

Some part of her had believed Nate's pictures had exaggerated the size of the creature he claimed was a werewolf. And after seeing Rusty—who was supposedly as big as they came—she'd been almost certain. But the two wolves she'd seen tonight were beyond huge, and she could easily believe creatures like this had spawned the original werewolf legends just like Nate had suggested.

She couldn't wait to tell Hunter about them—he'd be amazed.

Oh, God. Hunter!

He could still be out there with those wolves. Fighting the urge to get out and search for him on foot, Eliza started the car and slowly drove around the streets in between the warehouses looking for him. But there was no sign of him. Maybe he'd already gone back to the crime scene. She hoped.

When she drove by the place where he'd parked the SUV earlier, it wasn't there. He must have gone home. Thank God.

She considered stopping to tell the police at the house about the wolves she'd seen. While that might have been the logical thing to do, she wasn't feeling very logical right then. All she really wanted was to be with Hunter and make sure he was okay.

Besides, it wasn't like those two wolves were still hanging around. They were probably miles away by now. What could the police do, even if she told them?

When Eliza got to Hunter's house and saw that the driveway was empty, her first thought was that he wasn't there, but then realized he'd probably parked in the garage. Grabbing her purse from the seat, she got out of the car and hurried up to the front door to ring the bell. As she waited for him to answer, she nervously glanced over her shoulder into the darkness. She felt her heart race as panic started to set in again. Maybe she should have sat in the car and beeped the horn?

She was just about to press the little glowing orange button again when light suddenly bathed the front porch. A moment later, the door opened and she was gazing up into Hunter's golden brown eyes.

Letting out a sigh of relief, Eliza threw herself into his arms. Thank God, he really was okay. All the fear and anxiety melted away when his strong arms wrapped around her. She'd never felt so safe before.

"Hey," he said. "Are you okay? What's wrong?"

Still holding onto his shoulders, she reluctantly took a little step back so could look at him, but words caught in her throat. His hair was slightly damp as if he'd just taken a shower, and his clothes looked like he'd just been in the act of throwing them on when she rang the doorbell. He hadn't even bothered to button up his shirt, and his broad, muscular chest was exposed to her view. Damn, there should be a law against him coming to the door dressed like that.

It was amazing the effect he had on her. Seconds ago, she'd been freaking out, worried about him, and still shaking from her near-death experience. But a couple seconds in his arms and a glance at his naked chest, and her anxiety had disappeared to be replaced with another powerful emotion—desire.

Was it possible to become addicted to a man?

"Eliza, what happened?" he prompted when she didn't say anything. "I thought you were going back to the hotel."

"I-I was going to," she stammered, dragging her gaze away from his bare chest to look up into his gold eyes.

They were equally as mesmerizing as his chest, however, and it took her a moment to collect her thoughts. "But... Well... I saw you walking off toward the warehouses near the house where Wainwright was attacked. I didn't know what you were doing, so I followed you..."

His brows drew together. "You followed me? Why?"

She shook her head. "I don't know. I thought you were tracking the wolf or something, and I got a little worried."

He gave her an incredulous look. "Tracking the wolf? How would I do that? Just because I study them for a living doesn't mean I can track them."

Eliza felt her face color. "I know. It seems silly now. Of course there's no way you could track a wolf. Anyway, I lost sight of you back in those warehouses, and then, out of nowhere, a huge wolf jumped out at me."

"Oh, my God. Were you attacked? Are you okay?" Taking a little step back, he immediately started to check her over.

"I'm okay," she said, hastening to reassure him. "The wolf didn't actually attack me. But only because he didn't get the chance. Believe it or not, another wolf showed up and chased the first one off. They were both so huge— much larger than Rusty. I was afraid this second one was going to finish what the first one started, but he just stood there staring at me for a while, then walked away. That's strange, isn't it?"

"Yeah, it is," Hunter agreed. "But thank God you weren't hurt."

Pulling her close, he wrapped his arms around her

again. Despite how good it felt and all the things she was feeling for Hunter right then, she couldn't stop the little shiver that ran through her when she thought about how badly she could have been injured. Or worse.

"You're trembling," Hunter said softly. "Why don't we get you upstairs? A hot shower will make you feel a lot better."

She had to admit that sounded inviting. As he took her hand and led her up the stairs to his bedroom, she tried to push the whole episode with the wolves to the back of her mind. That was a lot easier said than done. The only time she seemed to be able to stop thinking about those glowing eyes and saliva-coated fangs was when Hunter was holding her.

"I'd feel a lot better if you'd join me," she said.

He gently ran the back of his hand over her cheek. "I could definitely do that. Let's get you out of these clothes and into the shower."

Eliza started undressing while Hunter turned on the water. After getting the temperature set right, he moved to help her. She waited patiently while he lifted her shirt over her head and undid the clasp of her bra. Hunter would have turned his attention to her jeans next, but she slipped her hands inside his shirt to push it off his shoulders and down his well-muscled arms.

She ran her hungry gaze over his smooth, muscular chest and rock-hard abs. She frowned at the deep, jagged scars on his right shoulder. She didn't remember those being there when they'd made love earlier. Then again, the bedroom had been kind of dark. She guessed she'd been distracted by how amazing the rest of his body was and how good he'd made her feel. But now that she'd seen them, she couldn't help wanting to know how he'd gotten them. Had some animal scratched him while he'd been studying them in the wild?

She opened her mouth to ask, but Hunter chose that moment to kiss her again, and as his tongue teased hers in the most delicious way imaginable, she forgot all about the scars on his shoulder. She could ask him about them later, she told herself as he unbuttoned her jeans and pushed them down over her hips. Much later.

When they were both naked, Hunter took her hand and led her into the step-in shower. Grabbing the bar of soap, he lathered it slowly between his hands before placing it back on the shelf. A moment later, he was running his soapy hands all over her body. Eliza doubted the places he seemed most interested in were all that dirty, but she certainly wasn't going to complain. On the contrary, she sighed with pleasure as he slid his hands up to cup her soap-covered breasts. He seemed quite fascinated with the way her nipples slipped through his fingers as he played with them, and she gasped as he tweaked the hard tips. He only grinned at her wickedly and gave them another playful squeeze before moving on to other parts of her body. The man was so unbelievably good at getting her hot and bothered.

Hunter lavished just as much attention on her bottom as he had given her breasts, turning her away from him and lathering her ass until it was completely covered in soap suds. The soap bubbles tickled as they ran down her ass cheeks, and she couldn't help but wiggle a little. That earned her a quick swat on the bottom, and she jumped in surprise. Not only did the smack send soap bubbles flying everywhere and make a very loud sound in the enclosed shower, but it also sent a surprisingly delicious shiver through her body.

At her startled expression, Hunter gave her a sexy grin. "I had to get the bubbles off somehow, didn't I?"

"Most people would just have used water," she teased.

He flashed her a grin. "True. But that wouldn't nearly be as much fun." He ran his hand over her bottom. "Besides, you have a very spankable ass."

She blinked at him over her shoulder. "I do?"

Hunter chuckled. "You do. Didn't anyone ever tell you that?"

She shook her head. "No. But then again, no one's ever spanked me before, either."

"Should I stop?"

Eliza considered his words, then smiled. "Actually, I kind of liked it."

Giving him a saucy little come-hither look, she turned around and arched her back, pushing out her ass in open invitation. Behind her, Hunter slid one arm around her waist to hold her steady, and Eliza felt her breath quicken in anticipation. But instead of bringing his hand down on her bottom like she'd expected, he ran his soap-covered hand over her ass in a loving caress. She sighed, only to let out a startled gasp when that same hand came down on her right cheek a moment later.

Then, before she even realized what he was doing, he lifted his hand and brought it down in several more quick spanks. He wasn't spanking her all that hard, but her wet skin made it sting more than she'd thought it would, and she was surprised to discover that it was creating a delicious tingle between her legs. Oooh, that was nice. Why hadn't she'd ever asked a man to spank her before? Because she'd never been with a man as sexy as Hunter before.

As Hunter continued spanking her, he alternated from one cheek to the other, bringing his hand down in an easy rhythm that soon had her letting out little "*ooohs*," and "*aaahs*," and she almost groaned in disappointment when he stopped spanking her to pick up the hand shower and use it to rinse away the remaining soap. She had to admit, the water felt extremely nice on her tingling ass cheeks, too.

Hunter stepped close to her, pressing his hard, muscular body up against hers. She let her head fall back against his shoulder with a soft sigh of pleasure as he trailed hot kisses down her neck. She especially liked the way his hard cock pressed insistently against her tingling ass cheeks. The spanking had definitely been fun, but this was even better.

Hunter slid his hand over her hip and up her stomach to cup her breast, his thumb and forefinger squeezing the nipple he found there. Wrapping his other arm around her waist, he ran his hand down over her taut tummy to the dark curls at the juncture of her thighs, and Eliza moaned as he gently found his way between her pussy lips to finger her throbbing clit. Reaching back, she placed her hand on his muscular thigh and slowly rotated her hips in time with his finger. The husky groan in her ear told her that Hunter approved of the way her ass was rubbing up against his hard cock.

Just when it seemed like he was going to bring her to orgasm with his finger, Hunter pulled his hand away from her clit and slid it up her stomach so he was cupping her breasts with both hands now. God, he was such a tease. Not that she was complaining. What he was doing felt absolutely wonderful. And yet, there were so many sensations it was difficult to concentrate on any one of them—his hands on her breasts, his hard cock grinding against her ass cheeks, his searing kisses on her neck. The combination was so intense she was almost dizzy from it.

Releasing a breast, Hunter slid his hand up to gently caress her neck, and she let out a sigh as his fingers traced small patterns along her extremely sensitive skin. She'd always known her neck was one of her erogenous zones, but this was practically orgasmic, and she let out an even louder moan as his teasing fingers moved up to her mouth to lightly trace the outline of her lips. She swore she could almost have an orgasm from that. But just as her knees started to get weak, he pulled his teasing fingers away from her mouth and slowly slid them down between her breasts to the damp curls between her thighs again. This time, instead of playing with her clit, he slipped his hand between her legs and slid his finger deep inside her wet pussy.

Eliza gasped, instinctively clenching around his

finger as he moved it back and forth inside her. He kept his movements slow at first, then gradually picked up speed until she could feel herself starting to come. But once again, he backed off, sliding his finger out of her pussy before she could climax. She groaned in frustration.

Refusing to let him continue his game any longer, Eliza reached down and covered his hand with her own, then positioned his fingers right over her clit and moved them in just the way she needed. Hunter quickly got the idea and made little circles round and round her clit with his finger. He started slowly, then gradually began to rub faster and faster, and after a while, she couldn't seem to focus on anything but what he was doing.

"That's it, baby," he whispered in her ear. "Come for me."

There was something about the way he said the words that had her body immediately obeying the softly spoken command, and as the first waves of orgasm coursed through her, she cried out in pleasure. The sensations were so intense she thought she might actually faint from how fantastic it felt. Thank God Hunter had his arms around her or she might have.

"Don't stop," she begged. "Please don't stop."

Hunter didn't. Instead, he continued to caress her clit until he'd wrung every last bit of pleasure from her. Only then did he stop and gently cup her quivering mound with his hand.

Eliza leaned back against him, her breath coming as fast as if she'd just run a sprint.

As the tremors of her orgasm slowly began to

subside, Hunter slid his fingers deep inside her pussy again. "You're so wet," he said hoarsely. "I need to be inside you."

His words sent a delicious tingle of anticipation through her pussy and Eliza could only let out a breathless "Yes," in reply as he reached for a condom.

Sliding his finger out of her pussy, Hunter grasped her hips. Giving them a little tug, he pulled her into the perfect position so he could slide his cock into her from behind. They both let out a long, deep groan of satisfaction as he sank himself inside her pussy her as far as he could go. But rather than thrust right away, he ground his hips in gentle circles. Eliza caught her lower lip between her teeth, her body shuddering at the feel of him pulsating inside her.

Abruptly, Hunter began to move, gliding in and out of her wetness with almost agonizing slowness. He was going to drive her crazy like this.

"Harder!" she demanded.

Hunter obeyed, the power of his thrusts pushing her up against the shower's tiled wall, and she placed her hands against it so that she could push back. Still holding onto her with one hand, he slid the other up to her neck, gently tilting her head to the side and kissing the curve of her shoulder. He pumped faster and harder, his kisses becoming more passionate until he was lightly nipping with his teeth. Something about it seemed to tap directly into her wild side, and she moaned at the erotic sensation.

Hunter was thrusting into her so hard now that he was almost lifting her off the floor of the shower, but still

Eliza found herself wanting even more.

"Just like that. Harder!"

With an animalistic growl, he redoubled his effort, forcing her up against the shower wall. She knew from the deep, husky groans he was making that his orgasm was only moments away, and she held her own back, wanting to come with him. When he finally explodes inside her, she let herself go, screaming out loudly as the climax that originated deep within her pussy rippled throughout her body. As her cries of pleasure echoed around them, she prayed the feeling would never go away.

It was only after her orgasm subsided that Eliza realized the water spraying over them was colder than it had been before. As Hunter leaned against her, she balanced on one leg and used the toes of her other foot to reach out and turn off the shower.

Hunter chuckled in her ear. "Those are some talented toes you have there."

She giggled, turning her head to the side to look over her shoulder at him. "If you think that was impressive, why don't you take me to bed and I'll show you what else I can do with them?"

In answer, Hunter lifted her up in his strong arms and stepped out of the shower. Realizing that he intended to head directly for the bedroom without stopping to dry off first, Eliza quickly reached out to snatch a towel from the rod as he carried her out of the room. Men.

Chapter Twelve

It was almost noon by the time Hunter woke up the next day. He didn't usually stay in bed so late, but considering he and Eliza hadn't gotten to sleep until after six that morning, it wasn't surprising. Beneath the blanket, his cock stirred at the thought of what he and Eliza had been doing all that time. Had he really only just met her a few days ago? Being with her felt so natural it seemed like they'd been together for years. He'd never met a woman who could arouse him so much just by being near. Or one with whom he felt such an immediate connection, both in bed and out.

The corner of his mouth edged up at the sight of Eliza sleeping beside him. She'd snuggled closer in her sleep and was laying half on top of him, her arm flung possessively over his chest. Not wanting to wake her, but unable to resist touching her, he reached out and gently brushed her hair back from her face. She let out a soft sigh, but otherwise didn't stir. She seemed so small and vulnerable like that. He frowned suddenly as his mind replayed what else had happened last night.

Hunter hadn't wanted Eliza to go back to her hotel, but the opportunity to track the other werewolf had been too good to pass up. It had never occurred to him that she'd follow. His gut clenched at the thought of what might have happened to her if he hadn't gotten there in time to stop the other werewolf. A minute or two later and... But he had gotten there in time. That was all that mattered.

Hunter had realized there was something strange going on with the rogue werewolf the moment he saw him with Eliza. The beast's attention was locked on her with an intensity that was palpable. That was how Hunter had been able to blindside the Were the way he had. But just because he'd caught the beast off guard, it didn't mean the thing was any less dangerous, and it had taken all of Hunter's effort to back the creature away from Eliza.

Worse, his attempt to keep himself between Eliza and the beast had left him open to attack, letting the other werewolf get inside his defenses to rip into his right shoulder pretty good. The wound had hurt like hell, but disengaging hadn't really been an option. Eliza would have been defenseless without Hunter there to protect her.

When the black wolf had headed for the forest, Hunter's first instinct had been to go after him and finish it, but he couldn't leave Eliza. He desperately wanted to take her in his arms and assure her that she was safe, but that had obviously been impossible in wolf form. And since he couldn't very well change back in front of her, he'd tried to communicate his concern for her the best he could. But when he'd turned back to her and seen fear in her beautiful eyes, and it reminded him once again how different they were. It pained him to know he could never let her see that side of him, but it had always been like that and always would. It was the reason he was still alone in the world—just like his father, his brother, and every other werewolf he'd ever met.

So, instead of nuzzling her cheek with his wet nose like he'd wanted to, he turned and loped off. He hadn't left the area, but instead had shadowed Eliza back to her car to make sure she'd gotten there safely. Once she was on her way, he'd gone back to the spot where he'd changed into a wolf earlier so he could transform back. Then he'd quickly put on his clothes and gotten the hell out of there before anyone had seen his bloody shoulder. That would have been just what he needed.

But even after he'd arrived home, Hunter couldn't seem to get the terrified look he'd seen on Eliza's face out of his head. He knew there'd be no way he could sleep without finding out if she was okay and had made it back to the hotel safely. For all he knew, she could have been so shook up that she'd wrecked her car. He'd taken a quick shower and just been pulling on his jeans when the doorbell rang.

Looking at the beautiful woman next to him now, he felt so protective of her that it made his chest hurt to think about it. He couldn't believe how fast she'd gotten under his skin, but he could sure as hell get used to being with her.

Whoa, dude. What the hell was he thinking? He was acting like he thought a relationship with her could actually go somewhere. Hunter shook his head at his own foolishness. If he thought she'd been scared when he'd stood in front of her in wolf form last night, it was nothing compared to how horrified she'd be if she found out *he* had been that wolf.

Of course, he didn't have to worry about Eliza ever finding out what he was because he would never tell her. Even if he thought she could handle the truth, there was no point to it. She'd be going back to San Francisco soon. That fact brought with it a pang of disappointment, but he ruthlessly shoved it aside. There was no sense in dwelling on something that could never change. No woman could ever accept what he was. He knew that for a fact because he'd been forced to learn it the hard way.

But that didn't mean he couldn't enjoy Eliza's company for as long as she was in Alaska. He wasn't masochistic enough to deprive himself of what little pleasure he could get out of the experience—even if it was going to hurt like hell when she left.

He was just thinking about some of the sights he wanted to show her after the rogue werewolf was taken care of when he abruptly realized he had a class to teach that afternoon. If he didn't get a move on, he was going to be late. Eliza was still sleeping so sweetly beside him that he hated to bother her. He's leave her a note telling her where he was going. But as he tried to slip quietly out of bed, she stirred, her eyes fluttering open to regard him sleepily.

Even half-asleep and with her long hair all tousled, she looked beautiful. He gently ran a finger down the curve of her cheek. "I didn't mean to wake you up, but I've got a class to teach this afternoon."

She propped herself up an elbow and brushed her hair back from her face. "What time is it?"

"A little after twelve," he told her. "But stay and sleep some more. I know you're tired."

"Are you sure you don't mind?" she asked.

"No, go ahead." He grinned. "Though I don't know how I'm going to concentrate on what the hell I'm teaching when all I'll be thinking about is you lying here naked in my bed."

She gave him a sexy smile as she reached out to graze her fingers down his stomach. "You could always play hooky."

Hunter sucked in his breath as her hand traveled lower. "I wish I could, but I can't. Tell you what. Why don't you come by tonight, say around six? I'll be home by then."

She leaned forward to trail kisses over his jaw. "I'd love to."

It was taking all his willpower not to say the hell with work and spend the day in bed with Eliza. "Actually," he said against her mouth, "you'd better make it closer to seven. I have to stop somewhere on the way home."

"Seven, then," Eliza agreed, kissing him again.

Unable to stop himself, Hunter slid his hand in her hair and covered her mouth with his for a long, hard kiss before he finally lifted his head with a groan.

"Oh, the hell with it. Maybe we do have time for a quickie."

Eliza pulled him down with throaty laugh. "Quickies are my specialty."

* * * * *

Lying back on the pillows half an hour later, Eliza watched as Hunter dressed. With a body like his, he should walk around naked all the time. Then again, maybe not. It would cause a stir among his female students. And some of the male ones, she was sure. Perhaps it would be best if he just paraded around the house like that in front of her.

Eliza frowned as her gaze settled on the scars on his shoulder. Last night they'd looked deeper, darker, and angrier. But now they weren't nearly as noticeable in the afternoon sun streaming through the window. Maybe the lighting had made them look worse last night. Or more likely, she hadn't been seeing straight. She'd been more than a little freaked out after getting attacked by that wolf.

Dressed now in jeans and a button-up shirt, Hunter came back over to the bed and gave her a kiss. "There are bacon and eggs in the fridge if you're hungry." He kissed her again. "I can't wait until tonight."

"Me, either," she whispered against his mouth.

Eliza let out a sigh as she watched Hunter go. God, he couldn't be more perfect. Of course, it was just her luck that he had to live all the way up here in Alaska. She was definitely going to miss him when she went back to

San Francisco. She wondered if it would be possible to maintain a long distance relationship with him after she went back home. Probably not. She'd never met a single person who'd been able to make something like that work.

But she pushed those dreary thoughts aside for the time being. She didn't have to leave for a few more days yet—she hoped. It all depended on her editor, but she had a hunch that after he heard about last night's wolf attack, he'd want her to hang around Fairbanks for a little while longer. Speaking of which, she was going to have to call him with an update.

Leaving the warm, cozy bed was hard, but Eliza forced herself to get up and pad into the bathroom. As she turned on the water and stepped under the spray, she had to admit this morning's shower wasn't nearly as much fun as last night's had been. The memory of Hunter running his soapy hands up and down her body was enough to make her pussy tingle. And the spanking he'd given her—damn, that had been hot. She'd never done anything like that in her life.

Turning off the water, she stepped out of the shower and wrapped a towel around herself. As she gazed at her reflection in the mirror above the double sinks, she noticed the faint outline of teeth marks on her right shoulder—another reminder of last night's lovemaking. She ran her fingers over them with a smile. She'd been right. Hunter really was an animal in bed.

Pulling on the jeans and shirt she'd worn the night before, Eliza ran a brush through her long hair before going downstairs to take Hunter up on his offer of breakfast. She passed on the bacon and eggs in favor of peanut butter on toast, though.

After she finished eating, Eliza put the plates in the dishwasher, then called her editor. As she'd hoped, Roger agreed with her about staying in Fairbanks. He practically salivated when she told him there'd been a third attack inside the latest victim's house and that she'd gotten a look at the body. Of course, she didn't mention the little part about almost getting killed by that same monster.

"Stay as long as you need to," he'd told her. "It sounds like you're really onto something. Just keep your eyes open for Clark Emery. He got hired by *Strange Times* and is on the way up there to scoop you. Don't let that happen."

She stifled a groan. Maybe she wouldn't run into him. "I won't."

"What are you planning to do next?" Roger asked.

Eliza didn't have to think too hard about that. In between bouts of mattress gymnastics with Hunter last night, she'd revisited her original theory and decided it was indeed possible that a person could be controlling wolves as huge as the ones she'd seen. The size of the beast didn't have anything to do with it. If a circus trainer could handle a ring full of tigers, why couldn't someone do the same thing with a couple of big wolves?

"Now that we have three victims, I know I can find a link between them and the werewolf," she told her boss, and this time, she didn't even have to bite her tongue when she said the word *werewolf*. While it might not be the traditional guy turning into a beast, she was still okay with thinking of the monstrous creatures she'd seen as werewolves. They were just too big to call them the same thing she'd call Rusty and other animals like him. "Once Alex and I figure out what that link is, we're going to follow it back to our man."

She didn't mention to Roger that the man wasn't a werewolf but simply a human using a wolf to kill for him.

The silent stretched out on the other end of the line for so long Eliza thought Roger had hung up. When he finally spoke, his voice was laced with concern.

"Are you sure that's a good idea? Don't get me wrong, I appreciate your go-get-'em attitude, but what you're talking about sounds dangerous."

"Alex and I aren't doing this alone," she said. "We're working with the cops and the professor I mentioned to you the other day—the one who's an expert on wolves."

Roger let out a heavy sigh. "Okay, but be careful. You're a reporter, not a cop."

Actually, she liked to think of herself as an investigative journalist, but didn't correct him. Besides, being called a reporter had been good enough for her grandfather, so it was good enough for her.

$$* \, * \, * \, * \, *$$

Telling Roger about working with the police reminded her that she still needed to let them know about the two big wolves she'd seen lurking around Wainwright's place. She made a quick stop by the hotel to change clothes, then headed over to the police department. She hoped Lieutenant Newman was there. Reporting what she'd seen might get her a few brownie point with the man.

On the way, she called Alex to let him know she'd talked to Roger and that they would be staying in Fairbanks for a while longer. She considered telling him about the run-in she'd had with the wolves, but changed her mind. He'd only worry. Better to leave Alex in the dark about her near-death experience.

"Fine with me," he said. "I can definitely use the per diem money."

"Well, then we'll consider that the good news," Eliza said. "In the not-so-good department, Clark Emery got a job at *Strange Times* and Roger thinks he's going to come up here to scoop us."

Alex snorted. "I don't think we have to worry too much about that. Clark's an idiot. He'll probably get lost leaving the airport."

Eliza couldn't help but laugh. "Nice to know, I guess. One other thing—I'm going to need the car for a while. Is that okay?"

"No problem there, either. Nate'll give me a ride."

"Speaking of Nate, how did everything go last night? Did you learn anything else at the crime scene after I left?"

"Not much. One of the neighbors told us he used to see Mark Dunham at Wainwright's place all the time— they were best buds or something. The neighbor wasn't sure why they stopped hanging out, but he didn't think it was a fight."

That was interesting. "Did the neighbor know of any other friends Wainwright suddenly stopped hanging out with?"

"Afraid not."

"Damn."

The whole reason for tracking down these people was to either warn them they were in danger, or figure out if they were the ones responsible for the killing. But with Aiken Wainwright's murder, they seemed to be at a dead end again.

"So, what's the plan now, boss?" Alex asked.

"I'm going to the police station to talk to Newman about some stuff. Then I guess we start trying to figure out the connection between these three men—it can't be that hard. Fairbanks isn't New York City. Somebody here had a beef with the victims, and somebody else here knows about it."

Alex told her to be careful, then said he'd call her if he and Nate figured anything out.

"Don't go running off into the woods by yourselves again," she warned, then cringed. She sounded like Roger.

Alex only laughed. Eliza wasn't sure the photographer was laughing because he planned on paying attention to her warning or because he was planning on ignoring it.

Lieutenant Newman wasn't at the police station, but rather than risk missing him altogether, Eliza hung out with Tandi while she waited for him to come back. The cop was in the break room eating a sandwich and reading a book. She looked up from her ereader and grinned.

"Guess I don't have to ask where you and Hunter disappeared to last night."

Eliza tried not to blush, but was pretty sure she failed. "What do you mean?"

"I mean that you look like a woman who spent the night in bed with her hot, hunky lover."

Eliza felt her face color another shade of red as she sat down.

Tandi laughed. "You're blushing!"

Eliza grabbed some chips out of Tandi's bag simply to have something to do with her mouth that didn't involve talking. She really didn't trust herself to speak right then. By the time she finished chewing, she remembered why she'd come looking for Tandi—and it wasn't to update the other woman on her sex life.

"What's going on with the case?" she asked. "Now that there are three victims who knew each other, Newman can't still be thinking it's just a wolf doing this, right?"

Tandi took a swallow of diet Coke. "What's he supposed to think? There's your idea—that there's some guy out there using a trained wolf to kill people. Or Nate's idea—that there's a werewolf out there. An old school cop like Newman can't handle either of those alternatives."

Okay, they did sound a little out there. "What about the fact that they went hunting together? That connection has to be worth exploring."

Tandi grabbed a handful of chips. "Some of the

other officers and I checked into that. Dozens of people went hunting with one or all of the victims at some point over the past several months. We need more to go on than that." She checked her watch. "I have to go back on duty. I'll give you a call later."

"If you see Lieutenant Newman, let him know that I'm looking for him," Eliza said.

Eliza pulled out her laptop to work on her story while she waited, but when Newman still hadn't come back to the station after two hours, she decided to pack up and go. She'd file a report with the sergeant at the front desk, then meet up with Nate and Alex to look for a new lead.

Of course, that's when Newman walked in the door.

"Ms. Bradley, glad I ran into you. Let me grab our PR person and we can talk about how the department should best handle informing the public about these attacks. After last night's killing, people are getting nervous."

That wasn't surprising. God only knew who else was on this psycho's hit list. "Actually, I'm here about something else. After I left the crime scene last night, I went walking around near the warehouses and almost got attacked by a couple of really big wolves."

The detective's eyes went wide. "You what?"

"Well, only one of them tried to attack me. The other one was more interested in fighting the first wolf. But the important thing is that there were two really big wolves hanging around only a few blocks from the house where that man was killed."

Newman frowned. "What the hell were you doing in the warehouse district?"

"I… Well…" She hesitated, not wanting to admit she'd thought Hunter was trying to track the wolf who'd killed Aiken Wainwright. "I thought I saw something, so I decided to check it out."

His mouth tightened. "That was foolish. You could have gotten yourself killed."

Eliza knew he was right, but she bristled at his words anyway. "I'm a reporter, Lieutenant. Sometimes taking a risk is the only way to get a story."

He shook his head. "I'm going to need you to show me where you saw these wolves."

"Only one of them tried to attack me. And does it need to be now?" She glanced at her watch and saw that it was almost five o'clock. "I have plans tonight."

"It won't take long," Newman said. "This is important."

Eliza sighed. It was obvious that he wasn't going to take no for an answer, so she might as well just give in and go over to the warehouses with him. She had no idea what he expected to see—it wasn't like the wolves were going to leave fingerprints. But the faster she got done with Newman, the faster she could get back to the hotel and get ready for her date with Hunter.

Outside, Eliza started for her car, but Newman said it would be easier if she drove with him. So much for having time to stop by the hotel before going to see Hunter.

"So, why am I showing you where I saw the

wolves?" Eliza asked as Newman pulled out onto the street.

He glanced at her. "Because the first victim—Jed Matthews— was attacked in the woods not too far from that area. It's possible these wolves could live around there."

Eliza frowned. According to Hunter, a pack wouldn't make its den so close to people. Then again, two wolves probably didn't really comprise a pack. So, what did it make them, then? Certainly not friends—not after the way they'd fought.

It was after five-thirty by the time she and Detective Newman got to the warehouse area, and it took her a while to get her bearings. It didn't help that all the buildings looked the same to her, but as they drove up and down the streets, several of them started to look familiar.

"This looks like…" Eliza started to say, but the words trailed off when she spotted two huge wolves squaring off against each other at the far end of the street. Even in the shadows cast by the buildings, she could tell they were the same ones she'd seen the night before.

Newman swore under his breath and stopped the car. "Stay here."

Eliza's eyes went wide as Newman got out and pulled his gun from the holster under his jacket. The thought that he was going to shoot the wolves both shocked and upset her.

The gray wolf turned his head to look in Newman's direction. Eliza felt her pulse skip a beat as the animal's yellow eyes caught the light. She was suddenly transported back to last night when the wolf stood in front of her as she lay on the ground trembling. She didn't know why, but that gray wolf had saved her life. If Newman shot at them, it was just as likely he'd hit the gray wolf as the black one. She couldn't let that happen. Before she realized what she was doing, Eliza reached for the door handle.

Just then, a shot rang out.

Eliza jumped, startled not as much by the sound of the gunshot as she was by the howl of pain that accompanied it. Frozen, she watched in horror as the two wolves broke apart and ran off. Which one had Newman hit?

For a moment, she was half afraid Newman would try to go after them on foot, but he shoved his gun into his holster and headed back to the car.

"Were those the two wolves you saw last night?" he asked as he got in.

Still too stunned by what she'd just seen, Eliza could only nod her head. All she could think about was whether the gray wolf had been hit.

"Well, I clipped one of them, at least, which means we've finally got a trail to follow," Newman said. "I'll get you back to the station, then get some hounds up here and see if we can't track the bastards down."

Eliza said nothing. She hoped it wasn't the gray wolf that had gotten shot. The animal had saved her life last night. That had to mean he wasn't a threat. She wondered if she should try and tell that to Newman again, but knew he wouldn't listen anyway. She doubted he saw any difference between the wolves. To him, they were both dangerous animals that needed to be killed.

After all the time she'd spent with Hunter and the wolves out at the sanctuary, the thought of an innocent wolf being killed for no reason made her feel really crappy, and suddenly she realized she needed Hunter to tell her the gray beast that had saved her life would be okay.

She couldn't get out of the car fast enough when Newman pulled into the parking lot of the police station. The drive to Hunter's place seemed to take forever and when she got there, she was relieved to see the garage door open and his SUV inside. At least she wouldn't have to sit around and wait for him.

Grabbing her purse, she jumped out and ran into the garage, only to stumble to a halt. Eliza stared at the dark red droplets on the floor in confusion. Blood. Why would there be blood on Hunter garage floor?

Following the trail of blood with her gaze, she was horrified to see that it led straight into the house. Even more alarming were the bloody handprints smeared all over the knob and the doorjamb. Her heart crawled its way up to get stuck in her throat.

Hunter.

Chapter Thirteen

The door was slightly ajar and Eliza cautiously pushed it open the rest of the way. "Hunter."

No answer.

Swallowing hard, she stepped into the kitchen, careful to avoid the blood on the floor. "Hunter," she called again, a little louder this time.

Still no answer.

A tiny part of her screamed that she should be calling Tandi and the cops, but she ignored it. She had to know if Hunter was okay first. So instead of pulling out her cell phone, she ventured farther into the room. Suddenly, she heard a noise coming from the direction of the downstairs bathroom.

"Hunter!"

Her heart settling into the pit of her stomach, she moved faster across the kitchen and down the hall. As she neared the bathroom, she heard the noise again. She ran the rest of the way and burst into the room.

Hunter stood in front of the mirror, blood running down from his shoulder to cover his chest and stomach.

In his hand, he held a pair of pliers.

"Oh, God!" she cried. "What happened?"

Hunter jerked his head up to look at her, his eyes wide. "Eliza." His voice was hoarse. Reaching for the towel that was on the counter, he quickly pressed it to his bloody shoulder. "I didn't hear you come in."

She dropped her purse on the floor and moved closer to him. "You're bleeding. What happened?"

He shook his head, avoiding her gaze. "Nothing. It's a scratch."

"A scratch?" Eliza frowned. "That's definitely not a scratch. What happened? Here, let me see."

Hunter's hand tightened on the towel, holding it in place even as she reached for it, and Eliza had to practically jerk it away from him. Now that some of the blood had been absorbed by the towel, she could see where it was coming from, and her eyes went wide at the sight of the hole in his shoulder. She'd seen enough pictures when she worked at the *Chronicle* to know exactly what she was looking at.

"You've been shot. We have to get you to the hospital."

"No hospital," Hunter said.

Was he already in shock from losing too much blood? "What do you mean, no hospital? Of course you have to go to the hospital. You've been shot."

He shook his head. "I'll be fine once I get the bullet out."

She stared at the long slender pliers in his hand, realization suddenly dawning on her. That confirmed it—

he was definitely in shock. No one in their right mind would try to take a bullet out of their own shoulder with a pair of pliers. "You can't take the bullet out yourself. I'm taking you to the hospital."

Eliza reached for her purse, but Hunter caught her arm.

"I can't go to the hospital," he told her again, his voice firm.

"Why not?"

His mouth tightened. "It's complicated, and I can't go into it all right now, but you have to believe me when I tell you that going to the hospital isn't an option. But if I don't get this bullet out soon, the wound is going to close with the thing inside me, and then I'll really be in trouble. I was going to do it myself, but now you're here, it'd be easier if you do it."

Her eyes went wide. "*Me?* What are you talking about? There's no way I can take out a bullet."

Hunter pressed the pliers into her hand. "Yes, you can. You have to. Besides, it doesn't feel like it's in very deep, so it should be easy."

Easy? Eliza already felt faint from the sight of all the blood. Hunter must be delusional from the pain. It was the only thing that would explain why he'd want her to take out the bullet with a pair of pliers. He'd seen the way she'd handled the sight of blood at the last murder scene.

She took the pliers from him and set them on the counter. "You have to stop this and let me take you to the hospital or call an ambulance. You could die if I don't."

"I'm not going to die from the bullet," he insisted. "But I will be in for a whole lot of pain if you don't get it out. Eliza, I need you to trust me on this. Everything will be fine if you just follow my directions. If you won't do it, then I will. You have to believe me when I tell you that I don't have a choice." He picked up the pliers and held them out to her. "I need you to decide quickly—I don't have a lot of time to mess around."

Eliza stared at the pliers. He was serious. She wanted to refuse, to insist he go to the hospital, but she knew that if she did, Hunter would only try to dig the bullet out himself, and she wasn't big enough to stop him. Without being able to see what he was doing, he'd only end up hurting himself worse. But still...

Hunter gently cupped her cheek. "You can do this, Eliza. I know you can."

She gazed up into his gold eyes, saw the trust in them reflected back at her. She couldn't believe she was really going to do this. Shrugging out of her coat, she tossed it on the vanity, then reached for the pliers.

"Shouldn't we sterilize these or something?" she asked.

He gave her a wry smile. "I don't think it matters. It's not like the bullet was sterilized."

That was true enough. She took a deep breath and stepped closer to him. Without the towel there to stop it, blood had started to run down his chest again.

"Even if I manage to get the bullet out, you're still going to need stitches, you know. And I'm telling you right now, there's no way I'm going to stitch you up. I completely flunked the sewing portion of home economics in school."

His mouth quirked. "Stitches won't be necessary."

Eliza wasn't sure what he meant by that, and she was afraid to ask. Knowing him, he probably intended to close the wound with a hot fireplace poker. That was something she really didn't want to think about.

Placing a trembling hand on his chest to steady herself, she lifted the pliers, but then hesitated. What the hell was she doing? She didn't know the first thing about removing a bullet.

The wound was blackened and ragged around the edges, and just looking at it had her feeling queasy. She suddenly flashed back to that frog in biology class the teacher wanted her to dissect. She'd been lousy at that subject, too—and had made a mess of the frog to boot.

When she hesitated, Hunter wrapped his hand around hers and guided it toward the gunshot wound. "Just go straight in. You'll find it."

Calling herself all kinds of stupid for doing this, Eliza slowly slid the tips of the pliers into the opening of the wound. The moment she did, the jagged hole began to bleed more freely. Hunter flinched.

She froze. "I'm sorry."

"You're doing great," he said. "Keep going. And don't forget to open the pliers up or you'll just push the bullet deeper. It's not far now."

His definition of "not far" was obviously different than hers because it seemed like it took forever to find the bullet. She already had the pliers in past the joint and the wound was bleeding fiercely now. Oh God, she was going to be sick.

"Just a little farther," he said softly.

She glanced up at him. "How do you even know where it is?"

He grimaced. "Trust me, I know. I can feel it. You're close."

She was about to protest, but just then she felt the tips of the pliers touch something. She swore she could almost feel them clink against something metallic.

"That's it," Hunter said.

Eliza hesitated. "Are you sure? What if it's something else? Something important?"

Like bone.

He clenched his jaw. "It's not. Just close down carefully with the pliers and pull back."

She did as he told her, ignoring the way her head started to swim when more blood gushed out. But the pliers slid out a lot faster than they'd gone in, and a moment later she was standing there staring at the misshapen bullet gripped in the tips.

Hunter let out a breath. "I told you that you could do it."

Abruptly realizing he was still bleeding, Eliza tossed the pliers down on the counter and pressed the towel tightly against the wound. "You're going to bleed to death. We still need to get you to a hospital."

He shook his head. "No, we don't. Now that the bullet is out, I don't have to fight it anymore. It'll be fine."

"Fine? Hunter, I may have gotten the bullet out, but it is nowhere near fine. The bullet may have hit something vital and now that it's out, you might start bleeding even more."

To prove her point, she jerked the towel away from his shoulder, only to go deathly still at what she saw. Where before the wound had been practically gushing with blood, now it wasn't bleeding at all. Even as she watched, the jagged hole seemed like it was closing up. And as she continued to gaze at it, the hole kept getting smaller and smaller. She swore she could see pink scar tissue slowly filling the ragged hole. In the span of less than two minutes, the horrible wound was completely sealed. It was still visible, and looked horrible, but it wasn't bleeding anymore.

Eliza stared at the scar. If she hadn't just taken the bullet out with her own two hands, she'd think the scar was days old. She reached out and gently ran the tips of her fingers over the place where the bullet hole had been.

Seeing the newly formed skin appearing right before her eyes made her think about the scars she'd seen on Hunter's shoulder the night before and she shifted her gaze to look at them. The marks that had been there that morning weren't just smaller, they were barely visible at all. She traced the faint lines.

"These were darker this morning, I'm sure of it," she murmured. "And even darker last night."

Realization suddenly dawned on her. It was too impossible to even think it, but she couldn't keep her mind from connecting the dots. "Last night, the wolf that saved my life got scratched right on his shoulder just like this."

"Eliza—"

"Then today, Lieutenant Newman shot a wolf. Now, you have a bullet wound in your shoulder."

She tried to tell herself it was a coincidence and nothing more. She might actually believe that if she hadn't just seen the bullet wound heal up right before her eyes.

Eliza slowly lifted her head to look at Hunter. "Oh, God. You're a...a...werewolf!"

"Eliza—"

One second she was standing there, and the next, she started feeling so faint she knew she was about to pass out. Everything in her vision began to swim around and go dark.

She felt Hunter steady her and help her sit down on the edge of the tub. "Breathe," he whispered in her ear. "Just lean against me and breathe. You'll feel better in a minute."

She didn't know how she could possibly feel better—the bottom had just fallen out of her whole world. Werewolves didn't exist—except now they did. Finding out that everything you thought you knew was wrong was kind of hard to process.

She looked at Hunter crouched down in front of her. He didn't look like a monster. He looked concerned and worried, even though he was the one who had a bullet pulled out of him. How could someone as amazing as Hunter be a werewolf?"

"You don't have excessive body hair or a unibrow," she said.

Hunter frowned. "What?"

"The classic signs," she explained. "You know, excessive body hair, overly long fingernails, one of those unibrow things, a violent temper…"

He sighed. "Eliza, I think we need to talk."

Was he flipping serious? "*Talk?* I just discover the man I've been sleeping with is a werewolf and you want to talk?"

"Yes. Come on. Let's go into the kitchen and I'll make you some tea."

Eliza had an urge for something stronger than tea, but she said nothing as Hunter took her hand and led her out of the bathroom. When she saw all the blood on the kitchen floor, she hesitated in the doorway.

Hunter must have sensed her discomfort because he said, "Stay here while I clean that up."

She did as he told her, waiting while he grabbed some paper towels off the rack and wiped up the floor before finally venturing into the kitchen. She leaned back against the counter and hugged herself. Her head was spinning. She didn't honestly believe Hunter was a werewolf, did she? There had to be another explanation, right? Werewolves didn't exist. But then why hadn't he denied it?

"So, are you a werewolf or not?" she asked softly.

He was silent as he set two mugs out on the counter. "Yes," he finally said, not looking at her.

Eliza closed her eyes. Oh, God. This so wasn't

happening. Hunter simply could not be a werewolf.
Maybe she was dreaming this whole thing. That made
sense. She'd come up to Alaska to do a story on a
werewolf, after all. But something told her this wasn't a
dream. Hunter really *was* a werewolf.

"Were you bitten by a werewolf like in the movies?"
she asked, not knowing what else to say.

He glanced up from the box of tea bags to give her a
look that was half amused. "No. Although a person will
become one if they're bitten. I'm what we call a hereditary
werewolf."

They never mentioned that in the movies. "Your
parents are werewolves then?"

Hunter shook his head. "Just my father. The gene is
passed down through his side of the family."

She couldn't believe she was sitting here having a
conversation about inherited genes. Hunter wasn't talking
about having red hair or blue eyes. He was saying he
came from a family of werewolves. This was too insane
for words.

"Does your mother know?"

A pained expression crossed his face. "Yeah. It was
kind of hard for my brother and me to hide it from her.
We couldn't control it when it first started."

Eliza blinked. "Your brother is a werewolf, too?"

He nodded as he poured hot water into the mugs.
"Twins. We share DNA, you know?"

They were both silent for a moment as they waited
for the tea to steep, but then she frowned in confusion.
"Wait a minute. If your father is one, too, why didn't your

mother figure it out earlier?"

"Because he kept it hidden from her," Hunter explained. "He was afraid of how she would react, so he never told her. He hoped they'd get lucky and that the trait would end up skipping a generation."

"It does that?"

He shrugged. "Sometimes. It's a recessive gene."

Eliza thought back to what she'd learned in her high school biology class about recessive genes. "You mean like being albino or something?"

The question was silly, but it was simply her rational mind trying to deal with something that should be impossible to cope with.

He removed the tea bags and set them on a paper towel. "Exactly like that, actually."

"What happened when your mother found out?" she asked.

"She left. We never saw her again."

Eliza couldn't conceal her surprise as he handed her one of the mugs. "She left her family, just like that?"

Hunter didn't look at her. "It can be hard for some people to accept."

He was talking about her, Eliza realized. He assumed she wasn't going to be able to deal with this, either.

She sipped her tea. Obviously, finding out your husband and children are werewolves would be a big deal, but she couldn't understand how his mother could have simply walked out on them.

"Her leaving must have been rough on you," she said softly.

His jaw clenched. "I got over it."

Had he? Eliza doubted that. It certainly explained why a great guy like Hunter wasn't married already. He probably purposely kept women at a distance, afraid they would bolt if they ever found out his secret.

"So, is it just the men who carry the gene, then?" she asked finally.

"In my family, yes. I'm not sure how it is with other hereditary werewolves."

She thought a moment. "Are there a lot of werewolves around?"

The corner of his mouth edged up. "I'm not really sure. It's not like we get together for conventions or anything."

Eliza couldn't help but smile at the thought of a werewolf convention. It probably wouldn't even raise an eyebrow back in San Francisco.

Hunter studied her thoughtfully. "Obviously I don't come out and tell people about this very often. Actually, I've never told anyone. You aren't freaking out as much as I expected you would."

She should be freaking out—it wasn't like he'd just admitted to being a vegetarian—but she was surprisingly calm. In fact, she had to congratulate herself on how well she was dealing with all of this. It wasn't every day that she found out the hot guy she'd been sleeping with was a werewolf.

Abruptly realizing Hunter was still waiting for an answer, she gave him a small smile. "I don't freak out very easily. It must be the reporter in me, I guess."

Hunter nodded, but made no comment, and Eliza found herself wondering if she'd somehow said the wrong thing.

Then it hit her. Crap. This wasn't just about Hunter worrying she'd reject him as a woman. He was worried she'd splatter his whole story across the front page of her paranormal magazine.

"Hunter, just because I'm a reporter through and through, that doesn't mean everything I hear ends up in a story. I'm not here in an official capacity, okay? I'm here because we've been sleeping together and I was worried when I saw all the blood. I'm not going to tell anyone what I saw, or repeat what I hear. You have to believe that."

At her words, the weight lifted from his shoulders as if it was a tangible thing. She thought she even saw him smile a little. But he didn't say anything, and as the silence stretched out she realized the wall he'd put up between them hadn't come down at all. She had to say something to make him realize she wasn't the enemy here.

"So, where do werewolves come from?" she asked.

"Where?" He shrugged. "I have no idea. I assume it's just a genetic trait that's been around since the beginning of time."

"Haven't you ever wondered?"

His mouth curved. "Not really. Have you ever wondered where your brown eyes came from?"

Eliza started to point out that it wasn't the same thing, but then realized it probably wasn't any different to him. "I guess not." She chewed on her lower lip. "The

211

other wolf—the one that's attacking people—he's a werewolf, too, isn't he?"

"Yes."

"Do you know him?"

Hunter shook his head. "No. He showed up round the time of the first murder. He's only been recently turned."

She sipped her tea. "How can you tell?"

"For one thing, the first two attacks came around the full moon. Learning to control the change takes months—more if you don't have someone to help you through it. Until a new werewolf learns that control, he or she is at the whim of the lunar cycle."

At least the movies got that right. "But there wasn't a full moon last night," she pointed out.

"Which means he's gained control of his Were half and can change whenever he wants now."

So a lot more people were going to be in danger. She set down the mug of tea. "I was right last night, wasn't I? You were trying to track him when I saw you by those warehouses, weren't you?"

Hunter nodded. "I was, but then he doubled back on me. That's when I caught your scent."

Eliza's gaze went to the faint scars on his shoulder. "I was stupid to be out there by myself. He would have killed me if you hadn't shown up. You saved my life." She gently ran her fingers over the marks. "I'm sorry you got hurt because of my foolishness."

Hunter shrugged. "Was wandering out in the dark like that foolish? Yes. But don't worry about the scratches—they were nothing. You more than returned the favor by getting out the bullet."

Eliza studied the wound on his shoulder. It continued to heal over even as she watched. "Why was it so important to get it out? You seem to be healing up fine."

He gave her a wry smile. "My shoulder would have healed, but the bullet would have kept tearing my muscles every time I moved. My body's defenses would have resorted to surrounding the whole area with scar tissue. I probably would have lost the use of my arm."

Oh, God. If she hadn't shown up when she did...

Hunter took her hand and pressed his lips to her palm. "I owe you a tremendous debt. I know how hard it was for you to deal with all that blood."

The feel of his lips on her skin made a quiver run through Eliza, and she bit her lip to stifle a moan. Hunter gave her a sexy, little half-smile.

"All these sensations you make me feel," she said softly. "Do they have anything to do with the fact that you're a werewolf? I mean, you don't like release pheromones into the air, or something, do you?"

He chuckled. "Not that I'm aware of. But I have to admit that I'd been wondering if you were releasing some kinds of pheromones yourself—something that would explain why you drive me so crazy. But I guess it's just good old-fashioned chemistry."

She drove him crazy, huh? That was nice to know. She rubbed her thumb back and forth over the back of his hand. "Are you immortal?"

The corner of his mouth edged up. "No. We tend to live a little longer than humans because of our bodies' healing abilities. But we're definitely not immortal."

She nodded, considering that. "What about silver?"

"What about it?"

"If the bullet had been silver, would it have killed you?"

"Ah," he said in understanding. "No, a silver bullet isn't any more deadly than the one you took out of me. If that one had hit anything vital, it would have killed me."

Eliza's gaze went to the bullet wound again and she shuddered. Not wanting to think about it, she decided to steer the conversation in a different direction. "Do you have any other powers?"

Hunter lifted a brow. "Powers?"

She nodded. "You know—like in the movies. Are you stronger than the average person?"

His mouth quirked. "Yes."

"How much stronger?"

"A lot."

Her gaze ran over his well-muscled chest as she realized that she should have already known that. "What about your senses? Are they better?"

"Yeah. I can see better in the dark. My nose is about the same as a wolf's. I can hear better, too."

She thought about that for a while before a horrible thought struck her. "How good is your hearing?"

He gave her a knowing smile. "Really, really good."

"So you overheard all the conversations I've been trying to hide from you the last few days, haven't you?

Like that phone call I got from my editor in the university parking lot?"

Hunter actually looked sheepish as he nodded. "And the conversation you, Tandi, and Nate had when they met us downtown the first night we went out to dinner. And the call you got from Tandi yesterday."

Eliza planted her face in her hands. Oh, God. He'd heard her and Tandi talking about her wanting to take him to bed. She wasn't ever going to be able to look him in the eye again.

"Did you sleep with me because Tandi was pulling ahead in the contest you had going on, or was it because you actually liked me?"

She jerked her head up, ready to defend herself when she caught the teasing grin tugging at the corner of his mouth. She stuck out her tongue. "Very funny. You know exactly why I slept with you."

He chuckled. "Yeah, I know. I couldn't resist."

She picked up her mug and sipped her tea. "What about red meat?"

"What about it?"

"Do you eat a lot of it?" It was something Nate had mentioned and she was curious.

"Maybe a little more than the average person, but my werewolf side makes my metabolism faster, so I eat more of everything, I guess."

The fast metabolism thing must be nice. Then she wouldn't have to worry so much about what she ate. "Well, at least he was right about the red meat."

Hunter frowned. "Who was right? And where did

you come up with all this stuff about werewolves? Other than Hollywood, I mean."

She gave him an embarrassed look. "Nate. Since werewolves are obviously real, he's not as crazy as I thought. Though the profile he came up with could use a little work."

Hunter crossed his arms over his broad chest, clearly interested. "This I have to hear. What else did Nate say about werewolves?"

"According to him, you should have excessive body hair," she pointed out, gesturing to his smooth chest. "Clearly you don't. And you don't have a unibrow."

His mouth quirked in amusement. "Thank God for that."

"And you don't have hairy palms, or overly long fingernails, either."

He made a sound that was half snort, half chuckle. "Hairy palms? I thought that only happened to werewolves who masturbate too much."

She ignored that image and continued. "And you don't have a violent temper. Honestly, Nate got more stuff wrong than he got right."

Hunter was still grinning. "Anything else?"

Eliza looked up at him from beneath her lashes, a naughty little thought suddenly coming to her. "Well, he did mention werewolves having an insatiable sexual appetite."

"Is that so?" Hunter said. "Well, I can't answer for all werewolves, but in my case, I'd have to say he got that one right. Although that could have something to do with you."

She glanced down to see his hard cock straining against the front of his jeans. Her pulse quickened. "Really?"

"Uh-huh." He leaned in close to nuzzle her ear. "In fact, I'm pretty sure it is."

Eliza caught her breath as he trailed feather light kisses along the underside of her jaw, and she had to put her hands on his shoulders to steady herself. Some small part of her mind told her it should matter that he was a werewolf, but it didn't. Maybe she was just being short-sighted, but she felt good with where she was right now, and thinking about it too much would only screw it up. Hunter made her feel things she'd never felt with another man before. What else could she ask for? Even now, her pussy was already beginning to purr just from him nibbling on her ear.

"Well," she said softly. "You'll be glad to know that you seem to have the same effect on me."

"That's nice to hear," he murmured, kissing the corner of her mouth.

She parted her lips, expecting him to give her one of those deep, searing kisses that made her knees go weak. But instead, he gently caught her lower lip with his teeth and began to suckle and tug on it in the most delicious way.

"Tell me," she breathed after he'd released her. "Are all werewolves this talented with their teeth?"

"I don't know," he said, nibbling on her lower lip again. "I've never kissed another werewolf."

For some silly reason, his words pleased Eliza. She didn't like the idea of him with another woman, especially a female werewolf.

"What do you say we get rid of these clothes and I'll show you some of my other talents," he asked between kisses.

* * * * *

Hunter knew it was entirely possible that Eliza would feel differently about him tomorrow once she had time to really dwell on what she'd learned. But right then, he didn't want to think about it. For tonight, at least, she still wanted him.

Sliding his hands beneath Eliza's top, Hunter lifted it over her head. Beneath it, she was wearing a red satin bra, and he almost groaned at the sight. As eager as he was to free her breasts from their confines, he couldn't resist catching them in his hands and teasing their hardened tips through the silky material. Eliza gasped at his touch, the sound soft and sexy in his ear as he rolled each nipple between a forefinger and thumb.

"Mmm," she breathed.

"Does that feel good?" he asked.

"Yes."

He gave each of them a firm, little squeeze. "What about when I do this?"

"Mmm-hmmm," she moaned.

Beneath his fingers, her nipples strained against the satin of her bra, and Hunter was suddenly impatient to feel them against his hands. Giving them another squeeze, he reached around to undo the clasp of her bra. Free of their fabric prison, her breasts spilled into his waiting hands. He cupped them gently, his lightly tanned fingers dark against the creamy flesh as he gently massaged them. She had the most perfect breasts he'd ever seen. Neither large nor small, they were just the right size to fit in his hands. Remembering how sweet their pink tips had tasted on his tongue earlier that day, he lowered his head and took one of her nipples into his mouth.

Hunter made little circles around the stiff peak with his tongue until she was practically squirming. Then he suckled on the ripe bud, drawing it firmly into his mouth and teasing it mercilessly. Eliza moaned and threaded her fingers into his hair, pulling him tighter against her breast. The husky sound made him smile, and he continued to suckle and nibble on that one nipple until he was sure she was about to go crazy. Only then did he release it to lavish the same attention on the other. But while he loved licking and suckling on her breasts, he had a crazy urge to taste another, even sweeter part of her body.

Lifting his head, Hunter released her breasts to slide his hands down her taut stomach to the waistband of her jeans. Tugging at the buttons, he pushed them down over her hips before doing the same to her tiny, red bikini panties. Rather than bending to take them the rest of the way off, he put his hands around her waist and picked her up to set her on the counter. Lifting her legs, he took off first one boot, then the other, dropping them on the kitchen floor with a thud. Next, he dragged off her jeans and panties, leaving her completely naked to his hungry gaze.

Despite his earlier hurry, Hunter was in no rush as he let his gaze run over her long, shapely legs. But the desire to run his hands over her silken skin was too powerful to resist for long, and he reached out to run his fingers lightly up and down one slender calf before dropping to his knees in front of her.

Eliza gasped, her fingers curling over the edge of the counter as he moved his mouth along the sensitive skin of her inner thigh. "Hunter…"

He looked up to give her a wicked grin. "Don't worry. No teeth this time—I promise."

She laughed, the sound soft and breathy.

Returning to his task, Hunter continued tracing a path up her leg with his mouth until he reached her pussy. The scent of her arousal alone was almost enough to make him come undone, and he stifled a groan as he inhaled the intoxicating fragrance. Gently holding onto her thighs, he slowly began to tease her with his tongue, tracing a path up first one side of her slick folds, and then the other. God, she tasted sweet. All honey and cream. Wanting more, he spread her legs even wider so that he could dip his tongue into her wetness.

Eliza breathed out a husky sigh as he plunged his tongue in and out of her pussy. The sound was such a turn-on and he ran his tongue up and down her folds again. While he got closer and closer to her clit with every swipe, he purposely ignored the plump little nub. He loved teasing her like this, and probably would have done it all night, but Eliza must have had enough of his little game because she threaded her fingers in his hair and firmly pulled his mouth to her clit.

Hunter went willingly, making slow, deliberate circles round and round her clit with his tongue before drawing the plump, little nub into his mouth and gently sucking on it. Eliza inhaled sharply. He chuckled and swirled his tongue around her clit again.

Keeping one hand on her leg, he trailed the other along the inside of her thigh all the way to her pussy. He ran his finger up and down her wet slit for a moment before sliding it deep inside and fucking her with it. Eliza cried out, her pussy clenching around his finger as he moved it in and out. She was close to coming already. For a moment, he was torn between bringing her to orgasm right then and teasing her some more. But when her fingers tightened impatiently in his hair, he gave in to her unspoken demand and lashed her clit more forcefully with his tongue as he thrust his finger even deeper into her pussy.

Hunter felt Eliza begin to tremble, the well-toned muscles in her legs tensing against him as she began to come. She writhed against his mouth, holding him firmly in place with her hand as if afraid he'd stop. But he had no intention of stopping. Tonight, he was going to make her to feel pleasure like she'd never felt before. Determined to do just that, he moved his finger faster, caressing her G-spot while he lapped harder and harder at her clit.

Eliza bucked against him, her screams echoing around the kitchen while her orgasm rolled through her. As her body shook and quivered, Hunter continued to move his tongue over her clit. Only when she gave his hair a tug, did he stop lapping and lift his head to look at her. She was leaning back against the cabinet, looking drowsy and completely satiated.

Deciding it was time to give the hard cock pressing against the front of his jeans some relief, Hunter kissed and nibbled his way up her stomach, past her belly button, and all the way to the tip of one breast. He would have stopped to suckle on the rosy red nipple he found there, but Eliza grabbed his hair again and yanked him up for a hard, hot kiss. With his mouth was firmly planted on her own, she slid her hands down his stomach to frantically fumble with the buttons of his jeans.

Groaning, Hunter buried his hands into her long, silky hair, plundering her mouth even as he felt her unbutton his fly. She shoved his jeans down just far enough to get at his rock hard cock, then tugged him free and caressed him firmly up and down a few times. Hunter broke the kiss to let out another groan. *Damn!* A few more seconds of that and he was going to be shooting his cum all over her hand.

Digging his wallet out of his jeans, he took out the condom he had there, then quickly covered himself. Gripping her bottom, he shifted her so she was sitting on the edge of the counter. Still holding her ass with one hand, he used the other to position his erection at the opening of her wet pussy. Even though he was eager to plunge himself deep inside, he couldn't resist rubbing the head up and down her slit a few times. But even that was too much for him, and he grabbed her ass cheeks with both hands to enter her in one deep thrust.

Eliza gasped, her arms and legs wrapping around him to pull him in even deeper. God, her pussy was so tight. It was all he could do not to explode inside her right then.

Taking a deep, ragged breath, he tightened his hold on her ass even more and pumped into her as slowly as he could. That approach worked for a while, at least until Eliza began moving her hips in perfect harmony with his. Each time he thrust, her pussy clenched around him, and despite his best efforts to take things slowly, Hunter found himself gripping her hips and pounding into her harder and harder.

Hunter bit down hard on his lower lip, refusing to give in to the tidal wave of pleasure that was threatening to push him over the edge. Just when he thought he couldn't hold back one more second, Eliza clutched his shoulders and cried out in ecstasy. Only then did he finally allow himself to come. His orgasm was so powerful he thought his legs might actually give out, and he pulled her against him more tightly as he sheathed his cock deep inside her.

His breathing ragged and throat hoarse from the harsh groans of satisfaction he'd just let out, Hunter collapsed against Eliza, burying his face in the curve of her neck. Her scent filled his nostrils and he inhaled deeply. Even if she stayed with him forever, he didn't think he would ever get enough of her.

Hunter wasn't sure how long they stayed like that, and he was just about to scoop Eliza up in his arms and carry her upstairs when he heard her giggle softly against the side of his neck.

He lifted his head to look at her. "What's so funny?"

Her blue eyes danced as she let out another little laugh. "As you were coming, I had the craziest image pop into my mind of you throwing back your head and howling like a wolf."

He chuckled. "If anyone could get a howl out of me, it'd be you."

She leaned forward to kiss him lingeringly on the mouth. "Want to go up to the bedroom and give it a try?"

Hunter's cock hardened again at the thought. In answer, he scooped her up in his arms and carried her upstairs.

Chapter Fourteen

"What's it like being a wolf?"

They were both lying in his big bed, their legs intertwined, her head pillowed on his chest, her long, silky hair draped over his arm. Eliza trailed her fingers up and down his chest. The wound in his shoulder was still there, but he knew it didn't look nearly as gruesome as it had earlier. When she'd asked how long it would take a wound like that to heal completely, he hadn't sugar-coated it. Something like a gunshot wound would take at least a week to heal on the outside, longer on the inside.

When Eliza discovered what he was, Hunter had been filled with dread. He'd never planned on her finding out, and once she had, he expected her to run out the door screaming. But instead, she'd stayed and asked him what had been calm, reasonable questions. It was a reaction he hadn't anticipated, but one he was grateful for. He'd spent his whole life fearing that when he met a woman he really cared for, she would automatically bolt if she ever learned his secret. Pretty much the same way his mom had left them and their dad. But he was coming to learn that Eliza wasn't like other women.

"Being a wolf is incredible," he finally said in answer to her question. "Exhilarating. Liberating. There's nothing like running free through the woods with the grass beneath your paws and the cold, crisp wind in your face. You can hear every sound, smell every living creature for miles."

"You sound like you really love it," she said softly.

"I do," he admitted. "But I'd be lying if I said there aren't some downsides to it."

"Like having to keep people at a distance because you're afraid they'll find out?"

Well, he'd already known that Eliza was perceptive. That comment just proved it again. "That's the big one, yes. Most Weres live alone for just that reason."

"But aren't werewolves like regular wolves? Don't they need to live in packs, too?"

"All werewolves feel the urge to be part of a pack, but it's tough for most of them to trust each other enough to actually make it happen. But like I said at the sanctuary, wolves—and werewolves—can have issues if they're alone all the time. I really think we're meant to live in packs just like regular wolves."

He winced even as the words left his mouth. Shit. He'd made it sound like he was begging her to join his pack. Not the most romantic line to use on a woman you were seriously falling for.

Eliza was silent for a moment as she ran her finger over his nipple. "Does it hurt? When you turn into a wolf, I mean."

He breathed a sigh of relief. Okay, so apparently he'd avoided that sticky foot-in-mouth moment.

"It did at first, mostly because I fought what was happening. Once you learn to give yourself over to the transformation, it doesn't hurt as much—unless you try to push it too fast."

"How old were you when you first changed into a wolf?" she asked.

"Sixteen," he answered. "It was on the first full moon after my sixteenth birthday to be exact. My dad hoped Luke and I didn't have the gene, but he still wanted us to be prepared just in case. Of course, we thought he was completely mental when he told us—until he shifted right in front of us. Even then, Luke and I didn't believe it would happen to us. We were wrong."

"That must have been hard to deal with at that age," she murmured.

"I'll admit, that first change was terrifying." Hunter remembered it like it was yesterday. "When I felt my body twisting and bending into the unfamiliar form of a wolf, I thought I'd go insane from the pain, not to mention fear. But dad was with us the whole time, keeping Luke and me calm. Well, as calm as he could. After that, it got easier. Within a few months, changing became as natural as breathing."

"But still," she said. "I remember that being sixteen was pretty tough. All those teenage hormones to deal with at the same time I was trying to figure out where my life was going. I can't imagine what it'd be like living with this kind of secret at the same time."

He chuckled. "Tell me about it. You think you had teenage hormone issues. Try being able to smell every girl in the school at the same time. My body was in a constant state of arousal, which can actually provoke a werewolf into changing when he's first getting used to the process. You don't know how many times I ran off to the bathroom to make sure I wasn't shifting into a wolf right there in class."

She lifted her head to look at him. "Just the scent of a woman can make you change?"

"Back then it could," he said. "Even now, the smell of the right woman—like you—can make my heart race and start chemicals rushing through my body that convince my Were side it should change. I ignore those impulses, but they're there."

She propped her head on her hand. "I have another question. When you're a wolf, do you do things that a normal wolf does?"

"Such as?"

Eliza shrugged. "I don't know. Like hunt other animals."

He ran his fingers lightly up and down her arm. "No. I've chased quite a few, but never with the intention of killing them."

"That's good. I'd hate to find out that I've been kissing a guy who's had a dead rabbit in his mouth."

He laughed. "No dead rabbits."

"What about needing to be part of a pack? How do you deal with it?"

He thought a moment before answering. It was a

more complex question than Eliza probably realized.

"I have my brother and my father. Even if we aren't together too often, the fact that we're there for each other is enough."

He didn't mention that since he met her, he'd been thinking of a completely different kind of pack—one between a wolf and his mate. It was crazy for him to even be contemplating that considering he'd known Eliza less than a week, but he could already see himself spending the rest of his life with her.

"Does being a werewolf make you more savage?" Eliza asked suddenly.

Still preoccupied with his feelings for Eliza, it took a moment for Hunter to realize what she'd just said, and when it finally did register, he frowned. "No. Why?"

"I was wondering if that was the reason this other werewolf is attacking people."

"No. It has nothing to do with him being a werewolf. If a violent person gets turned into a werewolf, they become a violent werewolf. This guy wouldn't be the first."

Her eyes went wide. "You mean there are other werewolves out that have killed people?"

He nodded. "There are some Weres who think that having the strength and skills we have mean they can take anything they want and kill anyone they feel like."

"Do you think that's what we have here?" she asked. "A serial killer who got turned into a werewolf?"

"Maybe, but I don't think of serial killers as being crazy and out of control. I think of them as being cold-blooded murderers. That's not this guy. I've fought with him a few times already, and he seems like he's insane. He doesn't behave like any Were I've ever dealt with before."

She was silent as she considered that. "How do you stop a person like that? I mean, you obviously can't tell the cops he's a werewolf."

Hunter sighed. "No, I can't."

"So what do we do?"

He wasn't sure if wanted to get into this with her, but he knew Eliza would keep poking until she figured it out. It wasn't like he could hide it from her forever.

"Even though we all tend to live solitary lives for the most part, all werewolves realize they're part of a bigger whole, so there are some unwritten rules we live by. They're predicated on the basic principle that we don't draw attention to ourselves because one Were exposing himself is a risk to all."

Eliza frowned. "Okay, but what does that mean to us?"

This part was going to be hard for her to hear. He had to choose his words carefully. "When an established werewolf like me learns of another werewolf violating our code, it's expected—required—that I deal with it."

Her frown deepened. "I don't understand what you're saying."

He supposed he couldn't blame her for not understanding—he'd been dancing around what he meant instead of just saying it. "I'll have to kill him."

"Kill him?" She swallowed hard. "Couldn't you just chase him off?"

"So he can go somewhere else and start killing there?" Hunter asked. "I wouldn't want that on my conscience. Would you?"

She sighed. "No, of course not. It's just that…"

"Just what?"

"I'm afraid for you," she said. "Going after him will be dangerous."

Hunter gently brushed her hair back from her face. "He's recently changed, and barely in control of himself. I have knowledge and experience on my side. I'll be fine," He gave her a small smile. "But it's nice knowing you care about me."

"Of course I care about you," she said. "I care about you a lot."

Hunter felt a surge of pleasure at her words. Maybe the thought of them having a future together wasn't so crazy after all. Maybe he'd finally met the one woman who would be able to accept him for what he was.

* * * * *

In that moment, Eliza realized just how much she really did care for him. It seemed crazy, considering they'd just met. Even crazier, considering she'd just found out he was a werewolf. But it didn't matter to her. It wasn't a simple issue that could be overlooked—like being messy or liking a different TV show—but it wasn't like Hunter was some cursed, evil creature who went around killing people. He simply had a genetic trait that allowed him to turn into a wolf. It was no different than if he had blond hair or blue eyes. Okay, maybe it was a little different. But she wasn't about to throw away what she had with him because of it. And while she wasn't quite sure she was ready to give a name to what it was she was feeling for him, she knew that it definitely wasn't something she'd never felt for any other man before.

Leaning forward, Eliza gave him a long, passionate kiss. Hunter slid his hand into her hair, kissing her back with the same urgency. She took her time exploring his mouth with hers, finding every delicious little nook and cranny before pulling away to nip playfully at his bottom lip like he'd done to her earlier. She didn't know if he'd like being on the receiving end, but the husky groan he let out told her he enjoyed it as much as she did.

Sucking on his lower lip again, she slid her hand down his rock-hard abs to wrap her hand firmly around his rapidly hardening cock. Remembering the attention he'd given her pussy downstairs in the kitchen, and then again when they'd first come up to the bedroom, she decided it was way past time to return the favor.

Giving his bottom lip another little tug, Eliza slowly kissed and nibbled her way down the steely contours of his chest and stomach until she came to his erection. Sliding her hand down to the base of his shaft, she swirled her tongue over the tip to lick up the bead of pre-come that glistened there. He tasted so good that she couldn't resist giving his penis a little squeeze. Cupping his balls with her other hand, she lovingly ran her tongue up and down his shaft. But rather than take him completely in her mouth, she closed her lips around the head and sucked gently, then flicked him with her tongue. Hunter sucked in his breath as if in anticipation of her next move, but she continued to tease the head of his cock, swirling her tongue round and round until he let out a groan of frustration. Deciding to finally take pity on him, she ran her tongue over the head of his cock once more before suddenly taking him deep in her mouth.

The sound Hunter made this time was one of satisfaction, and Eliza couldn't help smiling a little as she moved her mouth up and down on his cock. He was close to orgasm already. It was empowering knowing she could make him climax so quickly. But while she could have made him come for her right then, she wanted to tease him some more first. With that in mind, she pulled her mouth off his shaft and concentrated on his balls instead. Careful to keep her touch light, she lavished the same attention on them that she'd given his cock, gently fondling them with her hand while at the same time running her tongue over their velvety softness.

"God, that feels good," Hunter said hoarsely. "Don't stop."

Stop? She was just getting started.

Still cupping his balls, she traced a path up his shaft with her tongue again. Pressing her lips to the head, she glided her tongue over the tip, then took his entire length into her mouth. Hunter let out a ragged gasp as the tip of his cock touched the back of her throat before she began to move her head up and down again.

She kept her movements slow and deliberate, sliding up to the very tip of his erection before taking him all the way in her mouth again, going a little deeper each time. Hunter slid his hand into her hair, gently thrusting his hips in time to her movements and pushing his cock down her throat. Eliza whimpered. She absolutely loved it when he fucked her mouth like that. Knowing it meant he was close to coming, she wondered if she should back off and tease him some more, but quickly decided against it. She'd tormented him enough.

Grasping the base of his shaft more firmly in his hand, she moved her mouth up and down on him faster and faster.

"Just like that," he rasped. "You're going to make me come."

No sooner were the words out when he groaned. A moment later, Eliza felt hot jets of cum shooting down her throat. She took it all, relishing how delicious he tasted, and refusing to stop until she was sure she'd gotten every drop.

She lifted her head to find Hunter regarding her from beneath half-closed lids. His mouth edged up. "You're amazing."

Eliza smiled at the compliment, and maybe even blushed a little, too.

She bent to press another kiss to the head of his cock and was surprised to see that he was still semi-hard. Well, damn. Grinning, she crawled on top of him to straddle his legs. Bracing her hands on either side of his broad shoulders, she slowly and sensuously began to rub her clit against the head of his slightly erect shaft. The contact sent signals to every pleasure point in her body, and she closed her eyes, losing herself in how good it felt.

But rubbing against him wasn't enough. She had to have him inside her, and from the way his penis was hardening again, Hunter was obviously up for it. Dear God, she'd never met a man with his kind of stamina. There were definitely some advantages to dating a werewolf.

Grabbing a condom packet from the bedside table, Eliza carefully rolled it on his erection, then positioned herself at the proper angle so she could slowly and deliberately lowered herself onto his hard cock. A soft sigh slipped past her lips as he filled her pussy. No other man had ever fit her so perfectly, and she closed her eyes, savoring the feel of him.

Deciding she didn't want to rush this, Eliza lifted her hands and cupped her breasts. Her nipples immediately pebbled in response to her touch and she gave them a little squeeze between her forefingers and thumbs. Lying back on the pillows, Hunter watched her with a hungry look in his gold eyes that made her pulse quicken. She wasn't usually such an exhibitionist in bed, but the urge to put on a show for him was too great to resist, and she found herself lifting a hand to her mouth and slowly licking one finger. Getting it nice and wet, she then slid it down her stomach to the soft curls nestled between her legs, where she began to make lazy, little circular motions on her clit.

Hunter's eyes practically glowed with excitement now. Knowing he'd get an even better view if she leaned back a little, Eliza shifted and slowly rotated her hips in time to her fingers. The position not only pushed her breasts out at a sexy angle as she continued to play with them, but also made it easier to get at her clit, and she moaned at the sensations that suddenly assailed her. Catching her bottom lip between her teeth, she moved her fingers faster.

"That's it," Hunter told her huskily. "Make yourself come, babe."

At the erotic command, Eliza immediately felt her body start to tremble in that familiar way that said her climax was near. It started right under her fingertips, then moved outward, quickly enveloping her whole body, and she cried out as wave after wave of ecstasy washed over her. She was so dizzy from how damn good it felt she could barely even keep her fingers on her clit. Somehow, she managed, pushing herself to even greater heights. It wasn't until the area was too tender to touch anymore that she finally pulled her hand away and collapsed forward against Hunter's chest.

He let her lay there for a moment, allowing her to catch her breath before he slowly began to thrust into her pussy. Pushing herself up, she placed her hands on his chest and slowly rode up and down on him. The movement drove his cock deeper and deeper inside with every thrust, and she bit her lip with a moan.

Eliza was just settling into a rhythm when she felt Hunter's hand smack against her ass. She yelped in surprise. But as that same delicious warmth she'd felt when he'd spanked her in the shower the other night began to spread over her bottom, her lips curved into a smile.

"*Mmmm*," she breathed. "Do that again."

Hunter's eyes danced with amusement as he lifted his hand to spank her ass. Even though she knew it was coming, Eliza let out another squeal as the smack landed squarely on her already stinging ass cheek.

"Ride me," Hunter commanded softly, his hand coming down on her other cheek.

Eliza did as he ordered, moving up and down on his hard cock in time to the rhythm of his spanks. Each time his hand smacked against her ass, her pussy clenched tightly around his shaft. Hunter alternated from one cheek to the other, delivering smack after stinging smack until he finally grabbed her burning ass cheeks with both hands and pumped into her hard and fast.

Eliza gasped at the feel of his strong hands squeezing her tender bottom. "Harder!"

Hunter obeyed, thrusting so forcefully that Eliza couldn't have stopped herself from coming if she wanted to. Her orgasm hit her with such soul-shattering intensity she thought she might actually faint from the intensity of it. Beneath her, Hunter groaned long and low as he found his release. Knowing that he was coming with her only made her climax even better.

As the tremors rippling through her body slowly began to subside, Eliza opened her eyes to see a grin of complete and utter satisfaction on Hunter's face. Eyes glinting, he threw back his head back and howled.

Chapter Fifteen

Hunter didn't have any classes the next day. Eliza would have gladly stayed in bed, if for no other reason than she wanted to put off the confrontation with the other werewolf for as long as possible. She knew it was immature, selfish, and more than a little shortsighted, but she'd just found this amazing man and she didn't want anything bad to happen to him.

She was just wondering whether she could keep him in bed a while longer if she kissed her way down his chest and gave him another one of those blowjobs he liked when her phone rang.

It was Alex. "Hey, Eliza. Nate and I are down at the police department, and we thought you might want to see what's going on."

Hunter raised an eyebrow in her direction. "What's wrong?" he mouthed silently.

She cursed his exceptional hearing, but relayed the question to Alex.

"Your basic torch-and-pitchfork crowd is down here demanding the cops do something about this wolf."

The reporter in Eliza was desperate to see what was going on, but the woman in her wanted to keep Hunter firmly locked in this bedroom. Unfortunately, he was already up and getting dressed before she could give her opinion on the subject.

"We'll be there as fast as we can," she told Alex. "Get a few photos in case everything blows over before we get there."

"I don't think it will. These people look pretty upset. But I'm already ahead of you—I've taken plenty of shots already," her photographer said. "See you in a bit."

Fifteen minutes later, she was following behind Hunter's SUV as they made their way into town. She would have rather ridden with him, but she thought Alex might need to use the car, and since she was going to see him at the station, it made sense to drive both their cars into town.

She nibbled on a piece of peanut-butter covered toast as she drove. It was either that or bacon. She really needed to get Hunter to the grocery store. He barely had anything in his place that didn't come out of the meat department. She didn't even want to think what his cholesterol levels were like.

When they arrived at the police station, it was to find a mob of people gathered outside the building. Eliza quickened her pace to keep up with Hunter's long strides as they made their way across the parking lot. Lieutenant Newman was standing on the front steps along with several other cops, as well as a handful of men in uniform. When she got close, she saw that they were from the Department of Fish and Wildlife.

"...so we're urging everyone to stay indoors until we take care of this matter, especially after dark," Newman was saying.

"And how's that supposed to do any good?" called out a heavyset man from the crowd. "The damn wolf already broke into someone's house, didn't it? What's to stop the beast from doing it again?"

"He's right," someone else agreed. "We should be out hunting this thing!"

"Yeah!" came another shout, and another.

Damn, Alex hadn't been exaggerating. These people seemed like they were ready to light their torches and storm the castle any second.

Newman held up his hands. "Daryl, I've said this a dozen times already. We can't say for sure that the wolf broke into the victim's house. It's more likely the man heard a noise and opened the door to see what it was. Fish and Wildlife is already getting some people together so we can get out there and hunt this thing down before it can attack anyone else. But they need time to figure out the best way to do it. We can't go out shooting every wolf we see. Until then we need everyone to stay indoors after nightfall. And if you see a large wolf hanging around, call the police immediately. Don't go trying to kill the animal yourself."

Newman's words were rational, but it didn't seem like they were getting through to the crowd. If anything, they were only starting to make the people more upset.

Beside her, Hunter swore under his breath. "These

people are confused and frightened, and nothing the police can say is going to change that. We'll be lucky if they aren't all in the woods within an hour shooting at anything that moves, including each other."

Eliza was worried about that, but she was also worried about them shooting at Hunter when he went out to hunt for the other werewolf. That thought made her blood run cold.

Before she even realized what he was doing, Hunter jogged up the steps. Newman and the others immediately made way for him.

Hunter turned and surveyed the crowd, but he didn't say anything. He didn't have to. He simply moved his gaze from one person to the next until the crowd quieted. Hunter was a big man with a presence and a charisma that commanded attention. He didn't say anything different than Newman, but when Hunter said the police department would have a plan in place within twenty-four hours, the crowd believed him. And when he told everyone to go home and stay indoors, they nodded in agreement and slowly began to disperse.

As Eliza made her way over to Hunter, Alex and Nate fell into step beside her. She'd been wondering where they were. Before she could ask, Hunter spoke.

"I need to talk to Newman and the people from Fish and Wildlife. See if I can find out exactly when they're going to start hunting. Hopefully, I can keep them from killing a lot of innocent wolves," he said. "I'll be right back."

Eliza didn't want to see that happen either, but there

was one wolf in particular she didn't want getting shot, and that was Hunter. It wasn't like she could say that with Alex and Nate standing there, so she just nodded.

"Any new leads?" she asked Alex and Nate after Hunter walked off.

Knowing the killer was a werewolf and not human didn't change the fact that he was going after his victims for a reason. If they could figure out who was on his hit list, they might be able to get there in time to catch him.

"Nothing concrete." Nate said. "Alex and I talked to every hunter, fisherman, and hiker in town, while Tandi and a few of the other cops have been going through their files trying to find a firm connection between the first three victims and anyone else. We've come up with a list, but there are almost fifty people on it so far."

Damn. At some point Hunter and this other werewolf were going to go at it, and she dreaded that moment. But until then, this monster could kill a lot more innocent people, and she dreaded that too. She wished there was some way to figure out who this thing was targeting and warn them.

"Hey," Alex said. "You okay?"

She jerked her head up. The photographer was regarding, concern on his face. "What? Oh yeah, I'm fine."

"Tandi told us what happened out by Wainwright's place," Nate said. "How you were attacked by two huge wolves, and that you and Newman ran into them again yesterday. Newman isn't saying much about it, but from what little he has said, they were pretty damn scary—and that was in broad daylight. You went up against them in the dark and both of them were trying to kill you. It's understandable to still be shaken up."

"Only one of the wolves tried to attack me," she said. "The other was protecting me."

Alex frowned. "Protecting you?"

She nodded. "He fought the other wolf to keep me safe."

Alex and Nate exchanged looks. They probably thought she was insane.

"The werewolves were fighting each other?" Nate asked, lowering his voice.

Crap. Why the hell had she opened her mouth about that? But she couldn't stand the idea of anyone thinking Hunter was like that monster. She couldn't say that to Nate and Alex, though. They were both waiting for an answer, so she was going to have to tell them something.

"Shit," Alex muttered.

Eliza followed the photographer's gaze to see a blond man making his way toward them. She frowned as she recognized Clark Emery, the whiny reporter who had stomped out of *Paranormal Today* with his panties in a bunch. Contrary to what Alex said, he'd obviously found his way here from the airport just fine.

She was ready for Clark to start slamming them the second his mouth opened, so she was shocked when he gave her a smile and stuck out his hand.

"Eliza Bradley. I'm surprised to see you still up here," he said. "I thought you would have already turned in your article and been on your way home. Must be a juicy piece you're working. So, tell me—what's the story here?"

That was more than he'd said to her in all the time they worked together. Granted, it had only been a week or so, but still.

"Forget it, Clark," Alex said. "Roger already called and told us that you jumped ship to the dark side and are working for the competition."

Clark tried to look hurt, but it didn't work. It just made him look like he had gas.

"So I took a job with *Strange Times*. I have to pay the bills just like everyone else, don't I? That doesn't mean we can't help each other." He gave her another smile. "That way we both win."

Did Clark seriously expect her to fall for that? Maybe he'd been possessed by one of the aliens he was always writing about.

"Eliza, you never really got a chance to see Clark in action, but his standard MO was to wait around until someone else did all the leg work, then move in and take all the credit by getting his story in first," Alex said. "Even if it meant getting most of the details wrong."

Clark glared at the photographer, then turned to Eliza. "I'm not trying to scoop you. I came into this late and need help catching up. *Strange Times* hired me on a non-reimbursable probationary status. I need to give them something good, or they won't even pay for my plane ticket up. What do say to helping out a fellow reporter?"

She wanted to tell him to go to hell, but bit her

tongue. "Sorry to tell you this, but I think you wasted your time and money. Everything points to a regular old wolf going on a rampage."

She held her breath, half afraid Nate would jump in and contradict her, but he didn't say anything.

Clark folded his arms and gave her a superior look. "If that's true, what are you and Jimmy Olsen still doing up here?"

Eliza hesitated. There was one thing she could say that'd get this idiot out of the picture for good, but if it got back to her boss, she'd be screwed. On the other hand, Roger told her to do whatever she had to do to keep Clark from scooping her.

"We're hoping to turn this into a story we can use to jump ship to the *Chronicle*," she said. "You know—a city surrounded by untamed wilderness, living in fear of the man-eating wolf who kills at will. A piece like this could be our ticket to the big league. You of all people should understand that."

Clark snorted. "And they had the nerve to call me disloyal. At least I had the integrity to quit *PT* before I went to work for their competition. But then again, I never thought you were one of us anyway."

The other reporter turned and stormed off, leaving them standing there. Had Clark believed her? Regardless, she felt pretty dirty for admitting what she'd been thinking all along. Even Alex was looking at her out the corner of his eye.

"Do you think he'll leave?" Nate asked.

"Don't bet on it," Alex said. "Clark is sneaky as hell.

He's likely to show up at the worst possible time. Fortunately, he can't find his ass with both hands most of the time. There's definitely no way he's going to find these werewolves before we do."

If Alex had tossed out the word *werewolves* a few days ago, Eliza would have doubted his sanity. Now, all she wanted to do was convince him that they were still looking for nothing more than a man-eating wolf. Because her instincts screamed at her to protect Hunter's secret. But she couldn't lie to Alex—or Nate. And it wouldn't do any good if she tried. They'd moved too far beyond that point now. There was no going back.

"Let's hope you're right about Clark," she said. "Because this isn't about getting a story anymore. It's about stopping this monster before it kills again."

Nate opened his mouth to say something, but Hunter interrupted him. She hadn't even heard him come down the steps.

"They won't officially start the hunt until tomorrow, but they're under a lot of pressure to get out there now and make it look like they're doing something," he said, his mouth tight. "I'm going to go help come up with a plan. I don't want them shooting every wolf they see just to appease the public."

Eliza could tell that Hunter's mind was already on the task ahead of him, but she pulled him off to the side, then reached a hand up to pull his chin around, making him look at her.

"Be careful out there," she said. "You'll be with other people, but we don't know for sure if that will keep this thing from coming at you. You've tangled with him a couple of times already. He might try to attack you when you're not ready."

Hunter ran a finger along the line of her jaw, making her skin tingle. "Starting to think like a werewolf, huh?"

"No. I just worry about you and want you to be careful."

"I'll be careful—promise," he said. "Are you going to keep poking around with Nate and Alex?"

She nodded. "They've been working with Tandi and some other cops trying to come up with a list of people who knew the first three victims. But right now it's too big to be of any use. Maybe we can come up with a new angle that will help."

Hunter bent his head to kiss her. "Be careful yourself, and stay away from any heavily wooded areas. I don't want you stumbling into that thing when I'm not around to protect you."

She shuddered at the thought of seeing that big, black werewolf again. "You don't have to tell me that twice. I'm staying out of those woods—trust me."

Hunter promised he'd be home by six. "Do you want me to stop by and pick you up at the hotel, or here at the station?"

"I'll have the rental car, or get Alex to drop me off."

Hunter frowned. "Okay, but I don't you waiting around outside. If you get there early, you'll find keys to the front door in a fake rock to the left of the porch."

Seriously? She didn't know anyone actually used those stupid hide-away rocks. She would have teased him about it, but the Fish and Wildlife people were already heading out. She gave Hunter another kiss and reminded him again to be careful, then watched him jog over to his SUV.

"Seems like you two are getting pretty serious," Alex said from behind her.

She turned to see Nate and the photographer standing there with big smiles on their faces. "We're just friends."

Nate laughed. "Right."

"So, how are we going track down the werewolf's next victim?" Alex asked when it became obvious she wasn't going to say anything else about her social life.

"I don't know yet," she admitted. "First thing's first, though. I need to get something to eat because I'm starving."

* * * * *

Eliza was sitting in the same diner where she'd first met Hunter sipping her third cup of coffee and listening to Nate explain how he and Tandi had met when it hit her.

"What if we've been focusing on the wrong connection between these three men the whole time?"

Nate and Alex looked at her in confusion.

"Maybe they knew each other before they ever went hunting together. Maybe they went to school together." She looked at Nate. "You and Tandi stayed in touch with each other, so it's not crazy to think those men did, too.

If I'm right, it might lead us to the other people this werewolf might be after."

Unless he was done killing, and wasn't after anyone anymore. She'd discussed that possibility with Nate and Alex while they'd eaten, but instinct told her the werewolf wasn't done with whatever he'd set out to do.

Nate pulled out his phone. "I'll call Tandi and see if she can find out where those guys went to school."

It took Tandi almost an hour to get back to them with the information, but she was able to confirm that all three victims had gone to the same high school. She was pissed that she never thought of that idea. But then again, it could just be a coincidence. There were only about seven public schools in Fairbanks.

Eliza wasn't sure anyone at the school would talk to them without a warrant and a couple cops to back them up, but Nate said that wouldn't be a problem.

"I used to date the librarian," he said, leading the way.

Eliza lifted a brow. Nate obviously had way more game than she'd given him credit for.

A few years younger than Ned, the redhead hesitated when he asked to see the yearbooks, but then agreed—as long as they limited their search to old books and nothing related to current students.

The yearbooks were stacked on shelves in a small room off the main library. It took a little while to find the ones that correlated to the right dates. Once they did, it was just a matter of flipping through the pages, looking for something she hoped they'd recognize when they saw it.

"Bingo," Nate said.

He spun the yearbook around so she and Alex could see, then pointed at a photo of ten teens standing for a group picture. Underneath it were the words, *Rifle Team*. The school had a rifle team? Only in Alaska.

"These three are our victims." He pointed out each one according to the names listed below the photo. "Three guys who used to be on a school rifle team, then got into an argument while on a hunting trip? It can't be a coincidence."

There were seven other teens in the picture, including two girls.

"Is anybody else thinking what I'm thinking?" Nate asked.

"That depends on what you're thinking," Eliza said.

"That something happened to another member of this team, and now that person is getting their revenge?"

Alex snorted. "I think you're confusing a cheap, B-grade movie plotline with real life."

Nate's eyes narrowed. He opened his mouth to launch a counterattack, but Eliza cut him off.

"If we're right, this picture means there may be seven other potential victims out there. It'll take long enough just tracking down all of them."

"Maybe not," Nate said. "There's a good chance that some of these people don't even live in Fairbanks anymore. It should be easy for Tandi to find out."

When they walked into the police station half the cops were handling the calls coming in to the special hotline that had been set up, while the other half were taking statements from people who'd come in to report seeing a big wolf roaming around the streets of Fairbanks. Tandi was in the second group, and didn't look like she was going to be free anytime soon.

Eliza glanced down at her watch and swore when she saw that it was almost five-thirty. She'd wanted to get over to Hunter's place and check on him. While he hadn't come out and said he was going after the other werewolf, she had no doubt he would if the opportunity presented itself.

Alex must have noticed her dismay because he nudged her shoulder. "We aren't going to be able to talk to Tandi for a while. Go meet Hunter for dinner. We'll call if we get anything."

She felt horrible about it, but relieved at the same time. "Are you sure? You'll call if you figure anything out, right?"

Alex promised they would, then practically pushed her out the door.

Eliza was so focused on checking to see if Hunter's SUV was in the garage—it wasn't—that she didn't notice the car following her until she stopped. She groaned when she saw Clark Emery get out and slam the door. Crap. She really didn't need to deal with him at the moment.

"What the hell is going on?" he demanded as he strode up to her. "The police scanners are going crazy. People are seeing wolves roaming around town and the cops going crazy, but you and Alex spend your day at a local high school."

She glared at him. "You followed us?"

He ignored the question. "Whose house is this anyway?"

She was about to tell him to bug off when the expression that suddenly crossed his face stopped her. He was looking over her left shoulder like there was an axe-wielding murder standing right behind her.

The hair on the back of her neck stood up. She slowly turned around, knowing what she would see. The big, black wolf stood no more than thirty feet away, glaring like he hated the sight of them. More precisely, he was staring at Eliza that way. She could imagine why. Hunter had stopped him from killing her, and the thing obviously hadn't like that.

"Walk slowly toward the house," she whispered to Clark.

"Are you crazy?" he whispered back. "If we move, it will attack."

"He's going to do that anyway."

She wasn't sure why, but this time, the sight of the black monster didn't rob her of the ability to move like it had that night near the warehouses. Maybe it was because she knew there was a man underneath that salvage wolf exterior, or maybe she was at the point where the fear couldn't get any worse. Either way, when she told her feet to move, they did.

She and Clark slowly edged closer to the house, but hadn't gotten more than ten feet when the werewolf raced toward them.

"Run!" Eliza shouted.

She sprinted for the door. It was crazy to think she'd find the key in the hide-away rock before the werewolf got to her, but she had to try. She heard Clark behind her and all she could do was hope he kept up. She doubted the werewolf would even bother to toy with the reporter before he killed him.

She made it to the fake rock beside the porch, but the black wolf jumped between her and the door. Not that the door would have slowed it down much if they'd gotten inside. The one on Wainwright's place had been thicker than Hunter's, and it hadn't held at all.

She slung the fake rock at the wolf, knowing it wouldn't hurt him, but hoping it would distract him long enough for her and Clark to get somewhere safe.

"Go!" she screamed, shoving him off the porch and herding him around to the back of the house. If she remembered right, there was a shed back there.

As they rounded the side of the house, Eliza threw a glance over her shoulder. The werewolf was right behind them, running almost casually. She knew the thing was playing with them. If it wanted to catch them, it would have done so already.

"Get to the shed," she yelled.

She just prayed Hunter didn't keep it locked.

She was just about there when she felt a hand on her shoulder. Eliza barely had time to register what it was before Clark shoved past her with a curse. "Get the hell out of my way!"

The jackass practically trampled her in his effort to

get to the shed first. Eliza stumbled, but kept her feet. If she fell, the werewolf would be on her in a flash.

Clark already had the door open and she shoved him inside just as the werewolf nipped at her heels. She spun and yanked the door closed behind her. The whole building shuddered as the vicious creature slammed into it. Thank God the door opened out or it would have exploded around her. On the down side, there wasn't a lock, so she had to hold on to keep it from bouncing open as the monster outside smashed into it repeatedly.

Still holding onto the knob, she turned and looked around. The shed had the typical stuff she'd expect someone living up here in Alaska to need—hand tools, axes, a snow mobile, a snow blower, and a chainsaw, as well as lots of gas cans and oil containers stacked against one wall. Clark was cowering on the floor beside them.

"Get me something to wedge against the door," she shouted.

Clark didn't more. He just knelt there with his eyes as big as saucers.

Crap.

She let go of the door long enough to grab a nearby shovel and wedge it into the door jamb. It kept the door from bouncing open under the werewolf's impact, but that move only seemed to delay the inevitable as the creature outside started to rip the doors to pieces with his claws and fangs. Within seconds, he had one corner of the door off and was reaching inside with one of his paws.

She grabbed an axe off the wall and swung it at the

creature. If the thing got enough of its body through that opening, it would be able to rip the door open—shovel or no shovel.

"Dammit, Clark, help me!" she shouted as she hit the creature's front leg again. She was doing some damage—she saw the blood. But she wasn't doing enough.

She tossed a glance over her shoulder. Clark was practically curled into a ball on the floor, apparently content to let her to save him.

She searched the room again, looking for a better weapon. She would have grabbed the chainsaw and tried that against the werewolf, but she knew the thing was too heavy for her to pick up. Besides, she had no idea how to start one.

Then, as suddenly as the attack had started, it stopped.

Eliza stood near the torn-up door, her axe held high as she strained her ears for some indication of what the werewolf was doing. But all was quiet.

"Do you think it left?" Clark asked in a quivering voice.

She couldn't imagine why the thing would leave. It had just about torn the door apart.

Eliza was so focused on the door she didn't even realize there was a window on the side of the building until the werewolf smashed it in.

Chapter Sixteen

He'd followed the other demon yesterday after they'd fought and the human had shot at them. He and the big gray beast had tangled enough times for him to recognize that the other demon was more skilled than he was, so he'd hoped to strike while the thing was weak and slow. But the chance hadn't come because the creature had climbed into a vehicle and driven away.

He still drove occasionally, though he barely remembered how to do it. It seemed like a lifetime ago that he did those human things. Still, he had done it a few times since returning. But this time he couldn't—his vehicle was very far away and he hadn't wanted to break off the chase to get it. Instead, he'd followed the other demon as best he could, staying to the woods to the side of the roads, avoiding the lights and sounds of the others vehicles.

It had taken him all night and most of the next day to find the small road that turned off from the road and led to a house. He was ready to smash into the house and kill the creature before it could throw off its weaker form and face him, but the creature hadn't been there.

The long run had tired him and made him hungry, so he'd killed and eaten a deer. He remembered killing deer in the past, though he didn't remember eating them warm and raw, but it had satisfied his hunger. Then he'd laid down to wait for the demon. He could have changed into his weaker form—maybe slipped into the house through a window to wait—but he avoided the change whenever he could. He preferred his cursed form.

Besides, it hurt to change.

He'd heard the two vehicles approaching the moment they'd turned off the main road. He'd wondered if the second vehicle held the woman with the tantalizing scent he'd been thinking about so much lately. His mouth began to water at the thought of what she would taste like, but then other parts of him began to awaken as well, urging him to do other things. Those thoughts confused him, but as the woman's smell grew stronger, the urge to give in to those strange needs grew sharper and harder to ignore. Maybe he wouldn't kill her right away.

But then he'd picked up another scent he didn't recognize—a man's. The man was shouting at the woman, and he found himself moving toward them before he even realized what he was doing.

When they'd run, he'd chased them. It was fun hearing their hearts thud in their chests as the smell of the fear rolled off them. Then they'd hidden in that small wooden shack—and that had angered him. He tried to get through the door, but the woman struck him repeatedly with something sharp. He couldn't see what it was, and while it didn't really do much damage, it hurt like a son of a bitch.

That was when he moved around to the side of the cabin and broke through the window. The woman was still by the door, so he knew she wouldn't see him until it was too late.

He ignored the pain as the shards cut into him. He caught the woman completely by surprise and he delighted in the fear that spread across her face. Unfortunately, he'd misjudged the size of the window and wasn't able to work his way through it as fast as he would have liked. That gave the woman time to get it together and she ran across the small space to slash him with her weapon again. She cut into his face and shoulder over and over again, infuriating him so much that he almost broke his own shoulder in an attempt to snap at her.

The move slammed her back over a machine that he dimly remembered as a snowmobile. The axe flew from her hands as she tumbled head over heels into the stack of cans against the far wall. The containers scattered everywhere and his nose suddenly burned as smells from his previous life assaulted his senses—gas and oil.

He almost had his second shoulder through the window, but the damn woman found her axe and came at him again, swinging even harder than before. Before, he'd considered giving in to those strange urges he felt whenever he saw the woman, but now he just wanted to tear her to pieces. He was definitely going to enjoy hurting her.

He's so intent on the woman that he didn't even realize something was behind him until he felt teeth tear into his hind quarters.

* * * * *

Hunter was just wondering who the other car beside Eliza's belonged to when the rogue werewolf's scent struck him through the open window of his SUV. He was out of the truck before it had even rolled to a stop. He tore off his boots and jeans, then yanked open his shirt, scattering buttons everywhere. He shifted on the run, the pain so extreme that his consciousness sharpened down to a long, dark tunnel. But he pushed through it, enduring pain he knew would only be temporary in order to get to Eliza faster.

His sense of smell exploded into a vivid mural of sensations as he dropped forward to all fours. The tracks of pheromones and spores were so clear that he could almost see where the other Were had laid in wait, where Eliza had been when she'd began to run, and which way she'd had gone. He even picked up the slight increase in gas fumes that told him she'd made it to the shed.

He didn't recognize the other male scent that was with Eliza, but he knew the guy had run with her and that he'd been so terrified he pissed himself. That told Hunter pretty much all he needed to know about the man.

His ears picked up the sounds of growling, the cries of alarm, and the grunts of a physical struggle nearly at the same time his nose had found the scents. But his wolf mind always processed smells before sounds, so it only confirmed what he already knew—that Eliza and the man were in the shed, and that the wolf was trying to get in there with them.

He rounded the corner of the house to see the big, black beast trying to rip its way through the side window of the building. Someone was fighting against the creature from the inside, trying to keep it out. He growled deep in his throat when he heard the rapid thumping heartbeat he identified as Eliza's as clearly as if he could see her. She was alive, but he had no way of knowing if she was injured.

Hunter threw himself on the creature's back, closing his jaws down on the thing's spine. He bit deep, then yanked. The beast's thick fur prevented a killing grip, but he crunched down hard, feeling muscles give and bones crack.

The werewolf yelped under him and twisted the remaining portion of his body out of the window like an eel, breaking Hunter's grip and slipping sideways to get away. Hunter stayed with him, blocking his escape and slamming his shoulder into the thing in an attempt to knock it down.

Hunter was so damn furious he could barely think. All he knew was that this monster had attacked Eliza again. He growled in rage, surging forward to get his jaws on the black wolf's throat. He was so blinded by anger he completely forgot how incredibly fast the other beast was. Hunter's jaw's snapped down on thin air as the creature ducked under his attack and darted for the woods. The thing's rear legs almost dragged as it ran, testimony to the amount of damage Hunter had inflicted on him with his initial attack. The urge to go after the creature and finish him was almost overpowering, but he needed to make sure Eliza was okay.

He turned and ran for the shed, but a whisper stopped him in his tracks.

"Hunter," Eliza said softly. "There's someone in here with me. He can't see you."

Indecision like he'd never felt warred inside him. Normally, he'd never risk exposing his wolf form to another person. But the need to see Eliza and make sure the werewolf hadn't harmed a single hair on her head was stronger than anything he'd ever felt before. Strong enough to make him risk his life and his identity.

"Go," she begged. "Please."

He sniffed the air one more time to make sure the other Were's scent had faded, then turned and ran back toward the front of the house.

Hunter had picked up enough of the other man's smell to know it wasn't Alex or Nate, but he trusted that Eliza would keep the guy busy long enough for him to change and get his clothes back on.

When he reached his SUV, he pushed the shift again, staggering as the pain rushed through him for a second time. Two fast changes in the space of a few minutes, not to mention the exertion of the brief but savage fight dropped him to his knees and threatened to keep him there. He wanted more than anything to stay where he was and gasp his way past the bone-crushing agony. But he couldn't do that. He had to assume that whoever Eliza had been warning him about would be coming this way soon. He had to get up and get dressed. Being found naked and sweaty on the ground would provoke as many questions as being seen in his wolf form.

He climbed to his feet and dragged on his jeans. Ignoring his ripped up socks, he shoved his feet in his boots and gave the laces a cursory yank.

He winced as he lifted his arms to pull on the tattered remains of his shirt. His ribs felt like someone had hit him with a two-by-four. He was still aching from the change. There weren't enough buttons left on the shirt to even bother trying to do anything with it, so he left it hanging as he ran for the back of the house again.

Eliza was already outside the shed, carrying his axe and looking around carefully. The man—whom he didn't recognize at all—was hanging back near his snowmobile. It seemed pretty gutless, but Hunter could care less who the man was and why he was letting Eliza check to see if it was safe. The moment he saw her, all other thoughts evaporated.

He ran to her and grabbed her up in an embrace, kissing her, then looking her over and sniffing for any hint of blood that would let him know she'd been injured. That part would have been easier if she didn't smell like she'd taken a bath in gas, but he did the best he could.

"Where'd the monster go?" the man asked. He come to stand beside them, braver now that the danger had passed.

"What monster?" Hunter asked. "You mean the wolf that ran away as I drove up?"

"That was no wolf," the man said.

Hunter eyed the man's leather shoes and dress pants. Definitely not a local. "And you know so much about wolves, right?"

The man opened his mouth to respond to Hunter's jab, but Eliza stepped forward to make introductions before he could.

"This is Clark Emery. He's a reporter from another paranormal magazine in San Francisco looking for the werewolf."

Even if it wasn't obvious that Eliza disliked the man,

Hunter would have. He knew a toad when he saw one.

Emery eyed Hunter's torn shirt. "Where did you come from?"

Hunter gestured behind him. "From my truck, which is parked in my driveway of my house. Where did you come from and how the hell did you end up in my shed?"

"What happened to your shirt?"

Hunter looked down, then back up. "Nothing. It's how we dress up here. Is that a problem for you?" He leaned forward and made a show of sniffing. "You might want to go get cleaned up. I think that *monster* might have made you piss yourself."

Clark started to stammer something, but Hunter was done with him. He turned and took Eliza's hand, leading her toward the front of the house.

"You're hiding something," the reporter called out from behind them. "You know more than you're saying."

Eliza started to slow, but Hunter didn't let her stop. "If you plan on standing around my backyard for a while, be sure to let me know if that wolf shows," he said over his shoulder. "I doubt he went very far. In fact, he's probably out there watching us right now."

That did it. Before he and Eliza even reached the front corner of his cabin, Emery was running for his car. He threw Hunter a dirty look as he climbed in, but didn't say anything.

Hunter glanced at Eliza as he helped her up the steps. Her face was pale and she was shaking. Shit, she was going into shock. He unlocked the door and took her hand to lead her inside. That was when he noticed she was still carrying his axe.

"You don't need that now," he said softly.

Her hand tightened on the handle as she scanned the woods around the house. "Do you really think he's still out there watching us?"

"No. I just said that to get that asshole Emery to leave. The werewolf's gone. I promise."

Eliza kept staring out into the trees, her eyes wide and frightened. Dammit, he wished he'd never said those words to Emery. He reached for the axe again. This time, she let him take it. Thick, dark blood covered the blade and dripped down the handle. It was obviously the Were's—the smell told him that. Eliza had gotten her shots in on the creature, and had made them count.

But the giant wolf had fought back. The handle up near axe head was splintered and gouged. The damn beast had almost ripped it apart. If he had, Eliza wouldn't have been able to keep him out.

Hunter didn't like to think about that.

He set the axe against the wall just outside the door and gently urged her into the house. Once they were inside and the door was closed behind them, Eliza tucked herself immediately into his arms and squeezed him tightly—like he was some kind of life jacket she need to hold on to just to keep from drifting away.

He wrapped his arms around her and held her close, whispering words of comfort to her over and over. It took a little while, but Eliza's breathing and heartbeat finally calmed, the tenseness seeping away from her body, her urgent hold on him relaxing. That's when he knew she was going to be okay. Yet he still held her, needing to hold her close as much for his sake as for hers, needing to make sure she was safe, especially since it was his fault she'd gotten attacked. If he'd killed the rogue werewolf the other night, this would never have happened.

The son of a bitch must have followed him last night and laid in wait for him. When Eliza showed up instead, he went after her.

He was still stewing over that fact when she tipped her head back and yanked him down for a kiss.

"You saved my life—again," she said softly. "Thank you."

"I'm just glad I got here in time. If I was one minute later—"

Eliza pressed a finger to his lips. "You were there in time, and that's all that matters." She kissed him again, then pulled away to looked out the window. "Do we have to worry about him coming back?"

"Not tonight," he said. "I didn't get him as good as I wanted to, but I'm pretty sure I cracked a few bones and tore muscles, maybe even damaged his spine some. I know from experience how painful wounds like that are and how long it takes for them to heal. He won't be in any shape to make another move on us for a while."

Which was why he should be out there tracking the son of a bitch down right now. But he couldn't leave Eliza.

"Should we tell Newman what happened?" she asked.

Hunter shook his head. "They're already getting the

hunt together as fast as they can, and if we rush them, it's likely to make matters worse."

She grimaced. "I'm not sure how we could do that."

When he looked at her in confusion, she explained how Tandi and the rest of the police department was going crazy trying to respond every time someone thought they saw a wolf. She also told him what she, Alex, and Nate had discovered at the local high school. He wouldn't even have thought of that angle, but it was a damn good one.

"If this werewolf is targeting people who were in this club, one of them might have an idea who it is—even if they don't know he's a werewolf. We might be able to find this monster before he strikes again," she said. "Alex is going to call me when they track down the members of the club who still live in Fairbanks, but with all the calls the cops are getting, it might take a while."

"That might be a good thing," Hunter said. "The way you smell, you don't want to go out in public right now."

She frowned. "What do you mean?"

"Smell all that gas?"

She sniffed the air, then made a face. "Oh, God. Is that me? I fell over the fuel cans in the shed when the werewolf tried to get in the window." She took off her coat, then pulled her sweater over her head. "I'm never going to get the smell out of my skin."

He chuckled. "Don't worry. I know a few tricks to help with that. Get the rest of your clothes off and hop in the shower. I'll be right in."

Hunter stifled a groan as she ran past him and up the steps naked. That was definitely a sight he could get used to.

Going into the kitchen, he grabbed the dish soap from under the sink and a bottle of white vinegar from the pantry, then jogged upstairs. Eliza was already in the shower scrubbing herself vigorously with a bar of soap when he walked into the master bathroom.

"Here. Use this instead." He handed her the bottle of dish soap. "It'll cut through the oily residue and start separating the odor from your skin."

She gave him a skeptical look, but didn't argue.

While she worked on the front, Hunter took care of the back, concentrating on the places she couldn't reach as easily—mainly her ass and upper thighs.

She glanced at him over her shoulder. "How did you know dish soap would work?"

He ran his hand over her ass to help rinse off the suds. "It's what they use on animals caught in oil spills. It's gentle, but still gets the job done."

Eliza reached for a towel, but he stopped her. "One more step."

When she gave him a questioning look, he grabbed the vinegar and doused her down with the whole bottle.

She made a face. "I'm going to smell like a salad now."

He chuckled. "Be good or I'll break out the tomato sauce and use that on you."

She stuck out her tongue, but stopped complaining. By the time he followed up the vinegar with shampoo, then a head to toe lathering of regular bar soap, even his sensitive nose couldn't pick up the smell of gas anymore.

Eliza turned to face him, her wet skin glistening. "Do I smell okay now?"

Hunter couldn't help it. Even after what they'd just been through, seeing stand there like that got to him. He pulled her out of the shower and into his arms, not caring that he was fully dressed and she was soaking wet. He liked her like that.

He buried his face in her neck and inhaled deeply, pleased that her beautiful aroma was no longer hidden under that nasty gas odor.

"You smell better than okay," he said. "You smell delicious."

Eliza laughed as he swept her up into his arms and headed out of the bathroom. This time, she didn't even grab a towel.

Chapter Seventeen

"I could definitely get used to this."

Eliza stretched out on the faux bear skin rug and propped herself up on an elbow. Her skin was still slightly wet from the shower and the scrub down, but she wasn't cold. But she was never cold when Hunter was around. Then again, she didn't worry about anything when Hunter was around.

After being attacked by a werewolf, most sane women would still be shaking in her boots—if she was wearing boots, that is. Instead, Eliza felt calm and relaxed as Hunter got a fire going in the big stone fireplace that dominated one wall of the house.

Well, that wasn't exactly true. The more she gazed at her naked werewolf lover, the less calm and relaxed she felt. She swore there had to be something wrong with her. Who got this aroused after the kind of day she'd had? But seeing Hunter in nothing but his muscular glory was doing some crazy things to her body right now.

She bit her lip as he bent to place a few more logs in the fireplace. She had no idea that watching a guy build a fire could be such an erotic experience. Of course, it probably had something to do with the fact that she was getting a chance to stare as much as she wanted at that broad, muscular back, long powerful legs, and deliciously tight butt. Seriously, what more could a woman ask for?

Finishing up, Hunter turned and walked over to stretch out beside her on the rug. "I certainly wouldn't mind you getting used to it," he murmured in reply to her earlier comment.

"Oh?"

"Mmm-hmm." He leaned close to give her a slow, gentle kiss. "There's always room for you on my bear skin rug." He kissed her again. "Or in my bed." And again. "Or in my hot tub. Though I think we should wait until the other werewolf is out of the picture before we christen the hot tub."

Eliza couldn't stop her pulse from doing a little happy dance at his words. While she knew she shouldn't read too much into them, she couldn't help but feel a little thrill. She hadn't given it much thought, but if she was ever going to move to the great white north for a man, Hunter would certainly be the one.

Then something struck her. "Wait. Why do we need to wait to try out the hot tub?"

He momentarily stopped nibbling her neck to whisper in her ear. "It's outside on the back deck."

"Oh. I guess that makes sense." It was hard to think straight with him kissing her neck like he was. "We wouldn't want to be out there with him around."

Hunter murmured something she took to be an

acknowledgement. But then again, he might just be commenting on how good he thought she tasted. She couldn't be sure.

She arched against him when another errand thought popped into her head. "Hey. Since this is the land of permanent winter, why would you put your hot tub outside?"

He chuckled. "Because you can splash around as much as you want without worrying about making a mess."

She let that thought sink in for a while. It would be cold out there, but with Hunter, she had no doubt that it would be also hot as hell at the same time.

"You'd better be careful, or I might think you're serious and take you up on your offer," she said softly. "And I'm not just talking about your hot tub, though that definitely sounds intriguing."

Hunter pulled away to look at her. "I am serious."

Her breath hitched at the hunger that flared in his eyes. But before she could say anything, Hunter kissed her again, and as his tongue swept inside her mouth to take possession of hers, she surrendered to him with a throaty purr. She'd figure out where this thing between them was heading later—when her head wasn't shrouded in a blanket of pure, raw desire.

Sliding her hand up to bury her fingers in his hair, Eliza deepened the kiss and rolled onto her back, taking him with her. Yeah, that conversation could definitely wait until later.

As her nipples skimmed against his chest, part of her

wondered how it was possible to want him so much. She'd made love more times in the few days she'd been in Alaska than she had in two years with other men she'd dated, yet she was already longing to feel him inside her again. She was definitely addicted to him.

They made slow, sweet love there on the bearskin rug in front of the fireplace. And when they orgasmed together, the sensation was so beautiful and perfect that it brought tears to her eyes. Eliza burrowed her face in his neck, not wanting him to see. It would only make him think there was something wrong when in reality, everything was absolutely perfect.

Hunter lifted his head to gaze down at her. "Do know how incredible you are?"

She laughed and shook her head. "No, but feel free to keep telling me."

"I plan to—frequently. But if you don't mind waiting a little while until I say it again, how about we get something to eat? Making love to you makes me ravenous."

Eliza rolled her eyes. "Typical guy. Or is it the werewolf in you that makes you so hungry all the time?"

He flashed her a grin. "It's all you, I'm sure of it. Want to go to the diner for some bacon and eggs?"

Was he serious? "For dinner?"

"Sure. Lots of people have bacon and eggs for dinner. Why do you think diners serve breakfast twenty-four hours a day?"

Eliza couldn't deny the logic of that statement, but then again, she'd never thought too much about diners being open twenty-four hours a day in the first place.

She shrugged. "Okay, I'm game if you are. But why do we have to go to the diner? Can't we just have it here?"

"We could if I had any, which I don't," he said. "We finished all the eggs this morning. And you can't have bacon without eggs. Besides, food tastes better when someone else makes it anyway."

She ran her hand through her disheveled hair. Between the werewolf attack, the shower, and the lovemaking, she probably looked like a fright. "It's going to take me a little while to get ready. I'm a mess."

"I think you look beautiful." Giving her a kiss, he took her hand and pulled her to her feet. "Come on, let's go."

Thirty minutes later, they were sitting in one of the booths at the diner. Eliza was starting to think of this place as her home away from home when the same waitress who'd served her the first night took their order. Eliza just picked up her glass of water when Nate and Alex walked in. They came over the moment they spotted her and Hunter.

"We were heading out to your place when we saw your SUV in the parking lot," Nate said as he and Alex sat down. "We were finally able to talk to Tandi and tell her what we discovered. Out of our list of rifle club members, only five still live in Fairbanks, and three of them are already dead."

"Which leaves Ken Marberry and Tom Porter," Alex said.

"Have you contacted them already?" Eliza asked.

Nate shook his head. "We tried calling, but neither one answered. Tandi's on her way to talk to Porter right now, then she'll swing by Marberry's place. Alex and I were going to warn Marberry, but she didn't want us involved." Nate leaned forward and lowered his voice. "In case the werewolf is already there."

Hunter swore and stood up. "Give me Porter's address. If I drive fast, I can get there before Tandi gets herself in trouble."

Eliza pushed back her chair and got to her feet. "I'll go with you."

He stopped her with a look. "No. It's too dangerous, and you know it."

Fear gripped Eliza at the thought of him fighting the other werewolf, and she swallowed hard. She knew he was right, but it didn't keep her from being terrified for him all the same. "I could stay in the car. That way I'd be there in case you need me."

Hunter reached out to gently cup her face in both hands. "Eliza, it's too dangerous. A car door won't slow this thing down for a second. I need you to stay here with Nate and Alex. I'll be back as soon as I can."

She nodded, then stood there numbly as Nate gave Hunter the address to Tom Porter's place. Part of her wanted to insist she go with him, but the other part of her knew that if she did go and the other werewolf were there, she could end up distracting Hunter and putting him in even more danger.

"I'll be okay." Hunter gave her a long, slow kiss, then

grabbed his jacket. "I'll try and call you, but Porter's place is way outside of town and cell reception isn't always so great out there."

"Promise me you'll be careful," she said.

"I promise." He reached up to brush her cheek with his fingers. "I'm not going to do anything foolish. I have too much to lose."

So did she. It was hard to believe that she'd fallen for Hunter so much in such a short time, but she had fallen—hard. Her heart squeezed in her chest. She supposed she'd known from the moment they met over that bottle of ketchup, but she hadn't been able to let herself believe it could possibly be true until now. She loved him.

She opened her mouth to tell him, but he lowered his head to kiss her again. She knew everybody in the diner was looking at them, but she didn't care. She kissed him back even harder.

"I'll call you," he said as he broke the kiss.

She nodded. It wasn't really the best time to be declaring her love, anyway. Hunter had other things on his mind, and she wanted him to be focused on that. "Be careful."

He brushed her cheek with his thumb. "Always. If you could keep trying to call Marberry, it might help. I'm not sure what you'll say, but try to convince him he's in danger and that he should come into town and find someplace safe to hold up."

Eliza told him that she would, then watched as he ran out of the diner. Only after he'd gotten in his SUV and sped out of the parking lot did she sit down at the table with Nate and Alex. Now that the romantic scene was over, the diner had returned to its normal hum of conversation and clatter of dishes and silverware. Across from her, Nate was on his cell phone trying to call Marberry.

She could feel the men's eyes on her, but she couldn't look at them. She was too afraid they'd see the terror in her eyes. Fortunately, the food showed up, so she had something to occupy herself. One look at the crispy bacon and perfectly cooked eggs were enough to make her feel ill, though, and she pushed her plate in front of Alex.

"Hunter's worried that thing might already be at Porter's place, isn't he? That's why he didn't want you going out there with him."

She nodded.

Alex regarded her thoughtfully. "What's he going to do if it is?"

What could she say? She couldn't tell Alex that Hunter was a werewolf. "I don't know. I guess he just doesn't want Tandi out there by herself."

She could tell from the look on his face that Alex wasn't buying it, but before he could dig deeper, Nate interrupted.

"We might have a problem. Marberry's phone isn't ringing anymore. It says there's no service."

Alex frowned. "Do you lose phone service a lot up here?"

"Sometimes, but it'd be one hell of a coincidence for

Marberry's phone not to work when there's a frigging werewolf after the guy."

Understatement there. "Maybe we should call the police and tell them we think Marberry's in trouble," Eliza said.

The look Nate gave her was dubious. "And what will I say if they ask how I know he's in trouble?"

Damn. Nate was right. "You can say you were driving by his place and saw someone suspicious."

Nate considered that. "I'll give it a shot, but I'm not promising it will work."

It didn't, but not for the reason he'd been worrying about. The cops were so busy that the dispatcher put him on hold. He swore and hung up. "We're going to have to go to Marberry's place ourselves. He could be in serious trouble."

Eliza hesitated. Hunter wanted her to stay at the diner with Nate and Alex where she'd be safe, but if she did, Marberry could die. She'd make it up to Hunter later.

She grabbed her purse. "Let's go."

* * * * *

Hunter thought he was going to have to tie Eliza to the chair to stop her from coming with him. Thank God she'd listened to reason. He had no idea what he was going to find when he got to Tom Porter's place, but chances were it was going to be the werewolf tearing his way into the man's house.

He didn't want to think about what that meant for

Tandi. He didn't know her very well, but something told him the female police officer wasn't the type to avoid confrontation—even one with a werewolf. If she tried to take on the beast one-on-one, it wasn't likely to go very well.

Hunter tightened his grip on the wheel. He was driving faster than usual and the big SUV had already gone off the road more than once. The night temperatures had turned the day's snow-melt into ice and the road was a slippery mess, but he didn't dare slow down.

He slid through the turn as he pulled into Porter's gravel driveway and almost rammed into Tandi's SUV parked sideways across it. He tried to pump the brakes to keep control of his vehicle, but between the mud and slushy ice, that wasn't even a possibility. He swore and jerked at the wheel, barely avoiding the front bumper of her truck. He didn't have time to congratulate himself because while he'd missed her SUV, he couldn't escape the ditch beside it.

The left front side of his SUV dropped with a sickening thud and slammed into the far side of the ditch hard enough to make his teeth rattle. The next thing he knew, he had a face full of airbag and his truck wasn't running anymore. If he'd been an average man, he probably would have been knocked out, or at least been really frigging woozy. Fortunately, he wasn't an average man.

He was out of the SUV before the vehicle stopped rocking. The headlights were smashed and the front bumper was toast. His truck wasn't going anywhere for a while. But none of that bothered him as much as finding Tandi's patrol vehicle empty and the front door of Porter's house wide open.

Hunter sprinted toward it. He hoped to God the house was dark because Porter wasn't home, but it could just as well mean he was already dead. Where the hell did that leave Tandi?

The overpowering scent he'd come to associate with the other werewolf filled his nostrils before he reached the house. He put on more speed, itching to transform on the spot. One thing stopped him. If Tandi was still alive in there and he came busting through the door in his wolf form, she'd shoot first and ask questions later.

The scent was too strong for the werewolf not to be nearby, but the silence coming from the house contradicted that assumption. The guy didn't have the control to be this quiet.

Hunter slowed as he reached the door, then carefully slipped inside. While the house might be dark, he could see clearly. The couch and chairs were flipped over and the coffee table was broken, but he didn't see or smell any blood. It was hard to tell for sure over the werewolf's heavy stench, but he thought he could pick up traces of Tandi's scent.

A noise coming from the kitchen made him stiffen and he turned just as Tandi swung into the main room, her pistol in one hand, a flashlight in the other. Relief flooded through him, but he was smart enough to stay where he was and let her find him. He didn't want the cop shooting him by accident.

When her flashlight beam hit him, he thought Tandi was going to do just that, but she pulled her gun away at the last second.

"Dr. McCall! What the hell are you doing out here? I could have shot you."

"Eliza and I were at the diner when Nate and Alex found us and said you were on your way out here on your own."

Hunter was about to tell her how stupid that was when something grabbed his attention and wouldn't let go. The werewolf's scent was so strong that he'd assumed the beast had come in and found the place empty, then tore it up in a fit of rage and left. But if that was true, why didn't he smell Porter anywhere. Hunter should have been able to pick up the scent of the man who lived here, but he couldn't.

Because there was only one scent here—the werewolf's.

Shit.

Tom Porter wasn't the werewolf's next victim. He *was* the werewolf. And if he wasn't here now, it meant he was probably already on his way to Ken Marberry's place, if wasn't already there.

"Dr. McCall, what's wrong?"

He hadn't realized Tandi had crossed the room to stand in front of him until her light flashed in his face. "We have to get to Ken Marberry's place—now," he said. "It could already be too late."

Tandi frowned. "What makes you think Marberry is

in any more danger than Porter?" She played her flashlight over the room. "Judging from how tore up this place is, I think Porter is the one we need to be worried about. Looks like that creature busted in here and yanked Porter right out the door. It was standing wide open when I got here."

Hunter turned and walked out. "That creature didn't grab Porter. That creature *is* Porter."

Tandi's boots echoed on the wood as she ran across the porch. Then she was at his side, keeping up with him as she looked at him out of the corner of her eye.

"What are you saying?" she demanded. "That Tom Porter is a werewolf?"

Hunter didn't answer as he moved around her Jeep and climbed in the passenger seat. Damn, it was embarrassing to have to ride with her, but his SUV wasn't going to be coming out of that ditch anytime soon.

As if thinking the same thing, Tandi paused for a moment to look at his truck before silently getting behind the wheel.

She glanced at him as she shoved the key in the ignition. "I'm not even going to ask how you know that, but Nate said I should trust you, so I'm going to assume you're right and go from there. But if you're wrong, it means we're leaving Porter on his own with that thing."

"I'm not wrong."

Tandi cranked the engine, then spun the Jeep around in a tight circle, avoiding Hunter's SUV while throwing mud and slush everywhere. Once on the road, she reached for her radio.

"I wouldn't do that," Hunter said.

She paused, her thumb on the button. "I have to call dispatch and tell them to get units out to Marberry's place."

"Not unless you have friends you don't mind losing."

She threw him a sharp look, but didn't say anything.

"Tandi, if you send anyone there, they're going to end up dead. This thing isn't indestructible, but he's hard to kill, bloodthirsty, and probably insane."

She turned back and faced the road. Marberry lived even farther outside of town than Porter, but she was driving fast. At this rate, they'd likely be there in less than fifteen minutes.

"Can you kill this thing?" Tandi asked suddenly, and it was Hunter's turn to look at her sharply.

She was handling this situation a lot better than he expected most other cops would. He'd just told her that werewolves were real, that Tom Porter was one, and that they had to go take care of the monster on their own. And the only thing she'd asked him was whether he'd be able to kill it.

"Yeah, I can kill him," Hunter said. "But I won't pretend it'll be easy. Plus, for me to kill him, he has to still be there. The scent at Porter's cabin wasn't very fresh. I'm not sure he's spent a lot of time there lately. If Marberry is his last target, he may have already killed him and left. Nate said Marberry wasn't answering his phone when he tried to call him."

Tandi took out her cell phone. "Maybe Nate was

able to get in touch with him. Warn him trouble is coming his way."

Hunter could immediately tell Tandi had a lousy connection. He could barely make out Nate's voice. Tandi asked Nate if he'd reached Marberry, but she practically had to shout to be heard. Apparently, Nate couldn't hear her any better because he kept asking questions regardless of what Tandi said. Like whether she was okay, and if Hunter had found her yet.

"We're almost at Marberry's house," Nate said. "His phone kept saying it was out of service and we were worried he might have already been attacked."

Hunter's heart lurched in his chest. What the hell? Eliza promised him she'd stay at the diner.

Shit.

"Nate, no!" Tandi shouted into the phone. "Go back to the diner and stay there. Nate? Nate!"

Silence met her words.

"Dammit!" Tandi threw her phone on the dash and floored the gas. "If that thing is still there when they arrive, will it go after them or is it only interested in Marberry?"

Hunter wished he could give Tandi the answer she was looking for, but he couldn't help remembering how hard the werewolf had gone after Eliza and that other reporter. Like he'd already told Tandi—the beast was insane. It had gotten a taste for killing and it liked the flavor.

"It will go after them, even if Marberry is already dead."

Saying those words out loud tore something inside him and he didn't try to control the growl that slipped out. Tandi didn't seem to hear, or if she did, she didn't care. Hunter knew what he had to do, no matter the risk. He'd do whatever it took to save Eliza. He didn't care what happened after that.

"When we get close to Marberry's, I'm going to get in the back seat," he said. "I need you to stay focused on getting us there as fast as you can, no matter what you see or hear, okay?

The cop threw him a quick glance. "What are you going to do?"

Hunter unbuttoned his shirt while he kicked off his boots. "Just don't freak. And don't slow down until you get to Marberry's."

Chapter Eighteen

He'd stood outside the cabin for nearly an hour, dreaming about what it would feel like to finally finish what he came back from the dead to do. Would the demon remove the curse? He doubted it. He was going to burn, he knew that for sure. It was just a matter of who he took with him.

A car drove up and stopped in front of the house. A growl rose in his throat when he saw the dark-haired woman and the two men who occasionally traveled with her. He salivated at the thought of sinking his teeth into her. After the other demon had stopped him from killing her yesterday, he didn't think he'd ever see her again, but here she was—without her protector.

He didn't really understand why the thought of killing her aroused him so much. But it did and he no longer had the control or the desire to question why the demon inside him wanted to do what it did. He just went along with it. He found himself humming— well, as much as a demon can hum—as he crossed the road and circled the house searching for the best way in.

First, he'd kill the man who had doomed him to this curse, then he'd go after the other two before finally sinking his teeth into the woman.

* * * * *

It seemed to take forever to find the Marberry's house in the dark, and Eliza sighed with relief when it finally came into view. She was even more relieved to see a pick-up truck parked outside and several lights on inside. She still had no clue what they were going to say to Marberry. It's not like they could come out and tell him a werewolf was after him.

"Why not?" Nate had asked when she'd said as much on the drive over.

"Oh, I don't know. Because he might think we're insane," she'd told him.

Nate had said nothing for a moment, but then he'd nodded. "There is that."

As the three of them got out of Nate's truck, Eliza couldn't help but shiver a little as she glanced over her shoulder at the darkened woods surrounding Marberry's house. She'd feel a whole hell of a lot better if Hunter was with them. She hoped Nate was right about what he thought he'd heard on that garbled phone call—that Hunter and Tandi were on their way.

But since they weren't there at the moment that left the task of warning Ken Marberry to them. Lifting her hand, Eliza knocked on the door. Despite the truck parked outside and the lights, no one answered. A trickle of fear ran down her back. What if the werewolf had already gone through the backdoor and killed Marberry? Taking a deep breath, she knocked again, louder this time.

"Mr. Marberry," she called. "Are you in there?"

Still no answer.

"Maybe he's not here," Alex suggested from behind her.

Eliza shook her head. "He's gotta be here. His truck is here, and the lights are on."

She lifted her hand to knock on the door again when it abruptly swung open to reveal a huge, angry looking man.

"Who are you?" he demanded, his dark eyes suspicious.

She swallowed hard, her gaze fixed on the rifle the big man had pointed at her. "M-my name's Eliza Bradley. I'm a reporter."

His eyes narrowed as they sized her up. "What do you want with me?"

"I... We..." she corrected, glancing over her shoulder at Alex and Nate. "We have reason to believe someone may be trying to kill you."

Ken Marberry continued to eye them for another moment before he finally lowered the gun and gestured for them to come inside. Relieved at the prospect of putting a closed door between them and that dark, scary forest, Eliza hurriedly stepped inside, Alex and Nate close on her heels. The cabin was small, with the main room serving as the kitchen, dining room, and living room. Off to the right, was a door that led to the bedroom. Apparently, Marberry didn't believe in wasting electricity because there were only a two small electric table lamps lighting the place. The remainder of the light came from several kerosene lamps set about the room.

As she turned her attention back to the main room of the cabin, Eliza couldn't help but let out a little shiver. If she'd thought Nate's house was a little creepy, it was nothing compared to this place. Mounted animal heads stared down at them from every available wall surface. There were bears, foxes, and moose, not to mention wolves—lots of wolves. The flickering light from the lanterns almost made it seem like the taxidermied animals were glaring at her, the look in their glassy eyes suggesting they blamed her for their present predicament. She shivered again and looked away, only to find herself staring at boxes of animal skulls shoved up against the wall. She was shocked to see that there were more skulls on the kitchen table. God, that was beyond gross.

Eliza tore her gaze away from the skulls to see Marberry bolting the door. "Mr. Marberry, we think you and your friend Tom Porter are in danger. We know it sounds crazy, but—"

Marberry let out a harsh laugh. "Tom's not in danger. Hell, he's the one who's trying to kill me."

Eliza blinked. What was he talking about?

"We didn't mean to do it. We thought Tom was dead," Marberry muttered, pacing back and forth in front of them. "That's why we left him. But we should never have done it. Tom is back to get revenge on the rest of us for what we did."

Eliza shared a look with Alex and Nate to see that they looked as confused as she was. She turned back to Marberry. The man looked like he hadn't slept in days.

"Why would Tom Porter want revenge?" she asked.

288

Marberry stopped pacing to face her, a haunted look in his eyes. "A couple of months back, we all went hunting over in the Yukon, just north of Whitehorse. We go there every couple years. Well, this time, we found more than caribou and bear—we found a downed plane full of drugs and a whole shitload of money." He shook his head. "Tom wanted to leave it, but the rest of us outvoted him. We took the money and the drugs, figuring we might be able to sell them. Tom complained the whole time. He kept saying it'd bring us nothing but trouble. Turns out he was right."

He stopped to peek out the window before continuing. "A huge wolf came into camp that night, bold as brass, and tore into Tom's tent. The damn thing just ripped him apart. We'd never seen anything so savage before. We put over twenty rounds in the beast before it went down. Even then it still almost got Mark and me. We should have known then that something wasn't right with the thing.

"Tom was torn up real bad. We couldn't believe he was even still alive," Marberry said, his voice trembling. "We should have strapped him to a litter right on the spot and hightailed it out of there, but we didn't."

"Why not?" Alex asked.

"Because if we'd tried to carry him, we would've had to leave the drugs and money. And none of us wanted to do that." He shrugged. "So, we just stood there staring at him as he bled to death. Then I sort of mentioned that splitting the money four ways would be better than five. Nobody said anything at first, but they were all thinking the same thing. I don't know, but something took hold of us—greed, I suppose—and we made the decision to leave Tom there. We convinced ourselves he'd never make it anyway. We told ourselves we were just being practical. Why work that hard to carry out a man who was already dead?"

"So you just left him there to die?" Eliza asked. She couldn't believe someone could do such a thing, especially to someone they claimed was a friend.

"We did worse than that." Marberry shook his head. "We didn't want anyone finding Tom's body, then linking us to that plane through him, so we dragged him to a ravine and tossed him over the side. We thought the fall would end him for sure—he fell and bounced for a long time. But Tom always was a tough son of a bitch. He shouted and hollered at us from the bottom, begging us to help him, but we just walked away."

He swallowed hard. "I'd do anything to make up for what we did. The money and the drugs are still out back in my shed, and I'd give it all to Tom if he wanted it. But he didn't come back for money. He came back for revenge. We sent him to hell and now he wants to drag us back there with him. He's like some cursed hellhound come to take our souls."

As if on cue, a wolf howled outside. Eliza jumped, but before she could say anything, a wide-eyed and terrified Marberry grabbed his rifle, pushed past them, and bolted for the bedroom, then slammed the door behind him. A moment later, Eliza heard the sounds of the bolt action on Marberry's rifle being worked. She had no idea if he was waiting for the wolf or whether he was going to use the weapon on himself.

Eliza strained her ears, trying to hear whether the werewolf was moving closer to the cabin, but before she could even guess which direction the beast might be coming from, she heard the sound of breaking glass from inside the bedroom. A fraction of a second later, a gunshot rang out, followed by shouts and growls that echoed through the tiny cabin. Every instinct told her to get away as fast as she could, but instead she ran to the bedroom and opened the door.

She gasped in horror at the sight that met her eyes. The werewolf already had his huge mouth clamped down on the Marberry's neck and shoulder, shaking him like a rag doll. The man was screaming in terror as much as pain as the beast ripped and tore at him.

The big beast turned his black gaze on her, pinning her where she stood. The werewolf stared at her for a long moment, then without looking away, crunched down savagely on Marberry's neck, silencing him. Then he dropped his latest victim on the floor and lunged at her.

Her feet finally responding, Eliza screamed and quickly backpedaled out of the room. Alex and Nate did the same. Nate tried to shut the door before the werewolf could get through, but he only got it halfway closed before the beast's huge body slammed into it. The force of the blow knocked all three of them backward, but somehow, they managed to keep their feet, and as one, pushed back on the door with their combined strength.

If the werewolf made it out of the bedroom, none of

them would get out of there alive.

Crouching down, Eliza put her shoulder against the door and pushed with everything in her. She thought they might actually get the door closed, but just then, the wolf savagely smashed his head through the small gap remaining. She didn't even have time to move before the beast sank his teeth into her forearm. White hot pain shot through her, and she screamed as the creature yanked. He was going to pull her through the partially opened door. She couldn't let that happen.

Gritting her teeth against the pain, she balled up her fist and struck over and over again at the wolf's head. It felt like she was punching a boulder, and the boulder was winning. She opened her hand and raked her nails across his face instead. She caught him in the eye and he released her with a sharp yelp.

Eliza fell back, unable to stay upright any longer. It was like her legs had just stopped listening to her.

With the wolf momentarily distracted, Nate and Alex were able to finally get the door closed. Alex leaned against it while Nate grabbed a chair and wedged it under the knob. Eliza doubted it would hold for very long. She'd seen firsthand what the creature had done to Aiken Wainwright's door, and that door had been a lot heavier than this one was.

"We have to get out of…" Nate's words trailed off when he saw her arm. "Oh God, you've been bitten!"

Alex whirled around to look at her, his eyes wide.

Eliza tried to speak, but no words would come. She could only stare down at her savaged forearm. The skin burned like it was on fire, and it was all she could do to keep from crying as frothy blood bubbled out of the wound. She wrapped her hand around her arm, trying to stop the bleeding—and the pain—but it did no good. It felt like her skin was engulfed in flames that were slowing spreading higher. Within moments, every part of her body was burning just as fiercely as her arm.

"Come on," Nate said, taking her good arm and dragging her up. He urged her toward the front door. "That door's not going to hold him for long."

The words were barely out of his mouth when the bedroom door completely blew apart, scraps and splinters flying everywhere. Eliza stood there frozen as the werewolf slowly pushed the remains of the shattered door and chair aside and advanced into the room.

Nate and Alex moved in front of her, ready to fight, but she knew it would do no good. They weren't going to make it. Her only thought was of Hunter and of the words she hadn't said to him back at the diner. Now, he would never know how much she loved him.

* * * * *

Hunter was already in the back seat yanking off his jeans when Tandi announced they'd be there in two minutes.

Good to her word, the cop hadn't said anything when he'd crawled over the front seats, powered down one of the back windows, and started yanking off his clothes. That didn't mean she didn't look in the rearview mirror and try to figure out what the hell he was up to.

"Eyes on the road, Tandi," he warned. "I already put my truck in the ditch. We don't want yours there, too."

He didn't even bother trying to find a comfortable position on the seats. He just pushed the change as hard as he could.

Hunter had never shifted in front of a stranger. The only two people in the world who'd seen him do it were his father and brother. But he had to do it. Eliza and the others' lives could depend on it. They could be facing the other werewolf even now. He only prayed it wasn't already too late.

Dammit, he couldn't think like that. Instead, he focused on what he had to do—turn as fast as he could.

He heard Tandi gasp as his bones snapped, crackled and popped into their new shape. But he couldn't stop to tell her that this was *normal*, that he went through this level of pain every time he tried to assume his werewolf shape too quickly.

Regardless of what Tandi heard—and the insane view she was likely getting in the rearview mirror—she kept the Jeep on the road and moving fast.

Hunter was fighting to finish his transformation from man to beast, taking the last few moments to ensure he had full control of his body, when he felt the police vehicle turn suddenly. The move threw him to one side and his big paws scrambled for purchase on the cloth-covered seats. His huge frame filled the back seat of the Jeep so completely that he really couldn't slide very far, though he still felt the material shred under his claws. But he paid no attention to the damage as his sensitive nose picked up the scent he'd hoped he wouldn't find here.

The vehicle slid to a stop and he saw Tandi turn to stare at him wide-eyed before he launched himself out the open back window.

The Were's scent assaulted his nose first, quickly followed by the lighter but distinct traces left by Alex and Nate. But over all of them, one predominated—Eliza's. His mind screamed in panic as he realized why her scent was so clear and powerful, why it was hitting him so hard. She was bleeding.

Then the sounds of growls and splintering wood reached his ears. He raced for the house as fast as he could move. But his heart felt heavy in his chest as he ran. He was already too late. Eliza had been bitten.

* * * * *

Eliza ducked as the front window of the cabin exploded. When she opened her eyes, it was to see a huge, gray wolf land gracefully in the middle of the room.

"Hunter…" she breathed.

She saw both Alex and Nate give her startled looks, but she was too intent on Hunter to pay attention to them. Even the burning pain in her arm was forgotten as she watched the two werewolves square off. Her death had seemed like a foregone conclusion, and while she'd been terrified, it was nothing compared to what she felt now. Hunter was going to fight this monster, and for all his experience and strength, she wasn't sure how he could survive a brawl with something so vicious and insane with rage.

Hunter and the black wolf stared at each other for long moment, both of them baring their teeth in a snarl. Then, without warning, they leaped at each other.

They came together with a violent impact that made her gasp. The sounds of snapping fangs and deep-throated growls filled the cabin, echoing around her, and it was all she could do not to throw her hands over her ears.

Hunter and the other werewolf rolled around on the floor, their huge teeth finding purchase in each other's fur-covered flesh. They were moving too quickly to see who was getting the worst of the damage, but within seconds, blood appeared on both Hunter's gray fur and the other wolf's black coat. It wasn't long before it fell to the floor like red rain.

Eliza stood transfixed, all thoughts of her own pain fading into the background as she focused her attention on Hunter and the fight to the death he was locked in. She barely saw the front door open and Tandi come in until the officer lifted her gun and pointed it at the two wolves.

Eliza opened her mouth to beg the cop not to shoot, but the words died in her throat as she realized Tandi was aiming at the black werewolf instead of Hunter. Eliza had no idea how Tandi knew the gray wolf was on their side and she didn't care. She was just glad the cop wasn't going to shoot Hunter.

Eliza turned back to the fight to see Hunter and his

opponent twisting and flipping back and forth across the small space, smashing everything in their path. One second they were over behind the couch, and the next they were smashing into the kitchen table, crushing it to kindling and throwing the skulls and bones atop it halfway across the room.

One of the skulls flew through the air and slammed into the kerosene lantern hanging above the fireplace. The lamp fell from its hook and smashed against the floor. Fire instantly blazed up, spilling across the floor and against the far wall, where it ignited a set of low-hanging curtains. Within seconds, flames were spreading halfway up the walls of the room. Alex and Nate tried to pull Eliza toward the door, but she resisted. She couldn't leave Hunter. She wouldn't.

"Eliza, the whole place is going up!" Alex shouted. "We have to get out of here!"

She shook her head, heedless of the fire as it continued to spread through the small cabin. "I'm not leaving him!"

But just then, Hunter turned his head to look at her. There was no mistaking the command in his gleaming yellow eyes. He was telling her to go, she realized. The fact that he was willing to risk his life for her almost made her heart stop.

"Eliza!" Alex shouted, grabbing her good arm and dragging her toward the door. "Come on!"

Despair filled her, but she stopped resisting as they shoved her out of the burning cabin.

Tandi stayed just inside the doorway, trying to get a

shot at the black werewolf, but before Eliza and the guys had gone twenty feet, the cop came stumbling out of the cabin, coughing and choking. She stumbled, almost falling, and Nate grabbed her hand to lead her away from the burning building.

Flames followed them away from the door, coming out in a whooshing roar, and Eliza's heart sank even further. How long could a werewolf survive the kind of heat and smoke that were building up in the small house?

Alex put his arm around Eliza's shoulders. "We have to get you to a hospital."

"I'm fine," she told him.

"Alex is right," Tandi said. "Your arm is bleeding really badly. We need to get you to the hospital."

Eliza shook her head. "No. I'm not leaving until I know he's safe."

Alex and Nate exchanged looks, but they didn't ask whom she was talking about. They weren't stupid. They already knew Hunter was the other werewolf. The implications of giving away Hunter's secret should have made her uneasy, but right then, she couldn't think about that. Or about what the bite on her arm would mean, either. All she could think about was Hunter, and pray that he was going to come running out of the inferno any second.

But as the seconds ticked by and the raging fire continued to grow, a part of her began to doubt if her prayers would be answered.

* * * * *

Hunter knew he should be careful. He'd fought the other Were enough times to know that the man inside the monster was psychotic. That insanity made him unpredictable and dangerous. But knowing the black werewolf had bitten Eliza and what that bite would mean for her, filled Hunter with a rage that nearly drove him blind with the need to kill the creature. He'd thrown caution aside and launched himself at the thing, determined to end this once and for all.

The other werewolf fought even more ferociously than he had the previous times, like he didn't even care if he lived through the fight. But Hunter had experience on him, and a long drawn-out fight shifted the odds in his favor. He knew the other beast's fanatical strength would ebb soon enough. Or that he'd make a mistake and expose a weak spot at exactly the wrong moment. Either way, all it would take was one miscue and Hunter would finish this.

But then the kerosene lamp had broken, catching half the cabin on fire in seconds. He'd been so worried about Eliza getting out that the other Were had almost gotten away by trying to slip past him to the hallway and the back bedroom.

The flames might be leaping high enough to singe his fur and make it hard to breathe, but Hunter wasn't going to let the black wolf out of the cabin. If he did, the monster would go straight for Eliza.

Hunter wasn't going to let that happen, no matter the cost.

He and his opponent rolled savagely across the floor, using the flames as a weapon in addition to their fangs and claws. Hunter jumped to the side to avoid a falling beam and slipped in a patch of his own blood. He went down hard and the other Were took advantage of it. With a snarl, he snapped his jaws around one of Hunter's forelegs and crunched down.

Hunter bit back a howl of pain as the black werewolf began to crush down even harder. He knew he was about to lose his leg, but it would be a small price to pay. When the other werewolf yanked his head to the side to tear through the last of the bones and muscles, it would leave his neck exposed for a split-second. If Hunter could handle the pain, he would be able to lunge forward, get his jaws around the other beast's throat and finally end this. He probably wouldn't make it out of the flame-filled cabin after that, but he didn't care. Eliza would be safe, and that was all that mattered.

Then over the rush of flames, there came a crack from above. Hunter looked up just in time to see a heavy beam fall from the ceiling. He braced himself for impact, but instead of hitting him, the beam crashed down squarely on the other Were, savagely crushing the beast to the floor.

The insanity disappeared from the Were's gaze and for a moment, Hunter stared down into eyes that reminded him of his brother's or his father's. Eyes alive and alert with the intelligence of a man. The black creature released the hold it had on Hunter's leg and Hunter pulled away.

Hunter was torn. Even after everything that had happened, part of him wanted to try to free the trapped wolf. He and Luke could have ended up just like this if they hadn't had a father to teach them what they needed to know in order to survive. But the decision was taken from him when the wolf's eyes closed.

Another loud crack echoed and instead of one beam falling, the entire flaming roof rained down around him. Hunter ran for the window he'd smashed through earlier, his wounded front leg barely supporting his weight. Between the flames and the smoke, he wasn't all that sure he was going the right direction. That moment of compassionate indecision a minute ago might have left him with no time to get out.

* * * * *

A savage yelp of pain came from inside the cabin. "Hunter!" Eliza screamed.

She shook off Alex's arm and ran toward the cabin. Before she could take more than a few steps, hands gripped her, holding her back. Eliza didn't know which of her friends had stopped her, and she didn't care. All she knew was that she had to get away. She had to get to Hunter.

"Let go of me!" she cried, struggling to free herself. "Damn you, let go—"

The rest of her words were lost as the roof of the cabin collapsed with a loud, roar. Eliza froze, her heart seizing in her chest as the fiery rubble slowly caved in.

"Hunter!"

Something big and fast came leaping out from the billowing smoke. Out of the corner of her eye, Eliza saw Tandi aim her gun, only to lower it again as the shape resolved itself into a familiar gray color.

Eliza's heart began to beat again. Tugging free of the hands holding her, she started forward on trembling legs, tears welling in her eyes. Hunter's fur was matted, burned, and bloody in places, and he was limping badly, but he was alive. That was all that mattered.

Dropping to her knees in front of him, Eliza threw her arms around him, burying her face in the thick fur of his neck. She didn't care about the blood and the horrible smoky smell. He was alive.

"Oh, Hunter," she breathed. "Thank God."

He pulled back from her embrace to lick her face in reply, and she couldn't help but let out a laugh. It faded quickly when she saw him turn his attention to her injured arm. She'd been so worried about Hunter she all but forgot she'd been bitten. The wound wasn't bleeding nearly as much as before, and even the burning had subsided. It still hurt, but it was bearable. She held her arm still as Hunter sniffed it. A moment later, he gently licked the wound. The touch of his tongue was soothing and almost immediately, the remaining pain began to fade.

The shrill sound of sirens echoed in the distance, and Eliza tensed. Threading her fingers in the ruff of fur at Hunter's neck, she urged his head up. "Hunter, you have to go."

Hunter didn't move. The sirens were getting closer now. Eliza took his huge head in both her hands and gazed into his yellow eyes.

"Please. You have to go before the cops and firemen get here," she said. "I'll be fine. Go."

He hesitated again, but then giving her face one more lick, he turned and limped off into the darkened forest. Eliza waited until he'd disappeared from sight before she got to her feet. She glanced down at her wounded arm and gasped. Beneath the torn sleeve of her coat, the werewolf's bite was no longer open and bloody, but had already started to close over into a series of jagged, red scars along her forearm. Even as she watched the scars twitched and twisted, as if they were alive. They were smoothing out little by little. Something told her that in few days, they would disappear completely just like the bullet wound on Hunter's shoulder.

Chapter Nineteen

Hunter clenched his jaw as pain tore through his body—again. He'd never changed this hard, this frequently. He typically shifted into his wolf form once or twice a week, and he usually took his time, letting the change slowly transform his body. But over the last few days he'd changed so many times he couldn't even put an accurate number to it. It didn't help that his body was trying to heal from all the damage.

His wolf side resisted—its way of telling him it wanted to stay in whatever form it was in at the moment. He should be listening to his body and doing what it wanted. But he couldn't. He had to get back to Eliza as quickly as he could. She was injured and needed him. He gritted his teeth and pushed through the pain one more time, knowing that after tonight he'd be able to take a break for a while.

When the transformation was done, he was forced to stay there on the ground on all fours, breathing hard and fast, his arms and legs quivering in exhaustion. He just wanted to lay there on the ground and sleep for a week.

He thought of Eliza again and pushed himself to his feet.

Between the flashing emergency lights and the rolling flames from the cabin, the area was lit up like a freaking parking lot, but fortunately, everyone was focused on the house, not on the naked man slipping out of the forest.

He hurried over to Tandi's SUV and yanked open the back door, wincing as pain shot up his damaged forearm. He climbed in and dressed as swiftly as he could, which was hard to do while practically lying on the floorboards and nursing a sore arm. But there was something else slowing him as he did up the buttons of his shirt and tucked it into his jeans—fear. Eliza had accepted him as a werewolf, but would she accept herself that way? Would she deal with it or end up like the man he'd just killed, insane and out of control? He'd heard that happening to a lot of people in his time.

With a silent prayer, he shoved his feet in his boots and tied the laces, then waited until no one was looking in his direction before opening the door and getting out.

Hunter shrugged into his jacket and moved as quickly as he could to Eliza's side. She was standing with Alex and Nate, staring at the burning cabin. She turned as he approached. Without a word to the two men, she closed the distance between them and threw herself into his arms.

"I was so afraid for you," she said hoarsely, the words muffled against the curve of his neck.

"Shh, sweetheart," he soothed softly, stroking her hair. "Everything's all right now."

Hunter wondered if the words sounded as hollow to

her as they did to him. How could things be all right when she'd been bitten? But apparently Eliza must not have noticed because she only pressed against him more tightly. Closing his eyes, he rested his cheek against her silky hair. He wanted to hold her like this all night.

They weren't going to be afforded that luxury, though, and Hunter reluctantly lifted his head with a sigh as Lieutenant Newman made his way toward them. He had to dodge about a dozen firemen dragging hoses toward the burning cabin, but he continued on with a determined stride.

"What the hell happened here?" the cop asked. "Dispatch said there was another wolf killing."

Hunter's arm tightened around Eliza as he tried to come up with a story that was going to explain all this. But he was so frigging tired that nothing would come. He was about to shrug his shoulders and say he had no explanation for what had happened, but Eliza spoke first.

"There was a killing, but it wasn't a wolf who did it. It was a man named Tom Porter."

While the lieutenant stood there with his mouth hanging open, Eliza told him how they'd found a connection between all three of the first victims—the high school rifle team.

"After that, it wasn't too hard finding out there were only two members of the team still in the area. We figured someone was targeting the old rifle club, so we came out here to warn one of the members," she explained.

Newman's eyes narrowed. "Why didn't you call the

department and tell us what you found?"

Before Eliza could answer, Nate jumped in. "We tried, but your phone lines have been busy all day. We knew that if we didn't warn them, no one would."

"But when we got here, we realized that we had it all wrong," Eliza picked back up. "It wasn't an outsider killing the club members—it was one of their own. Tom Porter."

Hunter listened with just as much amazement as Newman as she told the cop about the victims taking a hunting trip to the Yukon, a downed plane full of drugs and money, and how the friends had decided to bring it back with them.

"Marberry told us the money and drugs are still in a shed behind the cabin," Eliza said. "He and the other men left Porter out in the wilderness to die after he got attacked by a wolf so there'd be more money to go around."

While Hunter knew Eliza was obviously omitting the part about how Tom Porter became a werewolf, it wasn't that hard to read between the lines and figure out what had happened.

It was possible that the Were who'd attacked Porter had been on that plane full of drugs and had survived the crash. Or he could have been a rogue werewolf who lived in the wilds. Either way, Hunter could understand how an event like that might drive Porter insane. To survive a wolf attack, then be abandoned by friends you'd known most of your life? That would be tough for anyone to handle.

"What Marberry didn't know was that Tom Porter didn't die out there, but had come back and was murdering them one by one," Eliza finished.

Newman said nothing for a moment. "How does that explain the fact that those men were killed by a wolf?"

Shit. Eliza might be weaving a good story, but that was one detail that couldn't be waved away—or explained.

"There never were any wolf attacks," Eliza said. "Porter made a weapon from the skull and jaw of a wolf—probably the one that attacked him in the Yukon. We were with Marberry when Porter crashed through the window and started swinging the thing at him. It was vicious looking. I can see how someone might think the wounds it made came from a wolf."

Newman frowned, but she hurried on before he could say anything.

"I'm guessing that Porter planned to take the money and the drugs for himself once all his friends were dead. But during the fight, one of the kerosene lanterns got knocked over. We barely made it out alive. Neither Marberry nor Porter did."

Though Hunter couldn't help but be impressed by Eliza's quick thinking, he wasn't so sure Fred Newman would buy it, but the cop merely nodded.

"That sounds too crazy not to be true."

Newman was a good cop, but the reality was that he just wanted this damn case to go away. Eliza had wrapped everything up and put a bow on it, and the lieutenant was more than ready to accept her wild explanation.

"She's lying! That's not what happened at all."

Hunter stiffened at the man's voice. His eyes narrowed at the blond-haired man hurrying over to them. Clark Emery. What the hell was that jackass doing here?

Fred Newman eyed the blond man curiously. "Who are you and what do you know about this?"

"My name is Clark Emery and I'm a reporter with *Strange Times* magazine. The people who were attacked weren't murdered by some guy wanting revenge. They were killed by a werewolf."

Beside him, Hunter felt Eliza tense.

Fred Newman was looking at Clark Emery like the man had lost his mind. "A werewolf?"

"Yes, a werewolf. You know, the monster made famous by Lon Chaney, Jr?" Emery pointed at Nate. "You know what I'm talking about. Tell him."

Nate snorted. "I don't know what you're talking about. It happened just the way she said. I'm pretty sure I would have noticed if there'd been a werewolf around."

"Bullshit!" Emery shot them a baleful glare, then turned to Newman again. "They're lying. If you don't believe me, give them a lie detector test. You'll see I'm right."

Newman's mouth tightened. "Watson," he called to an officer nearby. "Get this guy out of here."

"Wait a minute." Emery dug in his heels when the burly cop took his arm. "I can prove it."

Newman held up his hand, signaling Watson to hold up. "How?"

Emery stabbed a finger at Hunter. "Because he's a werewolf, too. He fought with the other werewolf yesterday. I was there."

Hunter felt Eliza's hand on his arm, trying to pull him away, but he slid his hand down her back and held her firm. There was no frigging way Emery could prove he was a werewolf.

Newman scowled. "Watson."

The large man started dragging the reporter away, but Emery squirmed out of his grip and charged Hunter, one hand reaching his coat pocket.

Hunter shoved Eliza behind him before Clark could take more than two steps. Newman moved just as fast, yanking out his pistol and pointing it at Emery, ordering him to freeze. Around them, every other cop did the same.

Emery skidded to a stop, one hand up in surrender, the other still in his jacket pocket. "Don't shoot! I don't have a weapon. I'm just going to prove he's a werewolf."

Newman's weapon didn't waver. "Take your hand out of your coat pocket, Mr. Emery—slowly."

Hunter had no idea what Clark had in his pocket, but he wasn't going to take a chance. If the reporter took another step, Hunter was putting him down. The hell with all the cops standing around.

Emery shook his head, but didn't take his hand out of his pocket. "It's not what you think. I have a foolproof method to prove someone is a werewolf. It's no danger to anyone except a werewolf. I'll show you."

"Slowly," Newman ordered.

The reporter wet his lips. "It's a known fact that a werewolf can't stand the touch of pure, blessed silver. Just the least bit of contact with the holy relic and he'll be screaming in pain."

Emery whipped his hand out of his pocket so dramatically Hunter was surprised no one shot him. The only reason they didn't was because he didn't have a weapon. Not unless he was planning to attack a bowl of ice cream.

Newman shoved his gun in his holster. "A freaking spoon."

"I wouldn't put those weapons away yet, officers," Emery warned. "You'll need them when I expose this man for what he truly is. He isn't likely to go quietly."

Emery lunged forward and swung the spoon at Hunter like it was a sword.

Hunter snatched the fancy silver utensil out of Emery's hand and deliberately closed his fingers around it. Out of the corner of his eye, he saw Eliza visibly relax.

"Satisfied?" he asked Emery.

The reporter shook his head, his eyes wide. "It's a trick. I'm telling you, he's a werewolf!"

Newman swore under his breath. "Watson, get this moron out of here. And if he gives you any trouble, arrest him."

Emery was still hollering about his first amendment rights as the cop led him away.

"What a fruitcake," Newman muttered, then looked at Hunter. "I'll need the four of you to hang around for a while so we can get your statements."

Hunter nodded.

As Newman and the other cops walked off, Nate came over to stand in front of him and Eliza. "You're a werewolf, huh? I knew it the whole time."

Before Hunter could reply, Nate wandered over to talk to Tandi.

"You don't think he'll say anything, do you?" Hunter asked Eliza.

"No." She smiled. "I think he's just thrilled to find out that he's actually been correct about werewolves all along."

She was probably right. Hunter looked at Alex. "What about you?"

The photographer gave them a wry smile. "Nah. I like the story Eliza came up with better. It won't get you the cover of *Paranormal Today*, but the local papers will eat it up for sure. Let me know if you'll need any photos to go with your story. I work freelance, too."

Giving them a nod, the photographer walked off to join Nate and Tandi. Eliza regarded the trio for a moment, then turned to face Hunter. It was the first time they'd been alone with each other since he'd gotten there.

She reached up to gently brush his hair back from his forehead, running her fingers over the cut there. There were a lot more of them, but thank God, the others were under his clothes.

"You're hurt," she said softly.

The corner of his mouth edged up. "It's just a scratch." He took her hand in one of his and gazed down at her arm. The bite was healing quickly, but it was still a series of jagged, ugly scars. Within a day or so the scars would be hard to see, but the effects were going to be far more permanent. "Your wound is a little bit more serious, Eliza. You've been bitten."

She nodded. "I know. And I know what that means."

Eliza had been cool and collected through all of this, so Hunter supposed he shouldn't be surprised by how calm she was being now. Still, he couldn't help but frown.

"Do you really?"

"Yes. It means I'll be werewolf."

His frown deepened. "And you're okay with that?"

She took a deep breath and let it out slowly. "I should probably be freaking out right now because I know how serious this all is. I know I'll have to spend the rest of my life worrying about people like Emery learning my secret—just like you've done. And then there's the change itself. That's got me a little worried."

He was about to tell her that he'd be there with her, but he didn't know if he could make that promise. He didn't even know if she was going to be staying around long enough.

When he opened his mouth to ask her, she shushed him with a finger on his lips. "But I'm also willing to admit that I can see some advantages to being a werewolf, too."

That surprised him. "You do?"

She gave him a small smile. "I know this probably doesn't mean much to you, but the fact that I'll be able to eat more without worrying about whether I'll fit in my clothes is a huge plus for me. The healing thing is really cool, too. You may not have realized it, but I'm somewhat accident prone. And I'll be able to see and hear better, not to mention smell when the milk goes bad."

It was his turn to smile. It was obvious she'd already given this some thought. "I guess knowing when the milk goes bad without having to taste it could be a serious bonus."

She grinned, then sighed. "But on the down side, I'll have to get over my phobia of nature if I'm going to be out running around in the woods all the time. That might be kind of difficult. I don't really like getting dirty. And of course, I'll have to get used to the cold weather if I'm going to be living up here."

Hunter stared at her, suddenly dumbfounded by the turn of the conversation. Was she saying what he thought she was? "Living up here?"

She looked up at him from beneath her lashes. "You did say you were serious when we talked about it before. Does your offer to share your bed include the rest of the house as well? I mean, I know you mentioned the hot tub and the bear skin rug, but I'm going to need some closet space, too. Actually, a lot of it."

He chuckled, the weight he hadn't known he was carrying lifting from his shoulders. He couldn't believe how lucky he was. Not only had Eliza accepted him being a werewolf, but she seemed to be handling her newly turned status pretty well, too. In addition to that, she wanted to stay with him. Pulling her into his arms, he gave her a long, slow kiss.

"You can have all the closet space you want, as long

as promise to stay with me."

"You might regret that when you see all the clothes I have." She kissed him again, then turned serious. "Really, though. I'm scared of going through that first change, especially since you said it was kind of frightening—and that it hurts. I don't really deal well with pain. You'll be there to help me, won't you?"

He cupped her cheek. "The first time, and all the ones after that, sweetheart. I love you, don't you know that?"

She blinked up at him. "You do?"

"Of course." He grinned. "I thought it was obvious."

Eliza's smile was shy. "I hoped, but I didn't know for sure. I like hearing you say it. And I love you, too, by the way."

He would have said something in reply, but she was already pulling him down for another kiss.

Epilogue

Eliza arched her back and sighed as Hunter ran his tongue along the slick folds of her pussy. That morning, they'd gone out for a run in the forest behind his house— their house, she corrected—moaning as he slid his tongue deep inside her. After running for hours, they'd shifted back to their human form, and well, one thing had led to another. Now, she was on her hands and knees in the grass and leaves while he licked her from behind.

She dug her fingers into the soft earth beneath her as Hunter swiped his tongue across her pussy over and over again. If someone had told her a couple months ago that she'd be making love with the man of her dreams out in the middle of the forest, she would have told them they were crazy. She hadn't been kidding when she told Hunter that the great outdoors had never really been her thing. But now that she was a werewolf, being outside was the most natural and exhilarating feeling in the world.

Eliza leaned farther forward and thrust her ass even higher in the air, hoping Hunter would find his way to her clit. He must have read her mind because a moment later, she felt his velvety tongue on her plump, little nub. She caught her breath as he made slow circles on the sensitive flesh. She always loved it when Hunter went down on her, but there was something about him doing it in this position that was decidedly primal.

Ever the tease, Hunter only licked her clit for a moment before going back to what he'd been doing before. Not that Eliza minded. The teasing always made her orgasms that much more intense, and she moaned once more as he ran his tongue along her pussy, then dipped it inside again. She might actually come just from that. But before she could find out, he'd moved back up to her clit again.

Instead of making little circles on the plump flesh like before, he flicked his tongue over her clit once, then twice, before closing his mouth over the sensitive bud and gently sucking on it. She gasped, sure she'd tumble headlong over the edge into orgasmville, but Hunter backed off before she could and once again made gentle, circular motions with his tongue. Damn, the man knew how to get her going.

Her clit was even more sensitive now than when he'd first begun licking her, and Eliza closed her eyes, getting lost in how good it felt. The forest seemed to disappear around her as she gave herself over to the sensations claiming her. It was like every nerve in her body was concentrated in that one little spot, and her breath started to come in little gasps as she moved closer and closer to climax. She was barely even aware of what he was doing as he lapped her clit with his tongue.

Her orgasm swept over her like a slow building tidal wave, and she dug her fingers into the soft earth, her cries of ecstasy echoing through the forest as Hunter's tongue coaxed every possible trace of pleasure from her body.

Only when every last tremor had left her did Hunter stop what he was doing. He moved, repositioning himself behind her. Her pulse quickened as he grasped her hips and teased the opening of her pussy with the head of his cock. His arousal was musky on the air, and she inhaled deeply, intoxicated by the scent. It was good being a werewolf. It was very good.

With a groan, he tightened his hold on her hips and plunged his hard cock into her in one smooth motion. Eliza gasped, her pussy clenching around him as he gently thrust. She rocked back against him, edging a little closer to orgasm each time her ass smacked against him.

Hunter growled and tightened his hold on her, pumping harder. Eliza dug her fingers into the earth and screamed her pleasure, glad there was no one within miles to hear and not caring if they did. Hunter climaxed with her, his groan long and low.

Afterward, Hunter stayed where he was, his cock still pulsing inside her pussy. Then finally, with a groan, he slowly slid out of her. Taking her hand, he pulled her down with him onto the soft forest floor.

"That was amazing," he breathed.

Eliza smiled. Sex wasn't the only thing that was amazing with her hunky werewolf. She never dreamed she could fall in love so fast or so completely, but she had, and she'd never been so happy in her life.

Things had moved at light speed since that night she'd been bitten. As Alex had predicted, both of the local Fairbanks' newspapers had immediately approached her, begging for an exclusive interview. Instead of agreeing, she'd done them one better. She'd written the story and offered it to the first paper that would give her a full-time job as a reporter. *The Daily News-Miner* had not only eagerly accepted the deal, but had printed her story on the front page, along with Alex's photos. They had definitely added a nice touch.

The *Miner* had offered Alex a job as well, but he'd declined. Apparently, chasing after ghosts, monsters, and legends was more entertaining than freezing his butt off in Alaska. He'd been more than happy for Eliza, though, and told her to look him up if she ever needed a photographer.

Even though she loved working for the *Miner*, she'd felt bad about bailing on *Paranormal Today*. They were the reason she'd come to Alaska and met Hunter. But after reading the story, even Roger Brannick agreed she should be working for a traditional news organization. He even agreed to not make her pay back the per diem and transportation costs the magazine had already covered— as long as she promised to send him a story every now and again. She agreed—as long as she could do it under a pen name. She was already halfway through a multi-installment piece on Alaskan monster myths for him, though werewolves were not one of them.

The werewolf version of their story still actually made it into print thanks to Clark Emery. He got his byline on page thirty-two of *Strange Times* right above an advertisement for a male enhancement supplement. Eliza almost felt sorry for the man, until she remembered what a jerk he was. She wondered what he'd say if he knew they had his silly spoon on the mantel above the fireplace.

As for Nate, he'd never brought up the subject of werewolves again. But the fact that one of his strongest beliefs had been confirmed was enough to encourage him to start chasing down some of his other paranormal theories. The last she heard, he'd signed on with an expedition to the Himalayas that was hoping to prove the existence of the Abominable Snowman. Eliza had been even more surprised to learn that he wouldn't be going alone, but that a certain female police officer would be accompanying him. Apparently, not only did Tandi have a serious thing for Nate, but she was also just as big into the paranormal as he was. Who knew? Well, as far as Eliza was concerned, they made a great couple. Kind of the real-word version of Mulder and Scully—with Nate being Mulder, of course.

Things had moved even faster where she and Hunter were concerned. After deciding to move in with him, Eliza hadn't even bothered going back to San Francisco at all. She'd quit her job at *Paranormal Today*, had her sister pack up her stuff and send it to her, then canceled the lease on her apartment. To say her family had been surprised was an understatement. They thought she'd either gone insane or been abducted by some snow-worshipping Eskimo cult. She'd finally convinced them that neither of those things were the case. Putting Hunter on the phone had helped. Her mother thought he sounded absolutely charming. The fact that he was a college professor didn't hurt. Her parents always wanted her to marry a doctor—even if it was one with a degree in animal behavior. Her whole family couldn't wait to meet him and were planning to come up for a big land-and-sea cruise next spring.

Eliza had been so busy getting that part of her life straightened out she barely realized how quickly time flew until Hunter reminded her it was almost time for her first change. She'd been nervous as hell, but it didn't seem nearly as frightening with him there to help her. When the full moon arrived the next night, she and Hunter had gone out to the woods behind their house, where they'd waited for her to turn.

"I'll be with you the whole way," he'd told her, and he was.

That first time had been painful. Even though she tried not to, her body had automatically fought what was happening to it. As it began to change shape, she'd instinctively held on to what her mind said was normal and fought the pull of her muscles as they tried to reshape themselves into their new form. That had just made it hurt even more. But Hunter's soothing words and gentle touch had finally gotten through to her, and she'd forced herself to relax and give in to the change. Once she'd done that, the pain had immediately lessened, and before she knew it, the transformation from human to wolf had been complete. Right then, she couldn't remember why she'd been fighting the change so hard. Being a wolf seemed completely natural.

Hunter hadn't changed into a wolf right away, but instead stayed in human form as she'd explored her new body. She felt a little self-conscious as he'd helped learn her first task—figuring out how to walk using four legs instead of two. That had taken a little longer to master than she thought it would. She'd always considered herself pretty coordinated, but she kept tripping over her big paws. It probably didn't help that Hunter kept laughing at her.

Once he finally gotten her going in a forward direction fairly smoothly, he'd helped her understand how to separate and interpret the hundreds of new smells assaulting her sensitive nose. Her sense of smell had been heightened already since being bitten, but in wolf form, her nose had been almost overwhelmed with everything around her. He'd taught her what smells were important, and which could be ignored. More importantly he taught her *how* to ignore them.

She'd been glad when he finally changed into wolf form, too. It had been really frustrating trying to communicate through yips and barks. Not that she'd been able to communicate with him any better after he changed, but at least he'd been at the same disadvantage. They'd spent the rest of the night running and exploring the Alaskan wilderness that was now her backyard. Hunter had been right. Being a wolf was absolutely exhilarating.

That first night spent together as wolves had been an incredible experience. She'd been so excited about the whole thing that she immediately jumped into his arms the moment they changed back, and they had made love right there on the forest floor. That had definitely been a first for her.

But she'd certainly gotten used to it, Eliza thought as she ran her fingers over Hunter's chest. They'd made love outside almost every night since.

"I could stay here all day," she said softly.

Hunter's chuckled was a deep rumble beneath her ear. "Me, too. But right now, I need you to hop up for a sec."

She frowned, but did as he asked. She watched in confusion as he reached into a hole at the base of the tree they were lying beside.

"What...?"

Her words trailed off when she saw the velvet ring box in his hand. Her pulse quickened.

He looked at her, his gold eyes more serious than she had ever seen them. He opened the box to reveal the most beautiful diamond engagement ring Eliza had ever seen. "Will you marry me, Eliza Bradley?"

She nodded, tears springing to her eyes. "Yes!" she laughed. "Yes! Yes! Yes!"

Grinning, Hunter took her left hand in his and slipped the ring on her finger. Eliza would have admired it right then, but he pulled her close for a long, slow kiss. When they finally came up for air, she held out her hand at arm's length to get a good look at the ring gracing her finger.

"When did you have time to put this out here?" she

asked.

"Last week when you were out doing that story at the museum," he told her. "I thought it'd be a romantic way to pop the question."

Her eyes flew to his face. "Last week? You left my ring here in a tree all week? What if someone had taken it?"

He chuckled. "Like who? The squirrels? They don't go for diamonds. They prefer emeralds."

She couldn't help but laugh again. "I suppose you're right. And it was a very romantic way to propose. I just thought this was a random place to stop and have sex."

He chuckled and nuzzled the sensitive spot behind her ear. "You don't know how hard it was to wait until we got here. But seriously, are you completely sure about this? I know we just met a few months ago."

Eliza pulled away to give him an incredulous look. "Of course I'm sure. In fact, I couldn't be surer. I can't wait to marry you."

"Just checking." He pulled her close for another kiss. "Wolves do mate for life, after all."

She wouldn't have it any other way. Now, the only question was how she was going to get her ring home once they changed back into wolves?

Read on for a Sneak Peek of my
military/paranormal/romantic-suspense action-packed
thriller HER PERFECT MATE (X-OPS Series Book 1)
Now Available from Sourcebooks in digital and
paperback online and in bookstores everywhere!

Landon almost laughed. Make himself comfortable. Right. He scanned the room, once again looking for something that would tell him where he was, but except for the immense television screen at the front of the room, the walls were bare. He didn't like the feeling he was getting. Special Forces qualified as black ops, sure, but an organization hidden in the garage of the EPA? That was another thing altogether. This had CIA written all over it and that wasn't going to work for him. He was a warrior, not a spook. And he was going to tell that to whoever was in charge when he or she walked in. Which could be a while, so he might as well try to make himself comfortable while he waited.

Pulling out one of the chairs, he sat down and prepared to settle in, but the door opened as soon as he did. He immediately got up, wanting to be on equal footing with whoever walked in.

Landon did a quick assessment of the man who entered. Average height, salt-and-pepper hair, expensive suit, wire-rimmed glasses. He looked like he should be teaching at an Ivy-League school somewhere.

He held out his hand. "Captain Donovan, I'm John Loughlin. Have a seat."

Landon did, then immediately went on the attack.

"You in charge here?"

If Loughlin was taken aback by the direct approach, he didn't let it show. "I'm the director, yes."

Director. Well, that just screamed CIA, didn't it?

"What the hell is this place?"

Loughlin leaned back in his chair. "First, let me tell what it isn't. It's not the army or any other branch of the military. Nor is it the NSA, the FBI, or the CIA Special Activities Division. It's called the Department of Covert Operations. DCO for short."

"Never heard of it."

Landon's frustration made him speak harsher than he normally would, but he didn't care. Loughlin didn't seem to mind.

"Very few people have heard of it, and we like to keep it that way. We were created after 9/11. Technically, we're a special organization within Homeland Security."

"That's great," Landon said. "But what if I don't want to work for the DCO?"

The man smiled. "We can discuss that later."

Which was code for saying it wasn't the kind of assignment he could turn down. Landon swore silently. This sucked. It was hard enough to get a good-looking evaluation report in the Special Forces since almost everything he did was classified and redacted. He couldn't imagine what they'd look like now. If he even got an evaluation report. It would be damn hard to get the Army Promotion Board to recognize a performance review when he wasn't assigned to a branch of the Department of Defense.

When he mentioned it to Loughlin, the man waved a hand dismissively. "Don't worry about that. Your records will indicate you've been transferred to the Department of Homeland Security. All performance areas on your evaluations will still be redacted, of course, but your service will be properly recognized."

Yeah, he was screwed big time.

"How long is the assignment?" Landon asked.

"There's no formal length of duty with the DCO. It really depends on your performance. Let's just call it indefinite right now."

Bend over, here it comes again, Landon thought. So much for ever making major. Anybody reviewing his records for promotion would figure he'd screwed up and been transferred into some rear echelon job to keep him out of the field.

"So, how did I get selected for this assignment? If I may ask." Then, because this guy was his new boss, he added, "Sir."

"We're not as formal here as they are in the army, Landon. Call me John. And to answer your question, the DCO keeps an eye out for people with your unique skill set. You were handpicked from a long list of candidates to serve in one of the toughest and most important assignments in the world. The DCO takes only the best and brightest."

He was really in trouble if the guy had to lay it on that thick.

"Unlike standard agents with the Department of Homeland Security, you'll have worldwide responsibilities," John continued. "You'll be paired with another agent who is just as highly trained as you are, only with a different set of talents."

Landon frowned. "I'll be on a two-person team? Doesn't that drastically limit the types of missions we can perform?"

"Not at all. We've learned from experience that a two-person team can perform more efficiently when it comes to the type of work you'll be doing."

"Exactly what kind of work is that? You still haven't said."

"We'll get into more detail later," John said. "But your primary job will be to cover your partner's back while they apply their special talents."

That was vague. What kind of special talents did this partner of his have? "That's it? You yanked me out of a warzone to pull babysitting duty?"

"That's not all you'll be doing, no. You'll be involved in direct action as well, but many times oversight will be a large part of your job, yes."

Landon sensed a "but" coming.

"However," John said, right on cue, "you do have one additional task. In fact, it's one of the most critical functions you can be asked to perform. Consider it the first general order for the DCO. It's something of a formality, but I have to discuss it with you. In the event your team is compromised and it appears likely your partner is about to be captured, it will be your task to eliminate them."

What the hell? John did not just say what Landon

thought he did. "I think I must have misunderstood. By them, I assume you mean the enemy we're up against?"

"No, Landon, you didn't misunderstand me. One of the most valuable services the DCO provides to the leadership of the United States is plausible deniability. Your partner possesses certain attributes that could prove embarrassing for our county if they were exposed. Therefore, it's critical that your partner never be captured. Part of your selection involved an assessment of your ability to follow out this particular job requirement."

Landon didn't think much of any assessment process that could determine he'd be okay with executing his teammate. What the hell had these assholes seen to make them think that? One of the founding principles of the Special Forces—the army in general—was that no one got left behind. There wasn't an army unit out there that wouldn't risk every single member in it to go back into enemy territory and rescue one of their people. It was the cog that made everything else work.

The idea that he'd be asked to kill his own partner was beyond distasteful. It was flat-out repugnant. Just what kind of attributes did his partner have that would make this person an embarrassment to the United States anyway?

He didn't care if he could turn down the assignment or not. Let them court-martial his ass. He was walking out of here right now. Landon started to get to his feet, but John held up his hand.

"I see this particular issue is difficult for you," he said. "Let me assure you we don't take this lightly,

Landon. The requirement has been evaluated at the very highest levels of authority, and it's been determined to be reasonable and required. That said, it isn't a common occurrence at the DCO. In fact, it's never happened, and we hope it never does. If it helps, you can look at it another way. It's your responsibility to make sure your partner is never put into a position where you have to kill them."

That wasn't much better, but Landon could live with it, especially since he sure as hell wasn't going to let any teammate of his get compromised.

"Is my partner aware of this order?" he asked.

John nodded. "Yes. All EVAs are fully aware of this stipulation and have signed the necessary documents to acknowledge and accept the consequence of their capture."

Landon had no idea what the hell an EVA was, but they must be seriously committed if they could work for an organization that would execute them.

John picked up the phone on the table and pressed one of the buttons. "Olivia, please have Todd and Kendra come in."

Since there were two of them, neither one was probably his new partner. Another team, maybe? He was about to ask John when the door opened.

The man and woman who walked in weren't dressed in the black uniforms Landon had seen earlier, so they probably weren't operatives. The business casual look they were rocking didn't give much of a hint as to what jobs they did. Neither did the clipboards in their hands.

John stood, so Landon did the same.

"Landon, this is Todd Newman and Kendra Carlsen," John said. "They'll be your training officers as well as be your handlers after you and your partner are certified for fieldwork."

Landon studied the man and woman closer as he shook their hands. Todd looked like he could have played linebacker when he was in college, but he was a little too soft in the middle to be lighting up guys on the field anymore. Kendra was cute, blond hair pulled back in a messy bun, reading glasses perched on her head, a spray of freckles across her cheeks.

He glanced at John. "What if my partner and I don't successfully complete the certification course?"

"You'll be debriefed and sent back to your unit." John smiled. "But something tells me you won't have to worry about that."

Landon hoped it wasn't the same something that told John he'd be okay with killing his partner. He'd never failed at anything and he wasn't about to start now, even if he didn't want to be here.

Kendra smiled. "Come on. Todd and I will introduce you to your partner."

It was about time. Landon gestured toward the door. "Lead the way."

Landon expected Todd and Kendra to take him to another conference room, so he was surprised when they led him into what looked like a workout room. Mats covered the floor and a heavy bag hung from a hook in one corner. Weights and workout equipment filled a good portion of the room. A woman was seated cross-legged in the center of it, her eyes closed, her hands loosely resting on her knees. At their entrance, she gracefully uncurled herself from the floor and got to her feet.

She was wearing a pair of black workout pants like his ex-girlfriend used to wear when she went to yoga class, and a form-fitting tank top. He couldn't help but notice her curvy, athletic body, expressive dark eyes, and full lips. With little makeup and her long, dark hair pulled up in a ponytail, she looked like the girl next door. Only more exotic than any girl he'd ever lived next door to, that was for sure.

He didn't care how tired and irritated he was, this was a woman he definitely wouldn't mind stopping to appreciate. Hopefully, one of his new training officers would introduce them before she left to give them the room.

"Landon, meet Ivy Halliwell, your new partner," Kendra said. "Ivy, Captain Landon Donovan, Special Forces."

They were going to have to pick his jaw up off the floor because Landon was damn sure that's where it was after hearing that announcement. No way this walking wet dream was his partner. She looked like she couldn't hurt a fly, much less do any kind of covert ops. They had to be messing with him.

"Your first mission is to put her on her ass," Todd said.

He'd had some big what-the-hell moments in his

life—most of them within the past twenty-four hours—but this had to be the biggest.

Landon narrowed his eyes at the man. "Excuse me?"

"Take her down."

Was this guy serious? This was his new partner and they wanted him to kick her ass? Ivy was about half his size and looked like she should be walking down a fashion runway somewhere, not trading blows with a trained combat killer.

Landon shook his head. "Forget it. I'm not going to take a swing at her, much less put her on her ass." He folded his arms across his chest. "You want entertainment? Maybe I should put you on your ass."

Kendra must have thought that was funny because she hid a smile behind her clipboard.

Ivy wasn't so subtle. She laughed outright. And damn if it didn't have a sexy sound to it.

"That's chivalrous of you, Donovan," she said. "You putting Todd on his ass is something I'd like to see, but he isn't going to let us leave this room until you learn the lesson you're here to learn. So, let's get this over with."

She didn't wait for a reply, but instead slowly circled around Landon on her bare feet. He instinctively turned to follow her. She moved with the sure-footed grace of a cat, making him think she was probably well-trained in one or more martial arts.

"Well?" she demanded.

He assessed her stance. "You're not ready."

Ivy rolled her eyes. "Tell you what. I'll make it easier on you. I'll hit you first. How's that sound?"

"That implies I'd let you hit me."

She shrugged her slim shoulders. "Oh, I'll hit you all right."

He laughed, but the sound was cut short as she twisted in a blur and her leg came around in a spinning heel kick that would have taken off his head if he hadn't backed away just in time.

"Shit," he muttered. He was way too tired for this crap. "Stop screwing around, okay? That kick would have done some damage if you landed it."

Ivy didn't heed his warning, though. Instead, she immediately followed up with the same kind of a kick, this time in the other direction. Landon quickly backpedaled to avoid her foot, only to smack against the wall. He dropped to one knee, instinctively thrusting out with his hands to both knock her away from him and put some space between them. But instead of falling back, she moved out of the way, avoiding his hands. For a moment he didn't realize what she'd done. Then it struck him.

She'd darted sideways while she was in mid-kick. That shouldn't even be physically possible.

Ivy landed lightly on her feet, a smile curving her lips. "I knew I could get you to take a shot at me, even if it was lame. Then again, I didn't expect much from another oversized grunt like you. I don't know why they keep pairing me up with guys like you all the time. Can't they find anyone with a brain?"

Landon rose from his crouch and moved to the center of the room. When she came at him again, he didn't want a wall getting in his way. "Guys like me?

335

You're trying to insult me now? Think that's going to get me to take a punch at you? What are you, a masochist?"

Her smile broadened. "I already got you to do that. And I'd only be a masochist if you ever got your hands on me."

He snorted. "Lady, that wasn't a punch. You'd know it if I wanted to hit you."

"All talk and no action," she scoffed. "Isn't that the Special Forces motto or something?"

Landon knew what she was trying to do and it wasn't going to work. She must have figured it out, too. She gave up on the verbal jabs and resorted to real ones, coupled with those damn spinning roundhouse kicks again.

He stripped off his camo overshirt and threw it across the room, so he could get down to serious business.

He blocked most of her strikes with his hands and the others with his shoulders, biceps, and thighs. He sure as hell felt them, but he got the feeling she wasn't hitting him nearly as hard as she could.

His plan was to lure her in close enough to get his hands on her. That way, he could put her down without being forced to throw a serious punch. She might be agile as hell, but if he connected with anything real, he'd break something. His best bet was to get his hands on her and pin her to the floor so he could end this stupid game.

That was easier than it sounded. Ivy was faster than lightning and could twist her body into a pretzel to get out of his grasp. He had her in a perfect jujitsu take-down position several times only to have her spoil it by not going down like she should have. He even planted his knee in her stomach and yanked her backward with him in a throw that should have landed her hard on her back, groaning in pain. Instead, she turned the move into some kind of gymnastic flip and came down as softly on her feet as if she stepped off a street curb.

Out of the corner of his eye, he saw the two training officers taking notes as they watched. Kendra was actually smiling. Landon clenched his jaw. What a couple of asses.

On the other side of the room, Ivy spun around to face him. Eyes narrowing, she ran directly toward him. He automatically braced himself for another blow, but at the last second she darted to her right, jumping at the wall and rebounding off it like she was an extra in some Jackie Chan movie, then ricocheting back at him, her right leg coming around in a roundhouse kick.

Instead of getting out of the way like any sane person would have, he moved closer, getting underneath her swinging leg and grabbing her shoulders. He avoided her foot, but ended up taking a knee to the left side of his rib cage. It hurt, but it got him inside her defenses. He was going to get a grip on her, and this time she wasn't going to get away.

That's when he realized her kick had only been a distraction. He'd been so busy watching her feet he hadn't even noticed her open hand coming toward him. He did a double take. She was going to *slap* him? His mind registered surprise for half a millisecond before her hand angled down to sweep across the front of his T-shirt.

Landon felt the fabric tug and swore he heard a

ripping sound. He even felt a sting. But he ignored it. Tightening his grip on her shoulders, he spun them both around, letting the momentum from her rebound take them down to the floor.

He twisted at the last second, taking the impact of the floor on his right shoulder before yanking her to his chest in a bear hug. If he'd been trying to kill her, he would have crushed a hell of a lot harder. Instead he squeezed just enough to let her know he could hurt her if he wanted to.

They came to a stop with him on his back, Ivy pinned to his chest. She didn't fight him, simply laid there with her face close to his neck, breathing deeply. Landon couldn't help but notice how soft her body was against his, and how nice it felt to have her on top of him.

His cock noticed, too.

Shit. This was going to be embarrassing.

"Okay, you two," Todd said. "I think we've gotten everything out of this demonstration I intended."

It took a moment for the words to register—probably because all the blood had left his head to rush to another part of his anatomy. Landon reluctantly loosened his hold on Ivy. He waited for her to get up, but she stayed firmly planted on top of him, which alarmed him. He thought she would have jumped up the moment he released her. God, he hoped he hadn't hurt her with that take down.

He gently tilted her chin up with his fingers. "Hey. You okay?"

Ivy blinked at him, her beautiful eyes filled with

something that looked almost like wonder. Then she gave herself a little shake. "I-I'm good. You?"

"Yeah. Fine."

"Good."

She gazed at him for a moment longer, then quickly pushed to her feet. She crossed the room to slip on a pair of flip-flops she had left there. When she turned back to him, her face was the perfect mask of composure he'd seen when he first walked in.

"No hard feelings, I hope?" she said as he stood. "That's just the way the DCO likes to introduce me to my new partners. I don't know why."

He knew why. The DCO realized the fastest way to get a man to appreciate the talents of his female partner was to have her kick his ass. At least she hadn't done it to him.

"Not at all," he said. "I suppose we can call this match a tie."

Her lips curved. "You think so?"

Reaching out, she flicked his shirt with her fingers, then turned and walked away.

Remembering the bizarre open-handed swipe she'd given him across the chest, he looked down to see four diagonal tears in his T-shirt. He pushed the material aside, frowning when he found four identical scratches on his chest. If he didn't know better, he'd think he got scratched by a cat—a big cat. They weren't deep or bleeding, but there was no mistaking what had made them—fingernails. Ivy's fingernails.

Not exactly standard-issue hand-to-hand combat

technique. He got the feeling nothing about this place was standard issue. Especially his new partner.

Look for HER LONE WOLF, Book 2 in the X-OPS SERIES!

Coming from Sourcebooks Nov 4, 2014!

ABOUT THE AUTHOR

Paige Tyler is a bestselling author of sexy, romantic fiction. She and her very own military hero (also known as her husband) live on the beautiful Florida coast with their adorable fur baby (also known as their dog). Paige graduated with a degree in education, but decided to pursue her passion and write books about hunky alpha males and the kickbutt heroines who fall in love with them.

http://www.paigetylertheauthor.com

OTHER BOOKS BY PAIGE TYLER

SERIES

The Buckle Bunnies Series

Ride of Her Life

Team Roping

Ride 'em Hard

The Badge Bunnies Series

Seducing Officer Barlowe

Two Cops, A Girl and A Pair of Handcuffs

A Cop, His Wife and Her Best Friend

Ride-Along

Hands-On Training

The Cowboy Series

Karleigh's Cowboys

And The Ranch Hand Makes Three

More Than a Cowboy (Special Two-Book Set)

Alaskan Werewolves Series

Animal Attraction

Animal Instinct (Coming Soon)

The Cutler Brothers Series

Cade

Madoc

The Cutler Brides

Modern Day Vampires

Vampire 101

The Friends Series

Spicing Up Her Marriage

Taking Her Friends Advice

It's Just a Job

INDIVIDUAL BOOKS

Western

Kayla and the Rancher

Paranormal

Dead Sexy

Just Right

The Magic Spell

Fantasy

Santa's Wayward Elf

Contemporary

Security Risk

The Postman Always Comes Twice

Good Cop, Bad Girl

Mr. Right-Now

Erotic Exposure

Unmasked

Sexy Secret Santa

If You Dare

Librarian By Day

Protective Custody

Spanking Sydney

The Real Thing

Not Really the Outdoor Type

The Wager

Maid for Spanking

The Girl Who Cried Wolf

Stop, or I'll Spank

Samantha and the Detective

Nosy By Nature

All She Wants for Christmas

The Trouble with New Year's Resolutions

Austin Malone, Private Eye

The Girl Next Door

Bridezilla

A Date for the Wedding

Sci-Fi

Cindra's Bounty Hunter

Pirate's Woman

The Ambassador's Daughter

Not the Man She Thought

Free-Read

Caught Red Handed

Made in the USA
Coppell, TX
21 December 2019